A PERMANENT FREEDOM

ALSO BY CURDELLA FORBES

Fiction

Songs of Silence (2002)

For Children

Flying with Icarus (2003)

Non-Fiction

From Nation to Diaspora: Samuel Selvon, George Lamming and the Cultural Performance of Gender (2005)

A PERMANENT FREEDOM

CURDELLA FORBES

PEEPAL TREE

First published in Great Britain in 2008
Peepal Tree Press Ltd
17 King's Avenue
Leeds LS6 1QS
England

ISBN13: 9781845230616

ARTS COUNCIL
ENGLAND Peepal Tree gratefully acknowledges Arts Council support

CONTENTS

The rainbow, sign of God's desire,
is earnest of the final fire

Edward Baugh, 'Colour Scheme' *It Was the Singing*

For
Julianne
Ariane
Kezia
Sam Fuller
and Laban

ACKNOWLEDGEMENTS

My deepest appreciation to Mervyn Morris, without whose encouragement I might never have dared.

I am grateful to Faber and Faber for permission to quote from Derek Walcott's 'Homage to Gregorias chapter 12 (*Collected Poems 1948-1984*), in 'Nocturne in Blue' and to Sandberry Press for permission to quote from Edward Baugh's 'Colour Scheme' (*It was the Singing*).

Aliun is purely my invention; however, information about his/her African connections Orunmilla and Mbaba Mwana Waresa, was gleaned from Professor John Mbiti's *African Religions and Philosophy,* Oxford: Heinemann, 1989. 2nd edition.

Up to a year after I had finished the manuscript, I was sure the name Aliun, which I found myself constantly alternating with a different spelling, Aluin, existed only in my imagination. One year later, exactly to the day, I decided out of a whimsical curiosity to inquire whether such a name did exist. I discovered that not only did the name Aluin, meaning 'supernatural being' or 'elf', exist, it had almost twenty variants, including a name as familiar as Alvin. Aliun, not one of the listed variants, was harder to find; I finally discovered it as a term at the centre of online discussion forums on illusionism: it appears variously as a title, signifying 'shapeshifter', and as the name of a device for levitation. So far I have not discovered its etymology. The websites listing Aliun the shapeshifter were in multiple languages, including Arabic, German, Spanish, Portuguese.

None of this was anything I could have predicted. For His secret interventions, I acknowledge the Higher Power.

There are allusions to the work of other Caribbean writers: to Derek Walcott's 'The Saddhu of Couva' (*Collected Poems* 1948-1984) on the dedication page; to the title of Dionne Brands' novel *In another Place, Not Here*, Jean Breeze's poem 'Riddym Ravings' and the title of George Lamming's novel *Of Age and Innocence* in Macóné, Macóné; to the figures of Melquíades the gipsy and Rebeca the fey child in Gabriel García Márquez's *One Hundred Years of Solitude* in 'A Permanent Freedom;' to the title of Marlene

NourbeSe Phillip's poetry collection *She Tries Her Tongue, Her Silence Softly Breaks,* in 'Say'; to the title of Walcott's play 'Malcochon, or Six in the Rain' and William Shakespeare's [he being Caribbean in all the ways that count] 1 Henry IV (4.2, Lord Vernon's speech in praise of Hal) in 'Nocturne in Blue'; to the title of Lorna Goodison's poem 'I am becoming my mother' in 'Requiem'.

Manifold thanks to Lisa Brown and Helen Gissing Cunningham for their patient reading of the manuscript and their insightful suggestions; to Camara Brown for hers when the manuscript was still in embryo; to Veronica Simon for the kweyól translation of 'The parrot fish! That is the one you must save for me!' in 'Nocturne in Blue; to Naeesa Aziz for confirming the translations of the Twi words and names for God★ in 'Stele'; to many friends: Paulette Ramsay, Joan Miller Powell, Carol Brown, Michael Bucknor, Barbara Rueben-Powell, Winston Anderson, Kezia Page, Colin Gillespie for, in some cases, encouragement; in others, dreadful questions tipped in fire. To Uncle Corny (deceased), my mother, Aunt Edna, and Miss Peggy, for their wonderful stories that keep showing me what is possible.

Untold thanks to all who pray for me.

★Twi words and names for God, and their meanings:
akwaaba: welcome
nya akokooduro: take courage *or* be courageous
aniwa hu asumasem biara: the eye sees the lessons
asomdwoee: peace
yebehyia bio: we will meet again
Onyame Agyenkwa: God, the Saviour
Onyankopon: God, the Almighty
Odomankoma: God, the Benevolent One

PROLOGUE TO AN ENDING

The woman stood at the top of the hill, one arm shading the sun from her eyes as she strained to decipher the figure toiling slowly upward. From this distance it seemed to bend almost level with the earth, and in colour was almost one with it, ochre brown, and dark at the sides with shadow. For a long moment she stood, curved slightly forward in the wind, a poised, stylized comma in an interrupted sentence. After a while he seemed to sense her eyes trained on him and he lifted his head and then his hand in salute. Only then did she seem satisfied for she smiled and, carrying her basket of cuttings under one arm, went back to the side of the house under the long awning of the conservatory, bending low among the rows of potted palms, ferns, orchids and hung greenery that made inside a cool darkness and a filtered light. She didn't look up from her work pouring new soil when his shadow loomed over her bent back and the cropped head bent to her cheek. But she rubbed her face with casual affection against the side of his. If her heart leaped a little, she kept it firmly buttoned over, under the old bush jacket that had been a man's.

'Hi, howdy.'

'Hi howdy. How you do?'

'So-so. Let me help you with that.' He let the crocus bag he carried over his shoulder slide to the ground with a soft thump and took the heavy bucket of soil from her hand. Carefully, he began grading handfuls into the empty pots waiting for the transplantation of the seedlings that lay on the ground, curved like babies in their silver plastic sacks. She watched him, the quick, capable brown hands moving in the fine earth of their own colour, the broad back in the tan shirt raggedly patched with the

9

damp of his sweat where he had laboured up the hill in the sun's heat. He tensed, reacting to her stillness, the way she had of watching like a statue alive, disconcertingly suspended and alert. Her eyes, missing nothing, caught the stiffening of his spine, the instinctive resistance to being shadowed.

'Earth man,' she murmured, teasing, offering reassurance. 'I saw you coming up the hill. You looked so at one with the ground, like a earthwork somebody throw up with a spade. I thought any minute you would sink right back into your hole – not a bump on the horizon. I wanted to draw you.'

He reacted with anger, his voice a flash of resentment at being so carelessly spoken. She thought she could look through him, ruffle the cloth of his skin and then smooth him with a careless tease. 'You don't seem surprised to see me,' he said, irrelevantly, since he never announced his coming, but coding his anger in these words.

She chose to understand, and moved away to sit at the rough wood table to the right where she kept her gardening tools. She pulled a plant towards her and began moulding earth with her hands, skilful and possessively intimate – the way she touched everything, as if she thought everything was one of her sculptures. Everything, everyone, he thought bitterly, his skin living the myriad caresses her hands bestowed, while her eyes looked out over him to places whose doors she had closed behind her, letting no one in. Even the touch of her hands was a kind of scorn – as if she thought she could feel out the meaning of him like feeling out Braille. But even as he thought this he knew it wasn't fair. It was the reflection of his own need, desire beating against the door of her strange innocence – wilful perhaps, but innocence nevertheless. It angered him that he, who had played a part in her reaching this place of freedom, still found it hard to accept his secondariness within it. It made him feel unworthy of his own calling.

'I felt you coming,' she said, calmly. 'This morning I woke up and I felt you in my head, bringing coconut water and hot cross bun.' She looked over at the side of his mortified face and couldn't help herself; she started to laugh.

Her laughter broke the tension. He started to laugh too. 'What else? I must be a madman. Whoever heard of bringing coconut water to country from town? Talk bout carrying coal to Newcastle.'

'Maybe is me who mad. I live up on this hill with all these trees around me and not one coconut. Who ever hear of country house without coconut?'

'Me. Plenty house in country without coconut. There, that's finished.' He placed the empty bucket in its exact corner, which he knew, as he knew everything about this place, and came to sit beside her on the bench. 'Move over.' But she had already moved, making room for him. She always made room, as long as it was only physical, and outside. She bent and passed him the two clay mugs she kept under the bench for midday drinks. Pressing his foot on top of the crocus bag he had dropped in the corner, he made two jelly coconuts roll out of its open mouth and with the same foot stopped them quickly before they could roll away over the dusty floor.

She tried not to, seeing his annoyance of a moment ago, but still she watched him as with a single deft movement he sliced the top off the first coconut and poured its contents into one of the mugs. The liquid, flowing, made a glugging sound. His hands were very capable and strong, yet finely and delicately made, the nails trimmed low and their crescent moons showing. They were warm and ruddy under the brown. He handed her the mug, their fingertips close and lightly touching. She watched him over the top as she swallowed the coolness sliding silk down her throat.

He cut and poured his own coconut, lifted the mug in salute. 'Well, here's to friendship.'

There was irony in his voice, which she chose to ignore. She touched her mug against his. The vessels jarred, clinked. 'How you do? Really.'

'I'm fine. Really.' He smiled down into her eyes, that tight, enigmatic half-smile that she knew too well, that said, don't ask me too much, lady, or you might get answers you really don't want to hear. 'And you? How is it going?'

She laughed. 'As expected, really. It's still all over the district that I'm a guzzum woman and not to be trusted. But everybody still come anyway, like Nicodemus by night. You should see the way people screechy up the hill and hear the excuses they come with.' With unerring mimicry, she put on the voice of the district moutamassy, 'Miss Maldene, you know, nayga people is a funny set a people, cyan trus dem. They don't know you, but the way they ready to whisper long story, ah say to meself, I not following these people here, you hear, I going right up that hill go welcome the lady to the district, and see, ah find you is a nice lady. Nice nice lady fi true, can't better. Miss Maldene, I hear dem talking bout how you bring obeah into the district, but I don't listen to dem, I say oonu too wicked and bad mind, not a thing more than the lady have a gift and she helping out her fellowman. Miss Maldene, me daughter have a sore foot from so long, I know it can't be no doctor complain, you think you coulda do anything to help her?'

They laughed together at the picture she painted, and she thought how incredibly warmed she always felt at his presence, how safe was his laughter. The thought disturbed her and she looked away from his eyes meeting hers in amusement across the table, but the moment was already translated, had blazed into a sudden heat she could not recall.

'Maldene,' he said, roughly, rising, hand blindly outstretched, but she was quicker than he was and by the time he got around the table she was at the far end of the conservatory, arms rigid across her chest, talking in her quick, abrupt way over her shoulder.

'You'd be surprised how many of them still turn up, despite the rumours.' She laughed again, without breath. 'People are so strange. They come wanting me to give them holy oil and tell them how many times to spin round and how many nights to sleep on grave to heal their sickness an kill their enemy. You can see that they really disappointed that all I have is herbs, an ah tell them, say the Lord's Prayer. So they make up their stories anyhow, to fill the need I can't fill – people soul want entertainment. Is a small district.' She finished, still laughing, still nervous, aware she had been talking too fast.

He stood by the table watching her, accepting the plea not to come any closer, listening. But his stance unnerved her. She tried to speak again and fell silent.

He said, irrelevantly and yet utterly to the point, 'Maldene, I'm leaving. Next Saturday.'

Fear and disquiet flared in the wide yellow eyes, their sharpened concentration magnifying that strange colour he thought so crazy in her cocoa-dark face. But the face itself was all wrong anyway, slanted and off-edge like an Egyptian adze, the asymmetrical front panel of a perfect, rounded, shaven skull.

'So it came through? So soon?'

'So soon,' he said, his voice gruff, almost angry, and then, with a shrug, 'But not really. It's been a long time since I applied. And I have been packed and ready.'

'Yes.' He felt gratification and pain that she looked lost, a cruel desire to punish her and a haunting desire to protect.

They stood there unmoving, she with her arms crossed defensively on her breasts, until he moved to close the space between them and, grasping the tops of her arms, brought her back to her seat, pushed her with gentle hands down on the bench. 'Sit down, Maldene. I'm not going to eat you, for God's sake.' The slight exasperation in the voice belied the gentleness of touch. This time he sat at the other end of the bench, straddling so that they were face to face, as on a seesaw.

She felt, with what she knew to be a quite unreasonable stab of resentment, that it was a gesture to imprison.

He said, 'Don't talk to me just to make conversation. Tell me because you know I really want to know how you are.'

'I don't make conversation with you,' she cried, defensive, declaring their friendship, denying this other, unwelcome thing between them. The whole shift of emotion between them was now a paradox. He had started off the one exposed, uneasy under her eyes. Now she was worried and afraid, and appallingly bereft. For so long she had felt safe when he forgot that he was a man. She had hated him for never being able to forget for long. Even when he said nothing, it was there, invasive; she kept having to deflect him with teasing conversation, fast talk. Now with this announcement that he was going away, to a cold country, in search of another life, she felt disrupted by anger and fear; her senses clamoured to perceive him completely as a man.

His sweat had dried but she could still smell him, very rainy, tumid and warm. He was a thickset man with cropped hair, black and shiny, wearing tan shirt and trousers and soft-soled tan shoes like a uniform, yet on him they looked turned aside from their

13

uniform's role, badly creased, neither neat nor right. They were two of a kind. She, too, was neither neat nor right. It showed even in the sculpting of her face. All askew.

This thought, oddly, eased her. She laughed in her nostrils, and was able to speak. 'The house by the sea has become empty. The Rastaman died, they say he lived there for over twenty years. But now it's empty.'

'And you want to have it,' he said, matter-of-factly. 'You've always coveted that house.'

She moved her shoulders in self-defence. 'Yes, but this is not selfish. If I could have afforded it – but anyway I can't. It would have been nice to have it as a dispensary. To keep this house... private.'

'Of course. You don't have to feel guilty about wanting space, Maldene.' She wished he wouldn't smile at her like that, like some blasted benignant king. Bloody man, you know me too well.

He laughed, and she realised that she had spoken her thoughts aloud. She leaned her forehead down on her upturned wrist away from him, resting her elbow on the table, shaking her head in negation. 'Damn you, Ramsoran. Nobody has the right to know me as well as you do. It's obscene, I even say my thoughts aloud thinking you're not there.'

'It's only because I'm there. Not because I'm not there.' His reply was deceptively mild, as was his hand rubbing her back in a soft to-and-fro motion of comfort and familiarity. She began to cry suddenly and he put his arms around her and gathered her close, leaning his forehead against hers as if the crying, too, was something that he was familiar with as an extension of them both, of who they were. 'It's ok,' he said, again and again, and then, humorously, 'It's not as if I'm dead. You can always come and visit me. Plane cross water, you know.' His laughter, like hers, was a way of acknowledging and containing all the things that could not be said, not because they were too much, but because she would again tell him no if he asked her to come with him, or change the fine balance of a long friendship with love's risk.

She looks directly at him now. They are sitting so close on the bench she can see the grain of pores on the light, streaked skin, he can see the faint line, almost like a moustache, where she had been born with a harelip, a guinea pig wound in the mouth, she said, and it had been imperfectly stitched up leaving a scar. For a long time she had kept saying it was the devil's mark, her cleft foot in the face, the way she had grown up hearing it spoken of, until she learnt from him another language.

Their foreheads lean against each other, rocking, and impulsively he kisses her on the guinea pig mouth. She jerks, turns her head away.

'Come on inside,' she says. 'Let me get you something to eat.' They are both trembling a little, as if an electric shock has passed.

Inside the cool house scattered with rattan, plaited rugs, impossibly more plants and her sculptures unashamedly useful as bowls, mugs, pots and plant-holders, he helped her make the simple meal of pumpkin soup and hard-dough bread with avocado and fresh-caught parrot fish she had bought in the market the day before, sensing his coming. What he thought of as her sculptures was really pottery that she fired and glazed in her own kiln, beautiful, unusual things with sometimes a wild, disturbing fire within them. She had no vanity about her work, and no sense of a value apart from the making of it; she sold the pieces to whoever wanted for whatever price they could afford. Or gave them away. For years she had stopped thinking of them as anything other than a hobby, occupational therapy, she said. So he was surprised when he saw the cloth covering the shape on the table where she worked in the kitchen, how sharply she cried out when he went to lift it to look, as he always had done. 'No!' He pulled up short, looking over his shoulder in surprise. She mumbled in odd embarrassment. 'I'm sorry. It's just – it's just that it's something new I'm doing, and I'm not sure of it yet. It's like nothing I've ever tried before.'

'Of course,' he said, gentle as always, but the puzzlement still in his eyes, a curiosity which she knew would come back at some other time, with the dogged persistence of which she knew he was capable.

She placed his bowl on the mat before him and sat down with hers, watched him lift his spoon to his mouth. 'Taste awright?'

…..

By the time they had washed and stacked the few dishes from lunch, standing side by side at the small sink, they had re-established an equilibrium that held steady against the sudden quick eruptions of particular moments – chance words, hands touching, the prick of laughter here or there.

He stayed late, until the sun had fallen well below the sky and the long shadows had begun their stealthy fingering on the slopes. It was a slow, quiet day during which they had only two visitations. The first was Miss Icilyn in pursuit of boiled noni juice and massage for her arthritis.

'Come back tomorrow for the massage, Miss Icy,' she said, handing over the bottle of dark brown liquid. Miss Icy was inclined to linger, making chat while out of the corners of her eyes she studied the nice-looking man who she knew of a fact had come to visit Miss Maldene several times before. Half amused, half wry, he watched her send Miss Icy on her way with the minimum of time wasted and the utmost of courtesy. She would survive, even here, and with goodwill, he thought. His heart eased a little about his going, and her aloneness. At the same time he felt his own dispensability. In the end, she has no need of me, he thought.

He was boiling the water for a last cup of fevergrass tea when a skittering of fine stones came against the windows, sharp rattlings like dry rain. He thought it might be the wind skittering branches against the sides of the house but it came again a second time and this time with whispers, giggles and the scampering of feet.

Laughing, she answered the question his raised eyebrows asked. 'It's only Miss Mirri's children from down the hill. They like to throw gravel because they know I won't do anything, but it is nice to pretend I will.' She put her head through the window and cried 'Grrr!', making a horrible face, and the children shrieked and sped off, laughing.

But her response was the invitation to a game and soon they came back; he could hear them outside giggling and shuffling, pushing each other with quick, urgent murmurs. 'No, you.' 'No, mi nah go. You go.'

She went outside, with him following, and the bevy scampered off again. 'Come,' she called out. 'Come and meet my friend.'

One by one they halted in flight, responding to the different invitation in her voice – was the game over or not over? There were three of them, little mites between the ages of four and six, the eldest a girl with huge wide-open eyes, curious, bold and sassy, clearly the leader of her two brothers. The little one stood rubbing one foot against the other, a thumb in his mouth and his fingers grasping his navel which was naked below his short merino vest.

'Ah, come on,' she coaxed. 'I promise I won't eat you this time. Only nex time. Jus come an say hi to my friend. This is Mr Ramsoran.'

Identical puzzled looks came over their faces. The name was too long for them to handle.

Giggling, they came, shy, bold, curious. He shook hands gravely. They looked at him with awe, this big man shaking hands with children as if he came from another country. Was he stupid or what? But still they felt important.

'So what is your name?' he said, addressing the little girl first.

'Aida,' she said, defiant. 'An dem a mi bredda. Dis a Big Man an dis one name Lionel,' she added with a proprietary air, obviously beginning to feel important as the eldest, the one addressed first, the one in charge. He was amused.

'So is you tek care a dem?'

'Hmmn hmmn,' she said, boasting.

'An is you tell dem to stone Miss Maldene house too?'

She didn't like that so much. Her eyes narrowing on his, she began to back off.

'Is she lead wi inna mischief,' the bigger boy said, accusing, plaintive, glad to wriggle out of any trouble that was forthcoming. 'Mamma seh she always a lead wi inna trouble.' Aida gave him a malicious look and shot out her mouth in a motion like sucking her teeth.

'Ah-oh.' He nodded his head up and down, pretending enlightenment. 'Ah see. So you nuh have nutten fi do with it? Is she lead yu all di time?'

The boy nodded, emphatically. 'Uh-uhn. Is she.'

'Cho man, ah don't believe yu. Ah don't believe she lead you. Big man like you? No sah.'

This was a new curve being thrown. Big Man drew bead, looked unhappy, confused.

'Mi know is untruth yu telling, man. Mi know is you lead dem,' he said jokingly, his tone balanced between mock potential admiration and mock reproof.

'Is me lead dem,' Big Man said, recuperating, dimly perceiving in this a hidden compliment of gender.

'Me don't throw stone pon Miss Maldene,' the little one piped up, perspicaciously eyeing the man's hand moving towards his side pocket. He was not surprised when a handful of coloured pencils came out. This one knew grown-ups. He was putting in his claim for rewards, ahead of time.

'All who tell lie no get no gift,' he said, mock serious, and Lionel's hand shot up in the air.

'Me teacher, me nuh tell lie!'

'Me neida,' Aida said boldly, Big Man muttering in sequence.

'Onnu sure?'

'Yes wi sure.' Lionel nodding his head up and down with the emphatic vigour of a puppet or a con-artist.

'Awright, mek sure, yu know.'

'Lionel lie!' Big Man said virtuously. 'Him throw stone too.'

'Is true, Maas Lionel?'

Again Lionel's head jerked up and down, his thumb making slapping noises against the roof of his mouth. 'Hu-huhn. But it nuh ketch him. Mi cyan trow good. A nuh fi mi stone lick him.'

Behind him, Maldene was choking with suppressed laughter.

'Awright,' he said, mock-relenting. 'Mi go gi oonu di gift so long as oonu promise nuh fi dweet again. Oonu promise?'

'Eeehn hn.'

Everyone got coloured pencils. He had bought the pack for his own use and forgotten them in his pocket, as he always seemed to forget things in his pockets.

'Oonu run gwan go play now.'

Whispering, heads close together, they scampered off to where the roof of their house appeared among the trees. He watched them absently, the remains of a smile forgotten, delight slowly fading on his face.

'See you later', Maldene called, waving. He looked at her face lit up with the light of the children's presence and his face grew cruel, and closed. Abruptly he turned and went back into the house.

She walked with him, for the last time, she thought, to where his car was parked at the bottom of the hill. They said goodbye without touching. 'I'll call you before I go, of course,' he said.

'Yes, of course.'

They stand awkwardly, face to face. Their separate thoughts fill the void.

He wonders to himself, as if thinking of another person, how easily he contains sadness, how easily his heart withholds judgement. He has said, 'You don't have to feel guilty about wanting space', but his heart knows it is her obsession with space that makes her refuse the risk, denying them both. He has no vanity, but he knows that there is also her fear, the fear that she will be harmful to him, though he has tried to persuade her it is not so. But he knows that beyond the fear is the tyranny of space. He knows too that she is unaware of how that obsession has structured her relations with the village on unequal terms: she sees herself as the vulnerable one, the outsider, but she thinks nothing of the fact that it is she who has arrived in this village so obviously from a more sheltered, more affluent life, that the simplicity of her living does not disguise the fact that it is from choice, not need, that she has done so, that in all of this it is the people of the district who are being asked to pay homage, that they must feel constrained to think that homage is demanded of them in any acceptance of her, in any appeal to her gifts. They would come to her because they were poor and her herbs worked, as did her mystique. If they undermined this with mockery, gossipy self-entertainment, it was a small price for her to pay. As it was, their level of acceptance, after a few months, had been remarkable, due in no small part to her own easy capacity to talk to people, to be at ease in any company. But equally it was due to the hospitality of country people who at some level always accommodated strangers, no matter in how complex and contradictory a way.

None of this will he say to her, knowing how fragile she still is. She will learn, in time; time, like God, is patient. He will always worry for her, alone here. He is glad for the young man, Boysie, who comes twice a week to help her with the planting and the distilling of the herbs; his presence at least must weave some safety-net of conversation. He is glad that people pass through in constant if unsteady streams, for he knows that the silence she craves is what most returns her to danger. She has chosen a village, the most gregarious of places, to hide away in, because she knows that here the barrier of class, the fine invisible thread of its filaments, is more effective than any policeman's barrier of yellow tape around the scene of a crime, in keeping people out while keeping them near. She is clever and yet blind, and this hurts him with a deep desire to protect.

She thinks to herself that she should by now be used to goodbyes, having made up her mind that learning to say farewell is the hope of any future that she can possibly have. But pain flashes unbearably around her heart while she absorbs his comfort. How beautiful he is – even down to the crude-cut mouth that seems to have been carved out of thick fruit.

'Well,' he says, at last, 'talk to you then.'

'Talk to you,' she murmurs. 'Walk good.'

She knows he will call when he arrives home.

Just so she knows he's safe.

She doesn't leave until the slightly battered Fiat – how could it make the journey to Kingston? but he would never get another, and perhaps it was just as well, with him leaving now – disappears around the corner between banks of shale, past the old standpipe and the guango tree with its roots twisted like mangroves, and then she turns slowly and goes back up the hill, ignoring the whispers that she can sense behind curtains. She calls to Miss Daisy and Maas Alton who have come out in their yards. They call back 'Howdy, Miss Maldene, yu tekking breeze? Yes, good night, Miss Maldene', but she can tell that underneath the everyday courtesies she is still to them a suspicion and a question sign. They are good, God-fearing people of a certain kind.

If they only knew what there really was about her to be suspicious of, she thought, smiling, a touch of malice on her mouth, where Jeremy had kissed her.

Inside the house she busied herself rehusbanding her few belongings into small spaces, as if they had been disturbed by

Jeremy's presence, putting her paintbrushes in turpentine to soak, uncovering the half-moulded clay model of his head on the dining table so she could look at him as she worked. It was only an image, and a fanciful one at that, but still it was better than his absence, and in wild contradiction its invocation of him brought her a measure of calm. It was only in her head she called him by his first name; to his face he was Ramsoran – which nobody else called him: his congregation called him 'Father' and his friends called him Ram. She was making his head and she needed to look at him as she worked, and yet she was tidying her house to tidy his presence out of it. With the dustcloth she was flicking outside clouds of disturbance he always left behind. Mixed-up, crazy woman, she spoke to herself, derisively. Mad-head woman. Not no guzzum woman. You of all people need to be set free.

There was not much housework left to do and she could not work on the sculpting – her thoughts were too disrupted. So she went to bed early, leaving the window wide open so that she could look out on the hill-and-gully ride behind the house where the peenie wallies' blinking interrupted the dusk and the sky hung already low, voluptuously weighted with stars. Her thoughts flickered like snake tongues: Jeremy, the children, Jeremy, the children, his going, the jail.

All of these things were plaited together, her mind turning in and out from one to the other.

It was strange, but she felt that perhaps if he had known her less well, if he had not known her story, it might have been easier for her to surrender the fight and marry him. But she felt that neither he nor she would ever be sure that she had not said yes simply to save herself, and she dreaded the thought of his feelings growing cold when he came to believe that she had merely been using him. Perhaps worse, she felt people would never forget that she had killed, and it would harm him, most particularly in his standing in the church.

Stranger still that she, who had never been healed, should now spend her life seeking to heal others, in spite of unbelief. She thought again of the children who routinely stoned her house, guzzum oomam come out, come out. It was a game, but under-neath, without them knowing it, they were also serious. Unbidden, the thought of her own child, of what he might have been if he had been allowed to live, came into her mind; she saw her life for a moment disembodied, as if she stood aside from it a spectator, and she saw him among the children of the district stoning her, guzzum ooman, come out, come out, eyes wide with apprehension and relish, unknowing, unaware of her as the earliest extension of himself or his life's possibility.

The child had been stillborn. The doctors said there was no connection between that and her frightened sixteen-year-old's frantic attempts to annihilate him with gallons of what she thought were abortifacient bushes – jackanna and chickweed and ramgoat national – boiled secretly in the night and mornings when she pleaded unwellness and stayed home from school in the silent house by herself, while her grandparents, unsuspecting, went to their work. She remained convinced that she had poisoned, if not flushed him out, or maybe strangled him, with all the bandages she had bound around her middle to hide him, or maybe both, and neither Jeremy nor the therapist had been able to convince her otherwise. She had felt, with the exigency of the unforgiving, that her life was a penance for his and, if anything, the calm integrity of spirit that she associated with her friend had not led her to trust him or his God, but to convince herself of her own stained set-apartness and inherent risk.

He had taken for granted that they would easily see each other again. 'Plane cross water' he had said; New York was only a plane ride away. But she was used to larger endings. She had killed. Not once, but twice, first at sixteen, and again, at thirty-two, exactly at the doubling of her age, which showed that the capacity was something in her and not an accident of youth's loneliness or terror. She had put paid to a woman who called herself her friend, and without compunction. When she first met him she had been in the jail, at Tamarind Farm, and at first for her, at that cynical time in her life, he had merely been the establishment official, the chaplain who did the rounds of the prisons, hawking his gospel of redemption to the unmovable unredeemed. Indeed, some of them had mocked him – she leading – singing, 'We shall not be moved!' But then he had become her friend. A man who seemed to have no respect for borders.

And in her own way, neither had she. This was the paradox that separated them. She had crossed impossible borders, made unspeakable breaches between continents of feeling and experience. His total acceptance made her feel guilty, where before she had felt justified. (The court, while not sharing her view, had felt there were mitigating circumstances; she had served only five years). But the advent of guilt linked this later action to the memory of the child, which she had fought all her life to forget.

After they let her out, she said she would go away where nobody knew her, where she could start over again, but more than this, where he was not. It pained her that he should be thought of as the priest who consorted too closely with murderers. She felt that here she could make expiation of a sort – the kind that demanded the ramification of boundaries, which he had set himself to breach.

She placed between them the stain of her own set-apartness and risk.

'Call me deportee,' she had once told him. 'There are some of us who don't need anyone to judge us, for we judge ourselves.'

He had been angry and distraught. 'So, would you do the same to me? Would you not have forgiven me?'

To this she had no answer. She thought not. And because it was so, she felt she could not love him, not now, not here, though perhaps in another time, but then she would have to be a different person altogether. As it was, she had no power to align herself alongside one such as he, whose large acceptance seemed to her to come from his own incapacity to do wrong. It would have been different if he had been a man who had sinned, who was without innocence. She could have embraced him then.

A man who always felt maimed, it stunned him that she should see him in this way; he could not understand. Striving, he said, 'But the power is not yours, Maldene, it comes from Another.' She thought vaguely that she would have liked to have his faith, but it remained to her a mystery – 'whose unfolding I think I am still waiting for,' she said, addressing the stars, and then, 'Gentil parfait knight. I think, though, I need a God who has sinned.'

At some point in the night she woke, sobbing, from a nightmare in which she went after Jeremy trying to call him back, but he could not hear. A long, futile journey in which she walked for mile after fruitless mile along a quayside littered with boats and flotsam bobbing on the water, Jeremy always two steps ahead of her, walking very fast, his face and body set with a dogged purposefulness like a sleepwalker's. It appeared to her that he was looking for someone, she thought it was her, she cried, Jeremy look, turn around, it's me, I'm behind you, but he could not hear. She lost him suddenly among the boats. She came upon a group of fisherman and said, 'Did you see a man pass this way?' They smiled and said, in the soft, admiring voices of men who like the look of a woman, 'Yes, dawta, him gone this way,' pointing to the left where the sea disappeared into the horizon. 'Him was walking after a girl, a nice pretty girl same as you.'

Waking, she wept briefly and violently. Wound in a tight cocoon, she stroked her body and said Jeremy, Jeremy, like a mantra, and slept fitfully, without dreaming.

He arrived in New York in the dead of winter, when there was no stain on the cold white sky but the pale promise of a rainbow.

STELE

When people started seeing things in the sky, the only person who wasn't moved was Aunt Stell. She had come over from Jamaica as a big woman and she had certain ideas.

'Warning,' she said, snapping the two sides of her mouth together as if fastening them with clips. And as we gazed at her expectantly, she opened them again to say, 'Too much wickedness on God earth. Brimstone and fire. Warning.' She snapped the mouth back together and would say no more.

But the expectation was fulfilled. Adele looked up from her writing in amusement. Touli and Brett snickered. Aunt Stell knew they had been baiting her but she didn't care.

Adele should have known better. You couldn't take everything Aunt Stell said seriously but she wasn't stupid. And all around us people were panicking. The hysteria rose to such proportions that there was a newspaper report of one whole town – inhabitants two hundred – taking off to keep vigil on a California beach saying they were going to wait for it there because it was the second coming. They were an extreme case, of course, but still there was a lot of speculation in the news and on the streets, and though most people didn't think it was apocalypse, most were worried simply because they didn't know what it was. NASA was watching it for scientific explanation, but so far they said it seemed to be just an unusual cloud formation.

Tony and Vas joked about how one time a coffin with two live johncrows paraded about Kingston for days, walking above ground, and nobody could figure out whose death or what it was. Tony and Vas were laughing because it was all a big hoax that somebody put on, through the newspapers to give it credence.

But this wasn't Kingston, this was New York and it wasn't 1940, it was 2003 and this thing wasn't a coffin, it was a riddle in the sky. And I, Lettie Binns, was as puzzled as everyone else.

I looked at Leeds' face to see what he was thinking there in his quiet corner, but his face was inscrutable. For a while I watched the lines grooved in his face without him knowing I was looking at him. I was the only one who knew what had happened to him. He hadn't wanted to spoil Christmas for the others. So typical of Leeds, I thought, my heart breaking. Another Makoni – guarding everyone else, risking himself.

I got up and went outside on the balcony to look and it was still there. Huge bat wings of a dirty gray-black spread out on the face of the sky so you couldn't see anything for miles. The thing looked both inimical and crucified. It hadn't moved in five days since the last change, when the writing appeared on the wings. The writing resembled Russian. But a Russian man who took a telescope and looked said no it wasn't Russian, because when he looked through the telescope it had disappeared; he didn't see anything – writing or wings. Some said Sanskrit. That too drew a blank. Finally a psychic was found who said it was the hurt of the world – which was what Adele was reporting when Aunt Stell snorted and said what she said.

Aunt Stell liked judgement while Adele's heart was towards pity, and that was why what the psychic said attracted her. The ancestor in our family that Adele wanted to be most like was Makoni.

Truth to tell, Makoni was the only ancestor we knew of in our family.

She had appointed herself, or been appointed, our protector. A teeny, tiny woman with most delicate hands. I had always imagined her tall and thin and sort of one-dimensional, wearing long calico skirts, like a slave woman in a daguerreotype. But she wasn't like that at all, when my aunt, whom we called the last aunt because she was the youngest of a line of about a hundred, described her. She was even light-skinned, not Africa-dark as I had imagined.

Her first appearance was to my great grandfather. Before he was married to my great grandmother, he was courting a woman in Four Paths, Clarendon, where he had travelled to from Rocky Point in Portland, looking for work. The woman's husband had just died. My great grandfather didn't know this; the woman wasn't wearing red under her clothes. So the dead husband, bitterly jealous, was visiting the woman at night.

My great grandfather stayed over at the woman's house one night, though his practice was to sleep in his own bed, even if the woman was sweet. But apparently this woman was above sweet, very sweet, and night caught him before he realized. She said, 'Why you don't stay? It too dangerous to walk out this time a night.' My great grandfather feared neither God nor machete man. But the woman was unusually sweet. So he stayed.

Late in the night the man came in the room, and he and my great grandfather wrestled. According to legend, my great grandfather was the strongest man in three parishes, but the man nearly killed him. At the point of his death, a woman appeared out of nowhere, chopped her hands crosswise, 'Pow Pow!' between them, quick sharp, and separated the two. She wrestled the man to daylight. My great grandfather went into a kind of trance until it was over. At the end she stood over him and took his hands in hers, which were like fleshed paper. 'Leave,' she told my great grandfather. 'And never come back here.'

The window was open, and my great grandfather said he saw the woman throw something like a rope of beads through the opening, and walk out of the room on it like it was a ladder. All this time the other woman, the sweet one, was asleep.

My great grandfather got breath back in time to call after the woman, 'Who you?'

'I am Makoni,' the woman said. 'I am your oldest cousin.'

For years my great grandparents trawled through the oral branches of his family tree, but could find no cousin called Makoni.

Seventy-five years later, the Bahamas aunt received a call from the last aunt, who had been adopted by strangers and taken to Canada at an early age.

'Who is Makoni?'

The Bahamas aunt, seized with the compulsion to piece out

narrative, called my mother in excitement. The last aunt's husband had recently died, and because she knew nothing of red panties, this one too refused to believe he was dead and would not leave his wife alone. The last aunt was tough as old leather, like her sisters, though they had grown up apart, and she put up a hell of a fight. But she remained convinced it was a fight she could not have won if a tiny, light-skinned woman, no more than five feet tall, had not appeared in the room and put the rabid man to flight.

'Who are you?' the last aunt cried.

'I am Makoni.'

'Makoni who?'

'You are safe now. Do not ask so many questions. I cannot stay to answer them. I have a long journey.' And she passed through my aunt's winter windows.

The aunt saw something flung against the moon like a ladder of rope, and had confused impressions of mingled bright colours and shadows like wings scrawled across the moon's face. She had no idea how this was possible since she lived in an apartment in Toronto with no skylight, and the windows closed night and day in the winter. Then my mother revealed to my aunt what she had told her own children fifteen years before. Makoni's visitations, she said, were always accompanied by signs: unseasonal rainbows (no rain), and sometimes the sign of a crucified bat. On the night she visited my great grandfather, the moon, turned a strange yellow-green, hurried madly through the sky, following him as he fled on midnight roads from the sweet woman's room, never to return.

I stood on the balcony for a long time staring at the thing, willing it to move. But it stood there like petrified rock, though in texture it looked like cloth. I imagined that it had been caked with something dreadful and then washed badly and hung out to dry with the stiff filth still in its weft. I think what worried me about it was that though it never seemed to move, it quite obviously did, maybe in some night silences when no one was awake (though isn't somebody always awake?), because twice at five day intervals we had woken up to find that it had shifted slightly in shape, though not in position, and the second time it had acquired this strange writing.

I wondered with dark excitement if it would change again tonight. Today was again the fifth day. 'I going stay up and watch you tonight if it kill me,' I told it, declaring war, and heard Leeds laugh behind me.

'You're very fierce, Miss Lettie ma'am,' he said. 'But there are certain things even in Nature that you cannot fight.'

'You think it's Nature?' I asked him idly, watching the thing.

'Don't you?' He gave me a funny look.

'I don't know what it is,' I said, sounding defensive even to my own ears. 'But I'm fascinated that so many people think it is not.'

He didn't answer that. Of late his face has grown more inward, more sad. From childhood, of all of us he had been the grave one, hardly sharing his thoughts, even with me, though the two of us had always been close. I have learned to read him by silence, the waves of his thought that I intuit from having been in his company so long. I reach up and catch them passing in the air. But tonight he is more distant from me, closed in on himself and the wrestlings he has had to wrestle with the thing that has betrayed him in his flesh. I look away, I don't want him to see me weep.

Suddenly Leeds said, 'Tell you what. I'll stay up with you tonight. See if anything happens – we can catch it.'

But we didn't. Catch it. And the thing stayed the same for the next five days and after a while people calmed down, in a brittle kind of way, and went about their business. NASA and the scientists still kept watch, doing their investigations. But the sky over New York stayed lowering and dark, and I felt, not Aunt Stell's judgement, but a great sense of sadness.

…..

It is strange how, when somebody remembers a thing, even a small piece of it, everyone else begins to recall other bits and pieces, until slowly a whole picture is made or a story told, matched like a bird's nest from fragments. And so it was at the big family reunion in New York, the year my illness was discovered. It was Christmas Eve, a huge fire had been lit, and two dozen or more members of the clan were sprawled around the blaze in various poses of stupefaction. Christmas had come a day early because some had to spend the next day with in-laws. So this

Christmas Eve the ham had been eaten, the sorrel drunk, the over-rich rum-filled cake sampled, and between the food and the fire, almost everyone was half asleep and more than a little dazed. Lettie, as usual, was the only one of us who still seemed more than half alive.

There had been a time when it would have been Lettie and me. Lettie and Leeds, the twin souls of the party. Now, watching her golden vivacity in the firelight, feeling my own life ebbing away in secret under my arm, I thought how far from that time I had travelled. I wasn't sleepy; I felt more like a ghost who had passed illicitly through material spaces.

In an effort to keep us all awake, someone called for stories, and the talk came to Makoni. Even I was surprised to learn how many she had visited in the interval between our great grandfather and the Canada aunt, which were the common stories that Lettie and I knew. It turned out that Canada had not been Makoni's first overseas flight – she had appeared at the death-bed of an uncle, Oscar, to 'help him cross over', according to the story told by Melina, Oscar's Guyanese wife. And this was in Birmingham, England.

My wound hurt rather badly, because of the cold. I sat in a corner, content merely to listen, but as I looked around at the figures sprawled, faces in various ways repeating bits of themselves across the room, I found myself suddenly smiling, thinking of Makoni and seeing her in a different light. As a child I had thought of her as a holy figure. But now I saw her as an aunt, and barely suppressed a laugh. In a family consisting of well over fifty persons in its immediate branches, nineteen were aunts. Powerful, mountain-breasted (Mount Everbreast, we nicknamed them), they descended like a flock of giant birds in any family crisis, took everyone in charge, swept through the situation like a hurricane, dealt with it swiftly and efficiently, and as swiftly and efficiently disappeared.

As a child I had seen them lifting off into the air like so many overweight ostriches, and thought they must be the only ostriches that flew or had cunning. In their wake a few feathers drifted down, all other signs of their coming swept by their wing beats from the scrubbed and shining yard – unless one counted a few broken bones or ears torn off and scattered where the aunts had twisted them.

This sense of having been dreadfully managed and beaten about was probably a small price to pay for the aunts' visitations. I think this was the conclusion we all came to, when everything had been taken into account. For whatever the aunts did worked – frighteningly, superbly. We dreaded and welcomed their coming, and breathed freely at their going. Lettie and I used to cling together after they had gone, shaking and exhilarated with longing and fright. Though Makoni's mission was in a sense the same, albeit she operated in another dimension, I had never before thought of her as an aunt, and I did so now probably because there were so many of them in the room and so many of their stories were circulating, like rum that made us all a little drunk. Still, even as I imagined her as one of them, she stood in a special place by herself, at the apex of a pyramid, and of course, not like any bludgeoning axe or crude rock edge, but rather a neat little rapier.

I liked Makoni. She had style. She knew how to make herself unobtrusive, even if she always seemed to leave her signature on the skin of encounters, saying, 'I am Makoni.' Though, to be fair, this was because the question was asked, 'Who you? Who are you?'

'But how the hell she get to Canada?' Sasha wanted to know. Her mother, Clarissa, an aunt, shot her the look that said, You may be in New York, young woman, but this is still a decent Jamaican household, so watch your language, Miss Ma'am.

Sasha pretended not to notice. 'I mean, seriously though. How do spirits travel?'

'I think she came on the plane. Leaked herself through the doorlocks like ink.'

'But how does she know where to go? Who tells her the address?'

'Telepathy, of course. She smells the cry for help.'

'And she probably listens in on conversations, reads people's letters. So she knows where everyone is.'

'Some of them are damn blasted out of order though, you know. They don't behave themselves.' This was Sasha again, refusing to meet her mother's eye.

'That one is true, boy. You remember the time Gramps came out of his grave in broad daylight and tried to steal Carib?'

That one I had seen with my own eyes. Carib is my brother. I was six years old. I remember screaming at the top of my voice, 'Mama, Mama, Gramps tiefing Carib, Gramps tiefing Carib!' and my mother running out of the house with a duster and a broom-stick, 'Let him go, you dirty rotten navel oul bazzat!'

That was a fight between them, papa! For a duppy, that old man could run! Their flight was headlong, a dizzying rush of movement like bad dreams represented in film. My mother managed to catch hold of Carib's hand just seconds before Gramps's shadow, a clear black outline like an invisible man, jumped into the grave and disappeared.

'Some of them are so blasted out of order,' Sasha repeated. 'In some ways it's a pity people aren't buried from home any more. Then you could plant the bitches. Pity they invented funeral parlour.'

'Young lady, it's all well and good for you to romanticize. You think washing, stuffing and dressing diabolus is any joke? You think anybody would have chosen to do it in the old days if they'd had a choice?'

'What's planting the bitches, Sasha?'

Aunt Clarissa nearly choked. The question came from one of the New York-born children, crouching for safety under his father's arm.

'Stick pins and needles in they foot bottom so they can't walk after they dead. And some of them, you have to cut out their trousers pocket or they throw stones, damage people.'

Sasha still wanted to know, stretching out the moment as though it was a philosophical question, how Makoni could board a plane and go exactly where she wanted, as if this was a normal thing where the dead lived.

'But it's really only like a door separating us and them, isn't it?' the Canada aunt finally said, since nobody else was answering Sasha, who had become querulous. 'I don't think it's all that different on the other side. I think when you get there, you go on doing exactly what you were doing when you were alive, until the day of judgment comes. So if you used to drink rum drunk, you would still be a drunkard, if you used to work over here, you go on doing that too; if you used to go to church, that's what you'll be doing there.' The Canada aunt is very pious.

Everyone laughed as if this was hilariously funny, but I thought of the cancer under my arm that the doctors thought could take me off any day now, and I thought of waking up on the other side to find I was still stuck in that dead-end job I had died, surely, in part, to escape – and I must confess I was a little shaken. I sat among the laughter and the chaffing for a while and then I put on my coat and went out on the balcony. I could hear the little silence that followed my departure, as if everyone was staring at the hole under my arm where the doctors had cut away my flesh, and wondering.

'Uncle Leeds is feeling hot,' the New York child said.

'Yes, Uncle Leeds is hot,' the mother told the child.

It was ok to let them think that way. The room was stifling, because we'd turned the fire up so high, trying to blaze away the winter.

On the stark balcony, scaled with ice, I found the cold's cruel fingers welcome on my face as I looked out over the snows and thought about my going. I was hardly twenty-five years old.

…

Lettie keeps telling me a different story. Lettie is the closest of my siblings to me, but even I sometimes can't figure her out. Lettie is ambiguous – somewhere in the process of growing up she got caught halfway between woman and child, and, since she never quite seemed to decide which to become, still hangs suspended there. Her speech and her laughter run between adult and child, and she still presents as truth things she has imagined. Men find her captivating, but worrisome. I wonder if she will marry. But Lettie is tough as any aunt, underneath. She can take care of herself. Now she insists that at that New York Christmas reunion there was Aunt Stell (though Aunt Stell died two years before) and moreover some big excitement about a big pair of bat wings that hung across the sky for days, acquired writing and then broke up into rainbow lights and began hurling itself through the sky like Aurora Borealis. She even says we both sat up one night watching to see how the thing secretly went through its changes, but we didn't see anything, just as no one saw the moment of the final change, though everyone saw its culmination. I have no memory of any of this, and frankly I am too tired to think where Lettie could have got it from. The end is coming soon and I'm thinking that I would like to travel a little bit more before it comes, though it is probably too late (Isn't it strange I've been to so many places but never Trinidad or Dominica or Guadeloupe or St Lucia or Montserrat – is there any more a Montserrat after the volcano?) and wondering who will be sent for me. Will it be Makoni? I think that what we all think about at the last is who will cross us over and please, for goodness sake, let there be something there, over on the other side, not the same tedious cycles that we have known.

In the morning, taking the train on a last ride to Connecticut, a short rumpled man in khakis smiles at me, 'Peace, brother.'

He looks as though he would say more, but I return his greeting perfunctorily and turn my face away. Perhaps, later, if he is still on the train, I think I might exchange a word or two, but for now I'm looking out the train window at that sliver of sky, thinking of Lettie's rainbows.

·····

A total eclipse of the sun drew thousands of sky watchers out of their homes between eleven a.m. and two p.m. yesterday.

At exactly 12:15: 08 p.m., the moon's shadow began to cover the face of the sun. The light from the sun slowly dwindled to a point as the moon moved over the last sliver. There was a moment of suspension, then suddenly the point went out and darkness descended as the sun's corona flashed momentarily into view, sparkling with jewel-like spurts of flame.

Lining beaches and roadways, standing on top of parked cars, trucks, buses and each other's shoulders, people in the crowds trained telescopes and pieces of darkened glass on the spectacle that lasted only just over seven minutes, yet had a profound effect on the course of Nature. Temperatures dropped below zero, cattle on a ranch in California stampeded, a man sat up suddenly in his bed and shouted 'Fire!' then fell back dead (no cause of death has yet been found) and a stare of owls was seen flying in broad daylight in Palm Beach, Florida. The sky was dark for the space of two hours but during this time an eerie light bathed the landscape; in the words of one bystander, 'as if the sun was rising and setting both at the same time.'

'It was awesome,' said Mary Levine from Fort Worth, Texas. 'I've never seen anything like it. It was like Aurora Borealis. My cat would not stop spitting. You could see he was disturbed.'

Total eclipses of the sun are rare, occurring no more than once every ten years over the entire earth. None has been seen in this city in the last hundred years. A total eclipse occurs when the moon passes completely in front of the sun, blocking out its light. Though the entire eclipse may last up to two hours, the actual complete eclipse, referred to as the Phase of Totality, lasts only a few minutes. In any one place where it is visible, it may appear for one minute or even less.

The next total eclipse that will be visible from this city will occur in 2051.

…..

Cruising at an altitude of 30,000 feet, Aliun looks down at the pages on which all these stories are written, and smiles. Strange to hear oneself spoken about in these ways, s/he thinks. Eaves-droppers truly hear odd things about themselves. But none of that is relevant, you know, Aluin says, forgetting Onyame's stricture not to be extravagant. Makoni, eclipses, science and scepticisms, beliefs, death and life, the veils between the other worlds and the living – in the end, it is me they are talking about, though they don't know it.

I will tell you the truth of how it happened, s/he says.

Onyame, the great Odomankoma, Onyankopon of your know-ing and not knowing, held colloquy in heaven, Zamani, the place of welcome. (You have travelled far, welcome; take off your shoes, welcome; here is a stool, sit; here is water, drink, pour wine, you are welcome; we will break bread, akwaaba, akwaaba, akwaaba). We always welcomed travellers, they who return with stories about the ways of men, and I grew curious, so that when it was decreed that someone should go to tell the new stories, because the old ways were changing, I was glad to say, Father of deities, Onyame Agyenkwa, here am I, O Lord, send me.

35

I say I volunteered, but whose will supersedes the Great Will?
I will re-tell the story. In the place of Zamani, in the heavenly places where colloquy was made, I was called upon to go to hear the myriad stories of the city's cry and make record. Nya akokooduro, you must go, Onyankopon aniwa hu asumasem biara. It is you, asomdwoee, it is on you the lot has fallen. It is written, Nokore, it has always been written. Here is the bowl, pour. Here is the staff, Yebehyia bio, go.

I took the staff, the sandals, and dived to survey the earth's deep. And that is how it happens that the first of the stories, this one that I am now telling, is mine, a tale full of chaos and replicating noise.

I must say they outfitted me bravely. For in that winter those who watched the skies looked up and said there was an eclipse of the sun; others said a shape like a great torn sheet or a great bat, a blackness of wings with talons, sprawled the sky and it was like and yet not like a hole jagged in the sky's surface; it was like and yet not like a covering redeeming a hole already torn in the sky. There was the excitement of science and telescopes and psychics and signs, but it was strange that, even so, few saw my coming or noticed my crucified face or the spread of my wings that stained the stenciled whiteness, few saw or understood the myriad ways of Aluin, God's sayer and sign.

For this I wept. Disappointment crusted my eyes, and I wept. On earth they said, 'Rainstorm, it rained.'

These issues from my first voyage of reconnaissance I brought back to Onyame in heaven.

'Something has gone wrong, Father of deities,' I said. 'Tears fall from my eyes. I fear I may be becoming human.'

'How so?' the Great One replied, hiding a smile, which I saw.

'Many of them did not see me. And when I tried to speak, to call to them out of the deep, they did not hear me. Tears have not fallen from my eyes before, Great Father. That is a human failing, not a failing of angels.'

'Your vanity is twice pricked. Dry your tears,' said the Great One, curbing as always the flick of my exuberance.

Extravagance, the Light said, refusing my choice of word. I was the Scribe of all scribes, and yet He always corrected my words.

'Your job is to make record. The rest belongs to Another. Now go and make a second reconnaissance, and listen.'

So Aliun again descended to earth and this time s/he listened. And s/he saw in that winter how the earth burned, so cold was the ice, and how the snows muffled hearts and made of every opened mouth a silence. But Aliun, with her/his ears now hearing, heard in that muffled sound ten million sounds, and each a thousand different sounds, and within each again a tale that it would take a thousand and one nights to unravel, and still they would be telling.

So Aliun wove a net of rainbows and caught within it all the stories of the great city, and s/he wove the net so that none of the stories could ever escape to be fully told and none could ever be delivered. And s/he took the net back to Odomankoma in heaven.

Odomankoma said, 'Good. You have done well. Now spread yourself across the firmament.'

Aliun spread her/himself between the poles of the firmament.

Onyame said, 'Now upend your net over the earth and pour out the stories.'

So Aliun poured them out.

And as their stories poured into my ears, my wings trembled and changed; the sound of quadrillions of words and questions and statements and angers and laughters and tears all seeped down through my tortured ears and recorded themselves on my wings in runes. Each story had its own colour so that my wings, once black, changed colour with each writing. People who looked up said, 'Look, the northern lights', but each colour and their running together was the sign of a shard in my spirit that I, Aliun, true form of Orunmila, muse of Mbaba Mwana Waresa, had been sent in this way to hear the stories of men and – ay, this is the rub – to weep their tears – such ignominy, Great One!

'Stop exaggerating,' Onyame said. 'Take your wings and tear them into pieces, one by one, and scatter the pieces over the face of the earth.'

So Aliun scattered them. And as s/he scattered them some pieces were trampled under people's feet and were lost, and others were rubbed out in the rain, and others snagged in the hair and open hands of those who looked up saying 'Rainstorm is weeping, is weeping', and yet others fled into the sea, where they became history.

And those who had caught the pieces in their hands and hair lost their eyes and became blind and began to search inwardly, tearing themselves, mistakenly thinking that the eyes had gone within them, and then at last, broken and maimed, they sat down in wayside places and began to try to decipher the runes with Onyame's help. Some were deciphered and some were not, as Onyankopon gave them grace, or not. Out in the distance fishermen with seaward eyes began to trawl the deeps where the greater runes had fallen, looking for history.

'Those who seek, will find,' Odomankoma said. 'Aliun, you have done well.'

This is the story of how stories came to earth. And how these tales of cities, caught in a single crooked hair, were half-written, maimed, and failed to be written:

MACÓNÉ, MACÓNÉ
or
Of Age and Innocence

Bus draws up with a screech; this driver drives like he's mad.
Glam girl hops on bus, looking like she knows she's not looking
bad. Spoils the look. Parades in front, tossing long hair made in
Taiwan. Driver drives fast, glam girl keeps slipping and stagger-
ing. Glam girl scoots on stiletto heels across bus floor, falls
abruptly on old man's lap, old man staring out of window with
empty eyes. Old man turns and looks at glam girl in his lap with
beadbright glaze. Glam girl mutters in chagrin, leaps up like
scorpion bit her, sits in empty seat in front of old man.

Old man's eyes start to look funny, all tender and lost. Gets up
and sits in elderly and disabled seat beside glam girl and his face
begins to smile a funny-looking smile. Looks straight into glam
girl's face but glam girl does not smile back, stares old man down
but old man isn't fazed, surveying glam girl up and down like a
picture he's making up his mind whether to buy or not to buy.

Woman in back of bus starts muttering, mutter is rising to a
growl. Woman must be Jamaican, only big fat Jamaican woman
make big noise in public when they see thing in foreign people
country they do not like. Other people know to keep quiet. Bus
is nervous, pretending not to see or hear. Black American and
Latino and American-White people mind own business but
dying to see and hear all. Bareface Latino man grins, the creep.
Glam girl changes her seat, old man follows her, smiling, eager
now, his face all lit, saying 'Macóné, 'Macóné.' Old man's voice
is tender, like girl and word is flowers that can bruise. Holds out
withered old hand to girl.

39

Muttering woman begins to bawl, 'Dirty oul bazzat, lef the young chile alone!'

Don't know why fat Jamaican woman behaving like that, because old man is not looking at girl in a bad way, he's looking like he's recovered a gift that was lost, beautiful-tender all at once.

Tall girl in back in dreadlocks and multicoloured headband rings bell, bus screeches to a stop; tall girl gets up, gives old man fierce hot look like compelling prayer. Old man follows tall girl off bus. Bus screeches on.

Mad Jamaican woman still screeling, 'Dirty oul bazzats!' Tall girl can see her mouth moving through the bus window, face screwed up as if spitting.

Tall girl's eyes are glazed and frightened. Old man walks looking backwards, smiling epiphany into memory of glam girl's face.

Off the bus, Grandfather, my Dado, walked ahead of me almost running, putting his weight on his good leg and dragging the hip-shodded one along like a heavy parcel. He stumbled on a pile of dirt by the sidewalk where the road was being mended, and then he began walking like an old man again. When I caught up with him he turned his head and looked at me as if I wasn't there. I felt that if I went up close and looked in his eyes, my image would not appear on his eye-baby. There would be nothing of me or anything else in there.

I wanted to take his arm and say, 'Come, Dado,' but I knew I would humiliate him forever if I did, so I walked wordlessly beside him until we came to the front door of Ta Lizzbet's house in Silver Spring, Maryland, USA.

My twelve year-old me shivers in and out of mind, filtering memoried fragments of self that coalesce again here, broken and clutched for safety. *Dado, Dado, it's me in here, Maxine...* When I'm scared or frightened and don't want to face things I make up stories like I'm watching a play or a movie and the person in it isn't me. It's a game I learned from Dado, my grandfather. (A knight is everything I've seen in my grandfather, and if I marry it will be to my grandfather's clone).

The childish habit remains. I still make up stories in another language, another voice. It will structure this story in ways I hope you'll understand.

....

I will tell you about my little brother. Emile fought incessantly at school when we first came here. Emile is an albino and when Ta Lizz said we were migrating I trembled for him, because I knew how much he had suffered on account of his colour. In his thirteen years, he had lived through a cycle of life like an old man before people would leave him alone, and now, in a strange, inhospitable country, he would have to do it all over again.

But Emile is surviving. He said, Maxine, I didn't fight over my colour, I decide long time, never again I going fight over my colour, for why? No dat deh skin mi haffi live inna fi di res a mi life? So my little brother, an old man at thirteen, fought not because of his colour, but because 'they' were rude about his country, about which 'they' knew nothing. I understood, without his explaining, that he fought over things that he thought he might lose by being here – above all, things like home.

Emile the joker, face backwards, mimes the first two fights, playing himself from the outside as he has been taught by Dado, the best of storytellers. The white boy said, grinning, 'Is it true that where you come from people live in trees?'

'Sure,' Emile said, smiling. 'And Sue has the biggest tallest tree.'

'Who's Sue?' the boy asks, puzzled.

Emile's albino eyes open wide wide, a sea of russet brown. 'You mean to tell me you so civilized and you don't know your own people? Sue is your ambassador to my country, man.'

Boy number two, black American from Silver Spring Maryland, boy of encyclopaedic knowledge, waving newspaper with feature on Bob Marley's anniversary, asks, 'So what is it like living in the shanty town capital of the world?' Emile doesn't know any shanty towns but he fights the boy anyway, trying to get Ta Lizz to send him home to Brown's Town, St Ann, Jamaica.

Instead, Ta Lizz answers the principal's summons to visit the school twice in one week, her face hard and set with terror (still life: cassava in black), and though my heart has long closed itself against

41

her, I find that her terror is also mine. Emile stops speaking, sitting many days on the edge of his bed as if the bed belongs to someone else, and Ta Lizz genteelly snarls and curses, trying to bully him into speaking so she will know he's not about to die on her.

She isn't the only one who thought that he would die. I did too. But the fall came and Emile went to senior high school after having been kept back a year, repeating grade eight – the Intake Centre director unmoved by Ta Lizz's outrage. 'No ma'am, I'm afraid we don't do it like that here. Gifted he might be, but no, not senior high, he's too young.' Placing children, especially boys, outside of their age group created too many problems for the county to solve.

Emile is unbothered. 'What you so upset for? I'll just breeze through because I know all the stuff aready.'

Emile wears his brightness like familiar clothes; school is a swop, the debt he pays to society so long as he can be left alone to do what he really wants, his carvings, his computer experiments, his researches into bizarre facts he finds in the books he devours.

Emile speaks down-South now like a native, and I almost caught him once with his pants down below his bum – like a native. At home that kind of dress is unacceptably low class and for that Ta Lizz would have killed him if I had not, though my objection is not to the low class thing but to the association with jail – your pants falling down because the warders took your belt away in case you hanged yourself or somebody else with it. Dado's strictures, 'What you practise to say is what you are, what you practise to wear is what you become,' filter out of my mouth into Emile's ears; he pulls his pants up to his waist. Like me, he knows he can't let Dado down. He understands that by proxy now I guard the ways for Dado, and I'm grateful to my brother for allowing this.

He has made friends, two Americans called Myron and Baal, boys who come home with him from school. I tell myself Emile will be fine, though my stomach twists in anxiety about him, even now.

…..

Macóné.

Macóné was our grandmother's name. She died young, after our mother, Ta Lizz's younger sister, was born. Dado says she was the most beautiful woman ever born, more beautiful than the moon and stars rising, than flowers when the rain is young.

The photographs that he has of her are faded and sepia. She does not look like the girl on the bus. She is neither glamorous nor pretty. She has high hard bones in her face, hard sharp eyes, a turban like a balm-yard Madda, and a prim smile. You feel she's doing her best to hold her true self in check, wary of the camera because she's not quite sure what it's up to, and that the smile is trumped up for the occasion.

When Dado met her she was a serious activist in the AME Zion church in Morant Bay, St Thomas, and had already preached once in America.

……

Is Emile bring it to Ta Lizz attention that Dado getting worse. Or not so much Emile, but Emile's shame. Ta Lizz standing in the kitchen having a fit of silence, Emile standing in front of her looking miserable and resolute. I say evening, Ta Lizz, evening Emile, and then I ask what's wrong.

Ta Lizz turn her face to the stove. 'You ask this boy,' she say, an her voice swell up with a vex she can't keep in so she turn around again and burst out, 'According to him, he not going for his grandfather again no evening, even if he is the first to get home.' She haul a pot from the bottom cupboard and bang it in the sink, and when she turn on the cold water over it the spray fly. 'So apparently, Maxine, any day you can't go, Dado must sleep in the street till Bertie and me come home all hours a night or morning.'

I turn to Emile and try keep my voice quiet so as not to antagonize him after Ta Lizz done pressure him like uptown Ole Higue. I say, 'What happen, Emile? Why you don't want to go for Dado?' and Emile just standing there looking miserable.

'Is not that I don't want to go for him. Is just that –'

'– You don't want to go for him,' Ta Lizz finish the sentence for him, with an ironic look on her face.

Emile say, 'Ta Lizz, it just too embarrassing. Ah tired of being

43

embarrassed on the bus. Ah jus feel bad! That's all. Ah jus feel bad.' Beyond that, Emile won't speak.

The conversation continues around the dinner table. Dado is in his room. It's a while since he ate with us.

Ta Lizz say, 'What you mean embarrassing you. How can your grandfather be embarrassing you. You shame of your old people or what, since you turn American?'

Emile's blood boil up like wine in him albino face. 'Don't call me American, don't ever call me American, ever, you hear me, Ta Lizz? Ever!'

Crisis nearly precipitate; the boy rude!

But even Ta Lizz realize this is time to tread softly. And funny enough is not me, but Mr Burton, Ta Lizz's stooge husband, Mr Burton who never display a assertive bone in him body, who, hearing the situation, refuse to set Emile free till Emile break an tell him the truth. Emile says on the bus today, Grandfather was looking at a girl funny, embarrassing the girl. Mr Burton finds this unsatisfactory, wants more, but Emile will not speak further. He turns away.

I excuse myself from the table and go outside. The evening sky is clear as crystal, lemon yellow and pale blue. It has the restless openness, the artificial feel of over-extended daylight. In a while it will be summer and the nights are falling later, so that it seems sometimes daylight will never end. It's one of many illusions we live with in this place every day.

It's the first time I am realizing that what happened on the bus that day was not a one-off, a fluke presentation of the it-could-have-shown-itself-in-a-million-other-ways variety, but some kind of syndrome that centred itself around women and Dado's memories of the past, particularly our grandmother, Miss Macóné, Miss Ma'am, all her titles – Miss and Miss repeated again, Miss Ma'am – a sign of the respect in which she was held by everyone who knew her. My grandfather didn't just want to go home, he wanted to go back to some still centre of memory that had been disturbed almost from the day we boarded the Air Jamaica flight out of Kingston to Baltimore. I resented Ta Lizz more than ever but I felt a niggling fear that it could not have been prevented, that it wasn't just what Ta Lizz had done in uprooting us but maybe what the American doctor had said, that Grandfather was getting old. But would it have happened so fast if we had been at home? I whisper the question to the skies, and give my own clear answer, no, because a clear answer means more than not absolving Ta Lizz, a clear answer means Dado can be cured.

All that summer after we arrived, Emile and I had tried to get him to come with us on our excursions round the city, but he always refused, preferring to stay in the sun by the window of the room he had been assigned, reading his books, listening to the radio, occasionally fingering his shell and Emile's carvings, looking out on the passing street. Sometimes he walked in the neighbourhood to catch the early morning air or the late evening sun, exercise his legs and see, he said, what America and his wife looked like.

He took his walks alone. I often wondered what he saw through the window: Brown's Town orange-ochre and green with its white bleached houses under the waking sun, the slow crawl of traffic and the morning sounds of people calling greetings? Or what was before his open eyes: Bradford Road, Silver Spring Maryland, with frail brick houses looking like they would blow away in a strong wind, their doorways never open (why are doors always closed in white people's countries?), all the year long? Did he see people of every race and tongue and kindred walking around, sometimes calling out from the upper windows of the houses to their children going to school, *Tomas, tiene tu chaquete; La Raine, come back for your lunch*, and the teenagers gathering between the rows playing loud music or messing around in the front but segregated, black with black and latino with latino (the few whites had no children), the whole place like a bunch of stripes held apartheid in parallel unmelding lines?

We were relieved when he started going farther afield, taking the bus into town. Until the night the police brought him in at one a.m., saying they found him at Rhode Island Shopping Centre unable to recall his name or address. They searched for him because of Ta Lizz's 911 call when we waited till eleven o'clock and he hadn't returned. It was then the doctor diagnosed old age, said Dado was going senile.

It is not unusual for people to get confused from old age; old age is that kind of disease, he (the doctor) said.

Emile and I were at school (I at university, the city's top HBCU, my aunt boasted to her sister Gretel, purely out of malice because Aunt Gretel's daughter Ann, who was born in the USA, wasn't so fortunate and had had to make do with one of the more mediocre schools).

Ta Lizz and Mr Burton almost lived at the dollar store they were trying to get started.

We could not keep him locked up in the house and he refused to be watched by a carer.

We reached a compromise in which he promised to stay in agreed safe places.

We learnt to find him in the evenings at certain haunts between the Metro station and Rhode Island Avenue, which had a mysterious fascination for him – was it the thought of islands? He seemed to like combing the same places, as if whatever he was looking for wound itself around and around, like a snail-shell, in a spiral tight and close to where his journey began.

I want to go and get the pills – the ones the American doctor gave my Dado for depression – and throw them away, but I know I can't. All I can do is resolve that Emile will never have to fetch him again. I'll start coming back from the library earlier, so I can find him in the first evening light and Emile can go and play his computer games with his friends or do his carvings if he wants, anything so long as he gets to become a boy again.

.....

My grandfather remembers things that never were. There was a time when he told us the history of things. Then, there was nothing he couldn't remember, exactly as he saw it then. And though he was the best of storytellers, he never got fiction and fact entangled, until now.

.....

When we lived in Brown's Town, St Ann, Jamaica, Ta Lizz ran a supermarket. The shop did well: in a quiet, small town, competition was comfortable, and Ta Lizz was cold-bloodedly efficient. We had our own house, Ta Lizz and Mr Burton drove their own cars, and if there was anything you needed that could not be had in Brown's Town you either drove into Kingston or Ochi, or some people like Ta Lizz flew to Miami.

Ta Lizz said we had to leave or lose our green cards, and Mr Burton said yes. So it was decided. Mr Burton was the kind of man who never had any say in his own house but made a lot of noise in rum bars about useless men who allow woman to run things. (Since we arrived he has been silent).

My aunt had arranged for us to get our green cards through her sister, Aunt Gretel, who is a *citizen* (this is how they all, people like my aunts, say citizen, in italics, meaning *America understood*, in the same way the unspoken subject 'you' is understood in an imperative sentence) – a *citizen* and lives in Maryland. A lot of money had been paid for these cards, and we could not put all our eggs in the fragile basket that was Jamaica. Better to put them in an oil rig.

All our lives, my aunt has prepared for imagined contingencies. Under Ta Lizz's jurisdiction, we do not run out of anything, we always buy in bulk and replenish long in advance. But also at home there was always this feeling among a certain kind of people that you would eventually go away, and such people asked, 'Have you got your green card?' or 'Have you got your visa?' as if a green card or a visa was something you owned that was kept in a safe place for you and when the time was right you would go and collect it.

My twelve year old me opened my eyes very wide and said, 'Which visa?' I wanted them to be very specific because there were as many visas as there were countries and there was no one visa that I should have or indeed any visa that I wished to have at all. It was all so ridiculous – if I wished to go somewhere, then I would go, but how was a visa something that I should possess, like a diploma or a permit to live?

I did not know then that later, here in America, I would face over and over the question, 'Are you from the islands?' and that I would open my eyes wide at people with a different question, 'Which islands? There are many islands, which "the islands" do you mean?' I didn't know either that people who were also from 'the islands' would ask me the same question in a fashionable kind of way and that, because of that question from people who were also from 'the islands', I would come back to the house in Silver Spring and cry into my pillow, longing for home.

In all the time we've been here, I've never called this place home. I say, in my head, *not yet, but soon, soon*, when people ask me 'Are you going home now?' and out loud I say, 'I'm going to my aunt's house in Silver Spring' because I know that this place, and not Jamaica, is where they mean.

When Ta Lizz got the green cards and people asked, 'Have you got your visa?' I was ashamed.

My grandfather tells us, Emile and me, the history of things that we knew but could not have explained before he explained them. He says *it*, this hunger for migration, this *unsteadiness of spirit* (these are Dado's exact words), is not the same as the spirit that governed other migrations before; *it* stems from the seventies when many people ran away because there was CIA in the country; we were friends with Cuba and CIA said we would become communist. If you hadn't known it before, it is only when Dado says 'CIA said' that you realize the CIA is not a disease but an active speaking agent of some kind.

An plenty people did believe dem an fraid. Bag a man – an ooman too – leff, pack up dem tings an sweep out like hurricane, gone a Merica. From then, some people live as if there was always something terrible round the corner, waiting, like an enemy or a disease. Others were made restless from the constant toing and froing that the migratory commuting opened up, like a great unshuttable door between America and our country, pouring people in and out on an invisible assembly line until it became as easy for some people to say 'I am moving to America' as to say 'See you later.' When the turmoil of the seventies died down, many tried to return and couldn't, because they had sold off all their property cheaply and those who now owned it were asking prices the would-be returnees could not afford to pay, even in their wildest madhouse dreams.

Statements like these were the frequent coda to the daily lessons by which Dado tried to teach us to value our country, which we already loved. My twelve-year-old me dreams in the sound of my grandfather's voice, his palm rubbing the plaits of my hair that fly up instead of lying down every time he takes his hand away. I am proud of my grandfather's knowledge, and our lineage. Dado's father was a Garveyite; Dado himself a diehard socialist and a fan of Michael Manley. Ta Lizz says his view is biased; Michael Manley ran the country into the ground. I decide to stick with my grandfather's version. I cut my eyes at Ta Lizz.

I grew up at my grandfather's feet learning everything that was counter to whatever Ta Lizz, my surrogate mother, tried to teach me. Ta Lizz was interested in elite schools and money. I dismissed her as a social climber. Dado's task was easy because I loved him fiercely with a fire that was equal only to the fire with which I did not love and despised my aunt. Dado taught us like he was running out of time and had some sacred mission to fulfil. He was a retired headmaster to whom we listened out of respect and because we felt pain for him, a headmaster without a school, a teacher without students; what else was there in life left for him? But soon we listened because we were compelled by his love for his country – deep and purple like star-apple – and his fire. (It was at Dado's feet that we learned that Emile, coming softly out of his chrysalis cloths, was a genius. Dado taught him to read when he was two).

I can never forget the look on Dado's face when Ta Lizz made her announcement at the dinner table that Sunday afternoon. One dead silence descend. Dado swallow hard pon the rice and peas in him mouth; you coulda see him cheeks and then him throat going up and down, like small earthquake lick him in there, and then him get up from the table slow an wander off outside, wid him face look vague and preoccupy. Even from then him did frail. We just sat there with our breath hold tight, expecting him to collide into some piece of furniture and fall down. I don't know why we thought that, because, despite him frailty and the hip-shodded hip and him dimmed eyesight, Dado was not a man to buck up in anything; him walk straight and true as razorblade. Him didn't buckup, him didn't fall down, him go out on the verandah and sit down in him rocking chair and we sit there watching him through the two leaf of the front door. Me and Emile let out wi breath 'fffff'. Mr Burton clear him throat 'hrrmm, hrrmm.'

Ta Lizz brusque. 'Dado old, mi know, him reach the age where him don't like move, is so old people stay.' Nobody say anything.

'Him wi get use to it and come right round. Clearly we can't leave him here,' Ta Lizz add, as if debate going on.

All my life I was going to do history and linguistics at UWI and I wanted to say, 'I'll stay behind. Dado and I can stay together.' But I didn't have the courage to be responsible for the old man on my own. He needed kidney dialysis twice a week – suppose something worse happened to him without warning? Not to mention the fact that I wasn't going to risk Ta Lizz looking inna mi face an putting mi down in that disrespectful way she had. 'You playing big? You really think you can live by yourself without a adult to look after you?'

But I *am* an adult, I said in my head to an imaginary Ta Lizz, in my coldest English. I am of voting age. And yes, I can live alone, in fact it would be a welcome relief, away from all this. But I know you'll take Dado with you and I couldn't live with myself if I abandoned him in that way. I said that in my heart, yet every day since Dado became ill I have been making it up to him for abandoning him, for not having the courage to say 'No, Ta Lizz, I not going.' I know Dado agreed to come here because of Emile and me – so he wouldn't lose us, so we wouldn't lose him.

'There are good universities in Maryland and DC,' Ta Lizz went on, as if I had spoken. 'With your academic record, and your SAT scores, you can easily get into any of them.' (She had forced the SATs on me and I was pissed shitty but Dado said I should do them so I did, contemptuously, and passed). And of Emile she said (Emile waiting there with a 'what about me' look on his face, picking his nails furiously under the table in that way he had when he was overexcited), 'You are at just the right stage. By the time we are ready to leave you will just about have finished grade nine so you can go straight into senior high.' It was one of the few mistakes of fact Ta Lizz ever made.

Before we left I took the bus to Puerto Seco and watched the sun sink low into the Caribbean Sea in a blaze of red and gold and finally, at the last minute before it went out, leaked silver and a haze of white that flattened in the water. I combed the beach and put sand, shells and a sea urchin in my bag. For Dado I took a big conch with pink inside markings and, deep in its whorls, the sound of the sea. My things sit on the window sill of the bedroom in Silver Spring, Maryland that I have been given to stay in (the sand poured into the cup of each shell). Dado's is too big for the window sill of the bedroom where he stays, so I put it on the chest of drawers, where it is flanked by the carved wooden figures of Brown's Town people that Emile makes for him from time to time.

Ta Lizz said we could throw a party to say goodbye to our friends but Emile and I said no. But in my own way I said *au revoir* to the sea and the sands and the lights of Brown's Town winking in the night, and when my friend Skye said, 'Will you write, call, will you miss me,' I did not reply. Such conversations are for people who are going away. I was not going away. I was merely turning my back.

.....

There is a boy. A long narrow American boy with hips like horses and a smile like some oversize light bulb – a down-South niggerboy's smile into which the lower half of his face impossibly disappears. Near up, he smells of something uncomfortable and Monsieur Jovan. I looked to see where he wore his pants and they were properly up, though his flanks seemed to shed them.

He is not a boy to whom I will speak.

We are in the same Caribbean history class at school – the city's kaleidoscope in miniature, its strict unmelding bars of colour and place and race, of who is American and in, and who is not and out – in a crisply shining blue-and-white classroom of plastic chairs, steely light and multi-coloured-black.

It is here that I learned how much my grandfather lived in the past and in places of memory that were only desire, long before his mind started reeling back to Macóné, Macóné. My grandfather spoke to us of Harlem, of Claude McKay and Langston Hughes meeting like equal men, of Caribbean fighting alongside American, each sharing what they knew to free each other's minds: Amy Jacques and Marcus Garvey, Martin Delaney, Sylvester Williams sharing black American space with W E B Dubois, and the other way round, too: Moses Baker, George Lisle inspiring Sam Sharpe in St Thomas, Jamaica, Nanny's roots – for Nanny was a St Thomas woman – my grandfather's father, and Macóné…

In that crisply shining blue-and-white classroom, glam girls looked at me with suspicion, with hate. You *natives from the islands*

51

think you are so it, so bright, so what are you doing here, if it was so great back there? Professor on first day of Caribbean history class, Advanced Seminar 1, criss-looking dougla lady with Trinidad in her voice, says write down or draw what comes to your mind when you think 'Caribbean'… Tears come to my eyes, seeing through the window Brown's Town orange-ochre green and white under the sleeping sun, the slow crawl of traffic and the morning sounds of people calling greetings, walking. Professor polls the jury, everybody saying sun, beach and palm tree, sun, beach and palm tree, shanty town and paradise, o my el dorado, crime and poverty, no problem, mon. Fat girl with smirking face glitters her eyes over at me – gives very long answer – let me read you. I spent a week in an all-inclusive in the Bahamas and I saw a lot of things, let me read you, service, servitude; it's what they depend on, service, the service industry, all they have, servitude, unequal access; do you know, people bleach their skins there, ashamed of their black. I wondered how that could be (as she says that, I see in my mind's eye the jars of bleaching cream in the black cosmetics section in the Giant supermarket, all made in the USA, or made in China for the USA, for American black people; don't they use them then?)… The girl hasn't finished. Let me read you: poor English, ignorance, and oh, mangoes; I saw for the first time mangoes, which I liked – so much juice!

Professor exclaims, Ah so much! So much!

Fat girl smiles happy; because I am an anthropology major, it is easy, if you know what to look for, you know.

Ah anthropology, of course, of course, professor's voice marvellously polite, too polite, hiding-gliding Trini picong like crab walking sideways… How you wrote the book on the Caribbean, all in one week, in one island of one country, in one hotel, oh my Lord!

Someone snickers – long boy with the hips like horses; fat girl bristles, bucks, rereads professor's tone of admiration, now slow-learning Trini picong, looks furious, mad, vex, refuses to speak for rest of session.

In the night, tall girl with dreadlocks throws up in bathroom basin remembering these stupid colonized black-white people with whom she has been lumped in school and hates her aunt the more.

No, he is not a boy to whom I will speak. He snickered and made fat girl furious; when his turn came he said I haven't myself been to the Caribbean but I have friends from there and I would love to go. Boy with hips like horses smelling of Monsieur Jovan and something uncomfortable keeps looking at me with warm secret eyes but I look away. I want no connections with this place, which pre-reads me by its own withered signs and has destroyed my grandfather by secret routes I do not know.

When it was my turn to be polled I told the professor I would pass.

.....

I do not know what to do so I begin to pray. I don't know if God will hear me because I haven't been to church since we came. But I try anyway. I figure I can't be any wickeder than I was when I went screaming rebellion to Ta Lizz's high society church in Brown's Town, my face set against both church and my aunt.

I kneel down by the bed but instead of praying I find myself bawling and I bawl till my face becomes a watermelon and for days my eyes are dry like salt.

But it look like the prayer-bawling work. Tonight Dado is better, my grandfather is almost himself again. For days he has been in this lucid spell. I am sitting with him in the room he has been assigned in Silver Spring, Maryland, he by the window from where he looks into space and me on the floor at his feet, and I'm teasing him, 'So Dado is what so fascinating in the street?'

It was a game we played, when he was well. Sometimes he answered, sometimes not. 'Life, child, life,' he'd say, and I'd say, 'Well, so long as is just life then, and not some new girl you find prettier than me,' and he would say, smiling, 'Where I go find girl prettier than my one dou-dou' and sometimes, 'So what you do wid yuself today?' stroking his palm to and fro on my locks, which bent momentarily and then flew up again the moment his hand lifted its pressure.

I start telling him about the day at school, making it up funny and lying to make him laugh. Emile's feet pound up the stairs in a rush, followed by his head a minute later stuck in through the door. 'Hi Grandfather, how ya doin?' Since finding friends, this boy is getting more and more black American.

Grandfather looks at him smiling, as if the sight of Emile's stretching limbs and windblown face makes him glad. 'Better for seeing you. But is when you going to stop battering the house down with them big running foot you have there? You auntie going have to put Goodyear tyre on you foot to keep up wid you.'

Emile laughs. The sound is happy in the narrow house. 'Got somep'n for you, Grandfather.' He comes into the room, bringing the feel of fresh boy and scattering energy everywhere, and of course I can guess what it is he is hauling out of his hopelessly convoluted pocket, another carving to make Dado laugh: Maas Joe Guthrie riding him mash-up horse with the gutter in her back so deep it look like Maas Joe sitting in a dugout between two banks.

Emile brings his cards and we play kalyuki and uno until Grandfather begins to look tired and we gather up the cards and the rest of the night saying, *Chups, love you Dado, goodnight. Sweet Dado, goodnight, goodnight....* I long for the days when he talked to us about Marcus Garvey and Amy Jacques and showed us how to play different faces, jonkunnu slipping in and out of roles that made us die with laughter, the way the Trinis on the university campus back home made us whoop when at carnival time they played mas and Emile and I went to look. But he seemed content to listen to the stories of our day and to smile at Emile's chatter and pass his hand occasionally over my hair, Emile's hair, and I hoped that God had heard my prayer and that somehow, in some helpless way, we were saving him.

.....

'Hi. Going my way?'

It's the boy from the class, his hips moving like brown horses, his shoulders blotting out a lot of space. Tall girl's hackles rise, a familiar feeling now. Boy sits at back of class with sideways turn of long body, too long to hold comfortably in blue plastic chair, doodling instead of writing notes, and looking at tall girl as he draws. Class after class.

'Don't know, since I have no idea what your way is. But if I am, believe me, it's purely accidental,' tall girl says in high English.

Tall boy mock-flinches, but faint heart never won fair lady. Tall boy backs up, stalls, comes back forward, 'Ouch! You pack a rough one, lady.'

Tall girl quickens pace, trying to outwalk boy. 'Oh yeah? Depends on what you're used to, boss-man,' tall girl volleys back, striding. But tall boy has long strides, hips like horses.

Tall boy grins light-bulb, down-south, nigger-boy smile, whole southern end of face disappears in sargasso smile. Tall boy says, showing impossible dimples, 'I guess. Used to feisty girls, but none quite so – direct.' Tall boy seems to choose words with care, scared of unleashing unexpected. Thought pleases tall girl. Tall girl smiles.

'Always a first time for all of us,' tall girl says.

'So it seems,' boy says. Tall girl not looking into boy's face but can feel boy grimacing. Boy stops abruptly, so abruptly tall girl almost bumps into boy. Holds out hand, saying, 'Hi, I'm Kurt, Kurt Kennedy.' Hand so unexpected tall girl takes it, then drops it fast like hot potato, feeling outplayed. Long warm hand, and firm, not limp kind of man's hand tall girl hates.

'Hi.' Tall girl keeps on walking, brusque like aunt.

Boy steps in tall girl's path. Bends head low and looks up in tall girl's face, looking comical, teasing. Face screwed up like in disapproval, but eyes smiling. Tall boy sexy as damn hell. Tall girl drops gaze, refusing. Tall boy insists, laughing, 'I'm Kurt. You heard that? Kurt.'

Tall girl seething. 'Heard you. Heard you the first time. Heard it in class a hundred times.' Tall girl has to stand still, boy blocking path. Tall girl vex as hell, because eyes lowered look coy and shy when tall girl wants eyes-lowered to mean, I don't want to look at you, scat.

'Oooooh, so you did,' tall boy mocks in exaggerated drawl of surprise. Half-straightens up so fast and sudden tall girl jerks head up in quick avoidance and collides with eyes so wide open and deep and shocking, like jolt from electric wire.

'So then, now that we've established that you heard, can we start all over again?' Boy straightens up and holds out hand. 'Pleased to meet you, Kurt,' tall boy prompts, like a cue in a play.

'You think you're irresistible, don't you?' tall girl snaps, ignoring hand.

Smile fades, like light on computer screen slowly going out after shutdown. Boy goes still, says quietly, 'We're in the same class. What's the big thing about saying hi? Is this how you island girls are?'

Are you *from the islands*? You're *from the islands* aren't you? In a thousand shops, fast food joints, Kinko's. Which islands? Is there such a place on the map?

Tall girl sees red. Tall girl ribbits, just like how madwoman ribbit in Jean Breeze Madwoman poem 'Riddym Ravings', step back, step forward, earth shake, earthquake, sprout horn, dreadlocks stark and stiffen like black tornado, like puffed out porcupine quill, thunder roll, earth black, ball of fire explode on tarmac, blue lightning zigzag flash, sky shatter. All of this go on in tall girl head, whole of HBCU resound with tsunami sound. Long scream come out in earthquake whisper, still small voice like God, 'Don't-you-ever-speak-to-me-like-that-again.'

Tall boy stun. 'But... but –'

'Excuse me.' Tornado brush past very fast, tornado run, tornado fly and boy voice floating behind, 'But what did I say?'

I swear to God I would dead firs before I give any Af Am boy the time of day. Even one with hips like horses running.

.....

Tonight I write a long letter to my friend Skye. I write and write until my fingers are numb. It is the first letter I have written since I came here. I have sent postcards and made phone calls, but no letters. I sit for a long time staring at this letter that I have written to Skye and then I tear it up and take it to the kitchen and flush it down the shredder in the sink. Suddenly there seems a vast gulf between Skye and me, between home and my friends and the me that was and the tall girl looking back at me in the mirror in the room to which I have returned from the kitchen in this place where I am supposed to be living.

I turn on all the lights in the room and stand in front of the mirror and take off all my clothes. I look at my belly and my hips and the shadow in between, my waist that is very tight as if it has been sewn in with grips. Like Macóné's face, I think to myself, but I do not smile. My breasts are fat and their centres very dark, much darker than the rest of my skin, a kind of purplish blue, like star-apples, like Dado's love for his country. The tall girl's face in the mirror is long and oval-shaped under the short dreadlocks that she usually wears caught up in a coloured band but which are now wild and stiff and loose on her head. When she catches them up her eyes slant and her cheekbones get sharper and more strong. She studies her toes and fingers, the veins in the shafts of her arms that are blue even under her cocoa skin. She has her grandfather's big veins. You can see blood in them sometimes. She tilts her head this way and that and stretches her arms in different directions so that her breasts hang down, or go sideways or point up; she walks this way and that around the room. She keeps the mirror in her sights and simpers at herself in various poses, mocking me, America and herself walking. She repeats all this with the lights dimmed.

Finally I put my nightie on and lie down on the bed staring dry-eyed at the ceiling.

·····

God was only playing with me. Or the two weeks of grace was the leap of light before the candle goes out. Because today Dado is in the hospital. The one for lunatics.

I say this brutally so as to leave myself with no illusions, and then I start to cry.

For two weeks he had started coming back from his journeys by himself, early, though because it was late fall it was pitch dark before he, or any of us, got home. Ta Lizz, increasingly worried sick and frightened, so that I could no longer hate her but swung between that and an unwelcome, uncomfortable feeling that we were linked by a similar pain, breathed a sigh of relief and felt that the doctor's medicine was working. He began eating with us again. Emile and I spent all our evenings with him in the room overlooking the street, playing kalyuki and uno, and when Dado spoke of the past now it was in brief but connected sentences that linked it with us and the present. Time seemed to regain its clear sense of a rosary: past-present-thought, past-present-thought.

Increasingly he spoke of Macóné. 'Strong woman you know,' he said chuckling. 'Tough as hell. Both of you look like her you know. Same high cheekbone and the fire in the eye.' The comparison always pleased Emile – achingly; he never tired of hearing it because as an albino he wasn't thought to look like anybody but himself. Dado constantly said, 'You look like her gone-to-bed – splitting image. An like yu mother. Boy look like him mother and add to that him grandmother bound to be lucky in life.' That had early given Emile a sense of confidence, even more than the knowledge that his people were Garveyites. We didn't remember our mother, but her pictures all over the family album showed her beautiful in the way Dado had convinced himself Macóné was.

'Boy, Dado, all the men must did think you well broad to court a woman like that,' Emile said in what had, over the years, become a ritual response, just so he could hear again the stories of Dado's and Macóné's courtship, the way she laughed at him the first time he waylaid her on the path to church, above the big river which had come over with mud in the June rains so people wore waterboots or carried a change of shoes to cross.

'But Johnny Seivwright, you can't be a serious man,' Macóné had said. 'Look how you frequent rumshop and throw dice, smoke cigarette and do all manner of evil, and you expect a Christian, God-fearing woman like me, testifying in her church, looked up to and respected in her community, to tek all you seriously?'

Dado said she had a full deep laugh that she buried in her throat when she was being derisive. Her ridicule stung him no end, but he was determined to win her come hell, come high water. 'Miss Macóné, as a good Christian woman you mustn't take that attitude, you know. The stone that the builder refuses becomes the head of the corner,' he told her. 'That is what your own same Lord said. You point up my small faults that can be easily rectified and ignore my myriad good qualities. That is not right, Miss Macóné. It is not something the Lord would approve.'

Even in those days when a school teacher was supposed to set a linguistic example, Dado generally spoke Creole, but he could put on his best English when the occasion demanded: if there was anything Dado possessed in abundance, it was a sense of style.

But Macóné, my grandmother, Miss Ma'am, was not im-pressed. 'Can be easily rectify, Johnny Seivwright? Then rectify yuhself and come and talk to me. God is not a God of half measure, is all or nothing, so don't expect me to compromise His standards as if you think I desperately looking man.' And she brushed him out of her way and continued striding down the river path in her tall man's waterboots with her head tied up like a Revival woman and her long calico skirts swishing as she walked. Dado was a short man, though thickset, Macóné at least six feet tall with wide shoulders and a man's voice. She was also much older than he, and shortly after they married she became the leader of a church, but he said throughout their marriage he never once felt intimidated.

He set himself to woo her in the most systematic way. He gave up the rumshop, the smoking and the dice, and started going to church. Not that he had been either a drunkard or a profligate; he was at the time, though very young, second in command to the headmaster of the primary school where he worked and well respected in the village for his intelligence and humility – a Mico graduate who had topped his batch year with the highest grades in the history of the college, yet never saw himself above people. He was equally at home in the rumshop where men congregated in those days to exchange news, views and heated debates on the state of the world, as he was on the podium of the local 4H club where he was President, or on the election platforms where he actively campaigned for the socialist party. His presence in the rumshop muted the tone of ribaldry and cut down on the openness with which men gossiped about particular women, though Dado said all it meant was that they attained a sharper wit in practising the art of linguistic disguise. He himself imposed no sanctions on anyone's speech – he didn't need to. It was a respect they accorded to his station as teacher of their children, as well as to their own sense of the school teacher as the keeper of their dignity. I couldn't help thinking it was also a form of deference to the personal dignity that marked Dado even then. He could knock back a white rum with the best of them, but he never permitted himself to get drunk.

First thing Dado did was to explain to his friends in Mr Wong's rumshop that he was going to be seeing them less frequently as he was planning to court Miss Macóné Bryce of the AME Zion church. The men shook their heads in mingled awe and commiseration, quizzed him as to whether he could stand the regime he would be getting himself into, but slapped him on the back, wished him luck, and promised their support. I wondered if even with the best self-control in the world they could have prevented themselves making some comment about what men referred to as the 'bedwork' – because to tell you the truth Macóné looked like the sort of woman who would give a man, even her husband, one rahtid lick if he 'behaved unseemly' in the bed or expected her to do the same. But of course I couldn't ask my grandfather about that and I could easily be wrong, because Dado said she was the most passionate woman he had ever known. (But he was talking about her preaching).

Anyway to cut a long story short, it took Dado six months of relentless pursuit, compromise and reform, ending in church membership, to win Macóné's hand. Together they made a formidable team. With her encouragement he moved on to further studies, got his own school and later moved up to the principalship of the secondary school where he worked until he retired. They were both community activists, helping to develop centres where people learnt skills, read, talked, shared, became politically aware and involved – a sort of joint extension of the rumshop and the church, though Macóné would have vehemently denied that connection, since as far as she was concerned nothing so immoral as 'that den of iniquity the rumshop' could enter into anything with which she or God was associated. I had a sense of her as a hellfire and damnation preacher with formidable organizing skills (which Ta Lizz had inherited) but Dado said the thing about Macóné was that she carried inside her a compassion that was larger than life itself. I sought, without success, to find it in her face.

Macóné died of cancer in 1962, the year of Independence, leaving Dado with three daughters aged six, four and three – Ta Lizz, our mother and Aunt Gretel. The occasion of her funeral was the last day Dado ever set foot in a church. He never discussed this phase of his life with us. But I think that the bottom fell out of his world and from that time on he disliked God. Which was odd, because though he never would himself (at least not as far as I know) he was always telling us to pray.

…..

Tonight Ta Lizz comes to my room, a thing that never happens, and says if push come to shove and Dado doesn't get well, she and Mr Burton will sort things out here and go back home. I look at her with shock because this can't be Ta Lizz talking, Ta Lizz never upsets her plans for anything.

'You would do that for Dado?' I say in wonder.

Ta Lizz's body flinches and shrinks into itself. She gives me a look and does not reply. The look makes me ashamed. I sit uncomfortably on the edge of the bed, not knowing what to say, how to cope with this Ta Lizz who might not be just my aunt but some other person whom I don't really want to know because it makes me ashamed and angry with her, the way I would if I were looking at her naked.

I swallow the question that comes unbidden to my mind: why did you bring us here, I mean, why, really? In some uncanny link that has sprouted between us, she seems to read my mind because she says, her eyes fixed on the window blind over the bed that is tearing away and needs replacing, 'You know, there are a lot of things young people don't understand. It's not so easy living all your life in one place, a small place, not being able to move because you have responsibilities, and is plenty things you would have done if you were young and could dream again.' Ta Lizz rose to her feet and became herself again, brusque and biting. 'One day you will understand the world in more than black and white, Miss Maxine. The fact that I make up my mind about things don't mean I don't have a heart. And you remember this – Dado was my father long before he was your grandfather.'

Then she left the room.

In an overwhelming heat of shame, it came to me that I'd never considered that she gave up the freedom Aunt Gretel had, to take care of us. I hated her for a long time because she made a promise to my mother, and her keeping it made me feel unwanted, as if I was her duty. I found her hard, uncompromising and lacking in reflection. But for a moment she had looked as if she would burst, obscenely, into tears, but then I thought of the small place to which she had condemned me, in this wide, provincial city, and my heart, which had begun to slip a little, went to close itself against her.

Long after she left the room I could feel a pulse beating like a drum, and I couldn't trace its source. I stared into the dark until it ran in a wash of colours before my eyes, and what Ta Lizz was and was not melted out in wavery, watery lines of indigo blue.

....

It happened almost without warning, but not quite. One day about two weeks later, he failed again to come home on time and so I went looking for him.

I found him sitting on the bench at the number 8 bus stop with his hands in his pockets, smiling ironically at the people passing by. Some people thought he was smiling at them and smiled back but Grandfather gave them such a rude look that they became embarrassed and walked hurriedly by.

I sat on the bench, put my arm around him and kissed his cheek. 'Hi, Grandfather,' I said in a black American kind of way. 'How ya doin?' I found it easier to talk that way when I needed to pretend not to cry.

He didn't answer. He didn't draw away either. I watched him watching his hands that were folded in his lap, thick-veined, and slightly trembling, as if they would leap away from his own gaze. After a while he said, 'They send you to car' me back.'

'No, of course not. I was just passing by on my way into town and I saw you so I just stopped by.'

'Just passing by, ehn?'

'Just passing by.'

'Hmn hmn.' It was his acknowledgement of an open and necessary lie.

We sat silent, letting this new necessity of lies between us sink in. Then I said, 'So where you off to, Grandfather?'

'Waitin for the number 8 to Wheaton.'

'Wheaton. Not Rhode Island Avenue?'

He looked irritated. 'No, mi not going to Rhode Island. Wheaton.'

'All right. Wheaton. Nutten nuh wrong wid Wheaton. I'll come with you.'

He didn't answer. He lifted his shoulder so that my arm fell away. The number 20 bus came and he got up and went towards it. 'Grandfather why you tekkin this bus,' I said. 'It not going to Wheaton.'

'Change mi mind. Going back.'

'But why?'

He didn't answer, just boarded the bus and showed his senior's pass. I went in after him and sat beside him where he sat in one of the seats that said 'Please give priority to elderly and disabled in this area.' The bus moved out quickly.

The next day it snowed. We were all at home because there was a weather warning. We joked around between the kitchen and the living room while Ta Lizz baked banana bread, the warm aroma against the winter white somehow affirming something about us as family. I had a rare feeling of us being truly together, even Mr. Burton who, uncharacteristically, was laughing and chaffing Emile. Ta Lizz took the bread out of the oven. Emile wanted his hot and piping, Ta Lizz laughed and said ok ok, go and get Dado, let's all have it together.

Dado wasn't in his room.

…..

When I'm scared or frightened and don't want to face things I make up stories like I'm watching a play or a movie and the person in it isn't me. It's a game Dado taught us, when we were young.

Today I am scared and frightened, but how do you find words to make a fiction to speak about terror and loss and what is suffered from behind a cloak of silence? Would Dado come out of his cloak of silence, his contours white as snow, and talk to us again? I felt he had paid the price for us all.

The old man was half frozen when they found him and the only thing that saved his life was that the coat of ice that had formed over his clothes had not yet quite solidified enough to seep through to the skin. It sealed him in like a glass case and after they had chipped it away with an ice pick in order to get the clothes off him and thawed him before the fire like a brown chestnut – the clothes he was wearing were all brown – they saw the blood. The old man's blood had dried like flowers of rust on the underside of his shirt near his heart and also near his seed, and at first they thought it was where he had spilled gravy eating sloppily on himself. But when the heat thawed him the blood started to run as if he had been a slit animal and so they had to run for tourniquets and call the doctor.

The old man bled all that night. It was as if the floodgates of his orifices were opened after a long drought and they were hungry to rain. The doctor said he had never seen anything like it, he knew of documented cases of people bleeding stigmata, but had never seen it with his own eyes. The old man bled from ears, nose, mouth, teeth, fingertips, anus, penis, and in the morning after several transfusions that refused to stay in, but chased his own blood out of doors, the old man lay blue and gray on the final set of sheets, with a look of peace on his face. During all of this he had neither spoken nor opened his eyes.

....

But in the morning, when there was no blood left to bleed, he opened his eyes and asked for his grandson and granddaughter.

Of course you'll say it doesn't fit. Not medically, not outside the realms of fiction. But still I hope Dado comes through on the other side. Though even if he does (white as Gandalf), he will still have paid the price for us all.

....

'Hi.' I would know that voice anywhere. But today there's no homeboy smile. He looks grave, and that gives him an odd, alien look as if he's someone else. He's looming over my table and I feel at a disadvantage.

'Hi,' I say, feeling foolish and wishing he'd sit down.

'May I?' He gestures towards the single other chair at the narrow cafeteria table. Did he read my mind? I find myself blushing furiously.

'Of course.' I'm relieved at how nonchalant I sound. I want to tell him to go to hell, sit elsewhere, but the cafeteria is crowded, it's the lunch break and there is so much noise and milling around that we are hardly showing.

His long body takes a long time to fold into the fragile wrought-iron chair. It needn't have taken so long, but he's a guy who does everything, even doodling, slowly, as if somehow slow is an important activity that should be practised. It makes him look not dunce, but graceful. I stare doggedly at the unappetizing bagel on my plate. He's having an oversize Coke and a double burger over which he splashes half a bottle of ketchup. There is silence while he bites unselfconsciously into his sandwich, and I feel ashamed.

At last he puts the sandwich back on the plate and says, very softly, 'I'm sorry if I offended you the other evening. It wasn't intentional,' and I find myself thinking stupidly what a relief he doesn't eat with his mouth open or talk with food in it.

'I'm sorry too.' I feel really bad. It's why I hadn't wanted him to sit here in the first place. 'I –' I begin another sentence and find I don't know what I want to say, so I finish lamely, 'It's a long story.'

He hesitates; I feel him hesitating so I look up at him quickly. Our eyes make four and I see that he's not unselfconscious at all but incredibly nervous. I am mad at myself because in looking down and then looking up and down again so quickly I appear to be batting my eyelashes in flirtation and that's the last impression I want to give.

'I don't mean to give offence, I'm really sorry, but I hope you won't mind me saying this – I've – sort of noticed you've been very quiet – more withdrawn than usual.' He's actually blushing, looking confused, as if he thinks I'll zap him one. 'I was just wondering if you're ok.'

I swallow panic. I don't want anybody to feel sorry for me, shit you. I don't want this conversation.

Suppose I were to tell you my grandfather is in a Maryland hospital bleeding in my dreams through the wounds of Christ, only in places Christ never bled, what would you say?

'It's a long story.' I feel, suddenly, very tired.

He smiles a little shyly, the light bulb subdued. 'I've got long ears and a long break,' he says. 'If you want to talk about it.'

Do I want to talk about it?

I am caught between languages, registers, tongues. I don't know how to talk across this rubbled canyon of words with me and you on different sides.

.....

Aluin cruises at an altitude of 30,000 feet, wings completely whitened now by the falling snow. S/he sees a boy and a girl standing on a parapet, high up above the city's gleaming wastes. They are dressed in silver and black and soon the waiter will bring their drinks. Other couples are seated in the candlelight; nobody is cold because the restauranteur has sealed the parapet in with heated glass so that they are in fact in a warm room, though they are freely looking out on the snow's wild beauties.

They're standing because she wants to see the snow under the lights up close, he to accommodate her but also because he can look at her profile unobserved, a long-boned, fierce and beautiful face like the face of an ancient female warrior. She will grow old with grace. He thinks that he will watch her face growing into grace over many mornings of sunlight, waking in the same bed, time tracing strong and delicate spider hands on her face so that it is veined like the life in leaves.

She looks out at the snows but she is thinking of him, he smells nice. Thinking no, not now, in another place, not here; it's too soon, and moreover the place is wrong.

Aliun smiles his/her extravagant smile and casts his/her gaze out like a net and catches in it an old man sleeping, breathing quiet in a hospital bed. The old man stirs, murmurs in the depths of a myriad sleeps, and peace, enigmatic, spreads over his face like a stain.

A PERMANENT FREEDOM

Alain

To say I was surprised to get an email from Denton Trent would be an understatement. At first I couldn't believe he had actually kept my email address all this time (and it must have been a long shot, for how could he have known that I still had that address?) Then I was simply pissed. 'Who the hell does he think he is?' I kept saying it without realizing, until Messina, who had been following me around the apartment as I paced up and down, arched her back and sank her claws viciously into my foot.

'Raas!' I said a Jamaican expletive that Denton used to say, and flashed Messina off with a snarl that sounded more like her than me. I hadn't spoken Jamaican in five years. It's the sort of thing you scrub out of your consciousness.

I fed Messina and went back to the computer.

I must have sat staring at the screen for upwards of an hour, not doing anything, before I got up and went for a walk.

It was the beginning of fall, that sort of in-between time when the leaves are just starting to turn and the world seems balanced on an edge where it could go either way, sun or dark, without anything being lost. Sad-ish, but invigorating at the same time. The air was nippy; I turned my shirt collar up and then turned it back down, deciding that I preferred the wind after all. Two joggers, a man and a woman, holding hands, trotted by me in the park, said 'Hi'.

'Hi.' I smelt their sweat as if had been put on ice, and the musky scent of the park foliage shutting down around its own secret core for the night. On a screen in the front of my mind pictures churned, picture pouring on top of picture as if out of some huge machine, until all was one vast moving blur, and the colour running in red.

I walked fast, until I could hear my own breath.

Did he know I was living in Maine again?

Dumb question. How the hell could he know? We hadn't kept in touch.

I wouldn't go, of course. That went without saying. Wouldn't even reply.

.....

At the end of a week I sent an email saying: So where are you?

Promptly the answer came. 'Don't worry about it. If you let me know your time, date and flight number, someone will be at the airport to meet you.'

But an address was included anyway. And a phone number, 'in case anything goes wrong, though I am sure it won't.' Oh really? Want to bet? And what makes you think a simple question 'Where are you?' means 'You've snapped your fingers, so here I come'? Man, you've got to be crazy.

The address shocked me because it showed he was back in the United States. How long?

I asked for a week off at the company, citing, for Pete's sake, family emergency.

.....

The plane was one of those thirty-seater turboprops, and it was full. I had an aisle seat in business class beside a shiny blonde girl who talked in a long cursive stream about the velocity of planes, how unmanageable airplane traffic was getting with so many people travelling, how hot it was inside here, couldn't they turn on the a/c, oh I guess not, not until we're airborne, and what a pity it was that they didn't serve refreshments except to business class on these short domestic flights, don't you feel sorry for those poor folk down in economy? Behind the burble I could see that she was nervous and making conversation in an effort to manage her panic. As the plane took off, her left hand clamped down quite viciously on my right forearm, reminding me of Messina's claws when she was hungry or wanted to be petted and I wasn't paying attention.

'Don't worry, it's all right, you'll be all right,' I said, patting her hand and trying to soothe her with what Denton used to call my brilliant smile, which he said was not my usual smile but the smile

I kept in reserve for vamping when needed. The girl immediately bridled, a quick wash of pink staining her cheeks, her eyes opening slightly wide in awareness. Shit. It was a reaction I almost invariably got from women when I forgot to be careful not to meet their eyes, and almost invariably it meant trouble. I cursed my own stupidity, Denton Trent and my inability to keep him where he belonged (buried, good, dead and plastered down) ever since that blasted email. He had worked some voodoo spell on me so that my thoughts took on a whole different configuration and were shaping themselves in variations around the one phrase 'What Denton used to say.' He used, of course, to say I had it wrong; it was Haiti that had voodoo, Jamaica had obeah. I cursed again and my blond companion's eyes widened again, this time with shock and hurt.

I had spoken aloud without realizing.

'Damn!' I was making a total mess. I tried again. 'Look, I'm sorry. It wasn't you – it was just something I remembered. Truly.'

'Oh, yes, I understand.' She was visibly relieved and all bright patter again. 'That happens to me all the time. You are there doing one thing or thinking about one thing and suddenly another thought just crosses over – just pops into your mind like that – it's like a crossing of wires, isn't it? Like electrical wires getting messed up in each other. Many times I've been talking to my friends and they say Amanda what on earth… you know? Asking me what I'm talking about, how on earth I got from point A to point B, you know? And I'm like, oh my gawd, I'm sorry, I was thinking about something completely different and I made the switch in my mind and was telling you the second part after the switch, I mean the part that's related to the second thought, but I didn't make it for you and that's why you got confused, you know?'

Oh God.

'Exactly,' I said, giving her this time what must have been a helpless smile. (What the heck. I wasn't going to see her after we got off this flight.) 'That's exactly the sort of thing.'

We talked a bit about crossover thoughts and telepathy. She grew more and more animated and the pink flags were flying in her cheeks now, and blue ones in her eyes. Her eyes were a kind of light washed-blue and protruded slightly; when she was animated they had little prisms radiating from them, like the hard core of diamonds.

'Yes, I think you can hear somebody thinking into your mind, if it's someone to whom you're really close – even if they're in another country, I'm positive. I had that with my grandmother… she's dead now… And my friends think I'm crazy in that as well. They have a way of saying, "Aw, come on, Amanda, I mean…"' That was the third time she had mentioned her name and given me that expectant look. I decided to call it a day.

I put my headrest back and ostentatiously stifled a yawn. The plane was now well above thirty-five thousand feet and riding smoothly so I felt I could abandon her with a clear conscience. 'Sorry,' I murmured apologetically. 'Have to take five. Haven't slept for two days, hectic work schedule, you know.' I said the 'you know' in the same conspiratorial tone in which she had sought understanding when reporting on her friends' exasperation at her self-declared craziness. She smiled unhappily and made a doubtful little moue.

I slid back in my seat and 'slept' unremittingly throughout the rest of the flight. Behind my eyelids I wondered what the hell I was doing, what was wrong with me, getting on a plane in answer to a cryptic email from a guy I hadn't seen in years, who had torn my guts out, pretty near massacred me. What the hell was this all about, what was *I* all about? Was he really ill, how ill was he, what exactly was wrong with him, or was it just a ploy to get me to turn up, to start something all over again? But why? Maybe his wife had left him or something, the bastard. If it was a ploy, it was a pretty clever one because it was bound to arouse my curiosity more than if he had simply written saying, Look, I'd like us to link up again for old times' sake. That, he would know, would not have got him very far. At the same time I thought, maybe I'm giving myself a little too much importance here. Did he say anything about being interested in that, you punk? Why the hell should he be, after all this time? But dammit, any way you looked at the situation, I was important in it, for whatever reason; the guy had asked me to come and see him, hadn't he.

Perhaps he was really ill. Perhaps he just happened to be telling the stark naked truth.

Part of what had always been hard to take, and at the same time wonderful about him, was that he never lied.

So what was wrong with him? The big C? Where was the wife? And what on earth did he think I could do, assuming he really was ill?

There were things I didn't want to think about.

I thought of his long beautiful legs and tight high buttocks, nigger bum, he said, in that laughing self-derisory but self-pleased way of his; the wide muscled chest and the long slope of the close-cropped head, like one of those Benin carvings they get out of Africa, the wild copper under his black skin. I made myself think about all that very carefully, by way of clinical experiment, and felt detached. So I thought about that spectacular body ravaged by illness and what he would look like sick. I hadn't seen him in five years. I wondered idly how I would appear to him. There was gray along the red strands (fire-engine red, my uncle's phrase) in my own hair now which I had been too proud or too vain to dye, but I had kept up relentlessly with the gym and I was still firm and looking good. I had no interest of that sort in him but it mattered.

There hadn't been anyone in a while.

There were things I didn't want to think about.

Let it go, Alain, play it by ear.

…..

The plane landed and I woke up in time to hold my bright blonde girl's hand through the terror of descent. Her fingers left shapes on the cloth of my sleeve.

'Thanks, thanks so much,' she was smiling rather wanly, defeated by the landing and my sleepy indifference during the last thirty minutes of the journey. I took that to mean the danger point was past. I wasn't in the mood to be dodging hints ('Are you staying in the city; perhaps we might run into each other again, you never know; the world is small…').

'No sweat,' I said pleasantly, briskly, swinging down my business-looking briefcase from the rack.

I took down her bag for her, said 'After you' and lingered behind her until the space between us filled with other passengers and she was lost in the crowd. But she surfaced again just as I entered the lobby and waved to me with a soft, hopeful smile. I nodded pleasantly and became absorbed in checking my wallet. That's how it is, my dear. Life is full of chance meetings and goodbyes.

…..

I knew her immediately. She was standing at the barrier, a little off by herself, as if to state her difference from everybody else. As if somehow her mission and her identity were a cut above the rest. I recognized her from the photograph, not from the picture of her I carried in my head despite the photograph. She hadn't changed all that much from the time the picture was taken. She had her hair long instead of in that low Afro cut that she'd had then. She should have done it the other way round. The heavier, fluffier hair made her look older; she would have looked better with it short. But women are strange creatures, especially about hair. She was slim and quiet looking. Not frumpy or fanatic looking or desiccated or oh my god holy as I imagined her. Just ordinary, rather dignified, in fact.

So she hadn't left him. She was still there. And here I was.

She came forward as soon as she saw me and held out her hand. 'Alain?'

'Yes.' I said it like a question. The question was my confusion about what was going on. Her hand was tiny and warm. She had a flat island voice, very inward and quiet. I think he had said she was from Grenada.

'I'm Marsha. I'm so glad you could come. Was the flight ok?' Her voice, though quiet, had a touch of intensity, as if from the extra effort needed to overcome a speech impediment.

I didn't answer. She kept on talking, walking as she talked. 'I got a parking space in the airport garage, I was lucky. Do you have your entire luggage or do you have to go to baggage claim? No? Great, let's go this way; it's nearer.'

The car was a forest green Saab. Pretty. Hers or his?

I kept silent until we were well out of the airport and on the motorway, with the wind singing in our hair through the half open windows. She drove very fast. I watched her hands on the wheel, fine and tensile, with a look of nervousness in the bone. Highly strung. A fanatic's hands. Her hands proved me right, even if her face didn't. Her hands looked the way I had imagined her over five and a half years.

'Now can you tell me what the hell, exactly what the hell is going on?' I kept my voice dangerously quiet, I wanted to punch somebody – myself for being here in the first place.

She didn't reply; her hands tightened very slightly on the wheel and the car picked up speed. Lady, are you planning to crash us or get yourself pulled over? She was going that fast, even for a bloody motorway. We went on in this silence for several miles. Then she put her right indicator light on and swerved off the motorway onto a side road that was also quite busy, but quieter. She drove a further mile or two until we came to a kind of campsite-looking place with a weatherboard sign saying 'Anglers Rest' in one of those old world scripts – Mistral or Matisse I think, I forget which. I used to know those scripts like the back of my hand. She swung into the gateway and parked under a stand of sycamore trees whose bark was already beginning to peel. Clumps of forty something-ish and older people in padded jackets were getting out of cars or walking towards a rustic sort-of-office further up, or across to the other side of the road where other cars were parked with the same kinds of people disappearing among the trees. Picnic expeditions, I thought, creek or lake further down, and the thought brought a pang of memory that was sharp and unexpected.

She unfastened her seat belt and turned in her seat towards me, her gaze serious, but clear and very direct. 'You must have guessed by now that Denton didn't send the email. I did.'

'No, actually I didn't. I wondered where you were,' I said grimly.

'I guess you're thinking this is some kind of joke.'

'I'm waiting for you to enlighten me.'

He had discussed me with her. Given her my address. We were one big happy family. Somehow that hurt like hell, and again unexpectedly. I didn't think my pride had stayed around that long. But it wasn't so much the thought of being discussed – that I suppose I expected, distasteful as it was – as the thought of them agreeing for her to write to me. I felt like a kid in the playground watching a hostile clique whispering about him and then laughing.

It wasn't how I remembered him, the way he had been. Suddenly I wanted to see him, the way he had been, not ventriloquized by this wife, his stranger.

She was saying, 'I'm sorry. I didn't know what else to do. I thought he needed you. He wanted to see you.'

'Wanted to see me? He told you that?'

She passed her tongue nervously over her lips. She nervous! Sheesh!

'No. No, he didn't tell me that. I guessed.'

I suddenly felt too tired to play catch up. I waited for her to tell me what she was going to tell me.

'He's really ill, you know.' She spoke quickly as if she wanted to get it over with or was afraid of my reaction. 'I didn't make that up.' Her eyes filled with tears and such a look of desolation that I felt panic; I wanted to get out of the car and go somewhere; I didn't want this lady falling down on me, please. Please.

She didn't cry. At least not audibly. She tightened her face and hauled her eyes and the tears in and shut them down as if she had blinds within. 'He's dying. The doctors say it is only a matter of weeks now. They did everything they could.'

The indicator light was ticking very fast. She had forgotten to turn it off. I watched it, fascinated. Then I said, 'What's wrong with him?'

'The big one.'

'Cancer?'

'AIDS.'

'But nobody dies so easily of AIDS these days,' I said stupidly, in a headlong rush. I could feel my stomach loosening. I had tested negative six months ago, but I could feel my stomach loosening. 'I mean, there are drugs,' I added, and my voice came out rough and angry.

'Yes, and he's had every kind of attention. We came here from Grenada as soon as we knew. Believe me, everything that could be done, has been done.' In spite of herself, her eyes teared up again. 'It was too late. He didn't test – he didn't think he had it, you see, he'd been extra careful.'

He had been extra careful. So there had been others; this guy hadn't been behaving himself. The mealy-mouthed bastard. And

74

she, what the hell was she? How could she sit there and say 'he'd been extra careful' as if she had been the doorkeeper of her husband's adulteries and it was bloody all right?

'Sometimes he gets... I don't know... not quite delirious, it's not delirium. He talks in his sleep. He kept calling your name; I thought he was calling for you, as if he wanted to tell you something. That is how it seemed to me.' She was silent, looking away. We were both silent, then she said again, 'That is how it seemed to me' as if trying to convey the sense of some irresistible knowledge that had weighed upon her and that, sweeping all in its wake, could not have been denied. A fanatic's sense of knowledge. I had never known anyone with a quieter voice. You almost had to bend to catch her words, and it wasn't because her voice was low; it was more because it was completely turned in on itself.

'He was worried about you. In the beginning... when he first knew, he wanted to get in touch with you... to let you know you should test too... he didn't get any answers to his letters, and your phone number had changed...' Yes, of course. I had dumped the letter without opening it. It wasn't something I could risk, not then, and after I heard his voice on the phone, the first message, 'Can you call me, Alain, it's important', and I felt as if a vegetable shredder was making neat little slices in my stomach, I wasn't going to risk that either, so I changed the number. I'd also deleted him from my email address book so he came in the junk, the morning a week ago when I decided to open the junk and see what the heck.

So, that's how long he's been ill. Not all that long. People don't die so easily of it, these days, I thought again, stupidly.

'Well, as you can see, I'm all right,' I said, though of course we both knew it wasn't about how one looked. 'So you didn't need to ask me to come. All you had to do was tell him look, Alain is alive and perfectly well and he tested negative even as we speak. So it can't have been him.'

'No,' she said, and then again, 'No, it can't have been you,' in a voice that puzzled me. Had she really thought... but she obviously knew that there must have been others. 'And yes, I could have done it the way you said, but I felt constrained... Say I'm ridiculous if you like... but I felt he should see you... that that's what he wanted.'

I sat for a while, not really knowing how to handle something so… *unheard of*, just trying to allow some energy to settle somewhere. Then I asked the next obvious question. 'So does he know? That I'm in a car with you on my way to see him?'

'I told him this morning. I said you wrote out of the blue (I've been doing his mail for him, you see) saying long time no see and you were going to be in the area so would it be ok if you dropped by. I said I thought it would be churlish to say no so I just answered on his behalf and said "sure."'

He was too ill to read his own mail. And this woman was stark staring quietly softly mad.

'Some storyteller, aren't you?'

She shrugged, faintly, as if to say there was nothing she could do about that, it was the way things were.

'What did he say?'

A fleeting, whimsical smile touched her lips, like a butterfly hovering and then gone. 'He said he didn't want you to see him like this.'

I thought of myself thinking about my gray hair and looking good because of the gym, and found that I wanted to laugh, hilariously. When women do that sort of thing they call it hysterics.

She was studying my face intently. I stared back, setting my face like a mask behind which my… *astonishment*… burned.

'Thank you,' she said at last, and started the car.

.....

It was only later, when we were almost there, that I said, with an abruptness that took both of us by surprise and made her hands jerk on the wheel, 'And you? Are you…?' I didn't finish the sentence but she knew what I was asking. And for some reason I found I cared in an indefinable way about the answer.

'Oh, I'm alright, I haven't got it,' she said in a choked voice, as if trying to hold back laughter. 'We… we didn't…'

She didn't finish the sentence. I said, 'I see,' though I didn't. I didn't understand anything at all.

.....

It's been two weeks. It's one of those chill evenings that are nevertheless full of light because of the glorious colour coming off the woods. The north window of my motel room faces straight up the Trail and it's like being drawn into the heart of a fire, molten red and gold. It is easy to forget that in another couple of weeks there will be nothing there but the still arabesques of dark, stripped branches.

I can't give a good reason why I have stayed. I can't say it was fundamentally an act of compassion or sentiment or even obligation. I think it's simply this: that a part of me, the part that lets things take the wind, that I had let go after I went on the corporate roller coaster, has suddenly come back 'to get his', as Trevolt McClettie might have said. Perhaps the corporate thing was never me, and so it was only a matter of time. Or maybe this radical sort of reorienting is what happens when you find yourself face to face with the fact that a guy you once knew, someone you've been intimate with, is going to die. Maybe things, selves, go in cycles and the time for a return to my old craziness is now. It's been five years of this particular cycle and I wonder how the hell I could have stood it for so long, but it was something I had needed. My ego had taken a beating and I guess I needed to prove to myself I could do something that no one had thought I could be good at. Including Denton, who had said I was feckless and immature, a wanderer by choice because I didn't care about anything. Corporate America was actually a breeze and I made a lot of money I didn't really need. No, I hadn't needed the job in that way; Trevolt knew this, and I guess that made him even more furious in response to my resignation over the phone (effective after a month of overdue vacation leave to be taken as of now – letter will follow). Piss off you Kiwi bastard I'll sue your effing ass for dereliction of duty, I'll take you for every cent you've got, you hear me. And moreover you can come and get your effing cat you hear me? I am not the keeper of any effing shelter for the effing homeless! He was screeching like a banshee and I could imagine him foaming at the mouth, spit flying into his oversize beard. It was the kind of histrionics Trevolt was good at and thoroughly enjoyed. Tantrums kept his adrenaline pumping; they were the energy his quirky but quite spectacular mind fed on. Throw her into the dumpster, I said. Trevolt adored animals so Messina was as safe with him as she would have been with me; possibly safer. She would miss me, was all.

Still I knew that it was a blow to him that I was leaving.

He will get over it.

…..

I didn't see him the first day I arrived. He was exhausted and sleeping, Marsha said, wait for the morning. She was buying time, of course, appalled at the unknown quantities of what she had done. I was in danger of getting drawn into her here-I-am, here-I'm-not force field and I didn't want that. I wanted to stay in a neutral space, not in their house, but it had been too late in the day to look for a suitable place and, as it turned out, I didn't move out till the following Tuesday, exactly one week.

They had one of those modern condos with a carefully culti-vated rustic look that spoke of money. He had said Marsha's people had money, and I had figured that he himself wasn't so badly off either at the time I met him, both of them professionals, and no children. The house was part of a complex that stood surrounded by forest and a long slope of wooded hills where, throughout the day, hunting guns barked. Rather spectacular scenery, the same I was looking at now from the window of the motel, more an inn, really, which I had found a little over a stone's throw away. The houses stood tall, making a statement, very new, with the raw shiny gold colour of new hay. I wondered whose idea it had been, his or hers. I had not found him a man for loudly elegant or glamorous places.

He slept downstairs in the small living room that had been converted into a bedroom. Sometimes he wanted to walk a little and he couldn't climb easily down the stairs. She slept on a truckle in an alcove from where she could hear him calling but they could still allow each other some private space. When I went in in the morning he wasn't in bed but sitting on a red chaise longue – one of those mock Edwardian things – in a padded silk dressing gown, as if he had made a special effort to receive a guest. He stood up when I came in, holding on to the couch with one hand, the other held out to me.

Nothing went the way I had expected. It wasn't as hard, or as easy either. He said in the slow, familiar voice, only it was a little husky now, 'I'm sorry, man, I wouldn't have wished this on you; it wasn't my idea.' He smiled, and it was wan, yes, but it was still his old aching smile, slightly lopsided as if it was falling off and you might have to catch it quickly in the cup of your hand. 'But Marsha…she…tries to make up to everyone for life…you know.' He said it not like a criticism but with affection, with the stress on 'you', as if yes I really personally did know, though of course he knew I didn't. That was his odd way of speaking, and suddenly it was Denton the way he always was, so that when he put out his hand I held it with one of mine and grabbed him roughly with the other, holding him so fiercely I forgot to breathe. His hand was very thin, like a crippled limb that had never had muscles. I relaxed my hold on it and then I kissed it and held him with both arms and his tears were wet on my cheek. He was a guy who always cried easily.

I made him sit back down on the couch and hauled up the African print hassock that clashed wildly beside it. His hand came up and wiped my face, smoothing my cheeks like a beautician giving a facial. 'What the hell you crying for, man? Somebody trouble you?' he said, mock growling.

We laughed, I a little tearfully; it was my eyes that were wet.

We sat there looking at each other and then he cried, in his diminished voice, with a kind of joy, 'So you all right, man?'

'Yes, I'm all right. I'm fine.'

'I'm glad,' he said, and then he was quiet.

I had been afraid of what I might find; had wondered if I would know him. But he was still himself. At least a little. He lay on his side watching me, his eyes very bright. 'So… tell me what you have been doing…all this time. Where were you that you got here so fast? I thought you'd have been back in New Zealand or the back of some other beyond by now. You stayed in the US!'

'Five years.' I told him in great detail about my job as an engineer building bridges for Meyers and Co in Portland, Maine. I was simply glad for the pure salvation of this talking. He listened intently, his eyes trained on mine throughout, his face moving in the way I remembered: with question, amusement, agreement, surprise, and a kind of hunger, as if he too longed for this ordinary relief, the freedom to talk as if life went on as it always had. He laughed soundlessly when I told him about Trevolt McClettie, with smoke coming out of his ears and his beard flaming while he streaked through the top-floor offices screeching like some modern-day Cassandra when one or other of his staff hadn't done things exactly the way he had in mind.

'Mean bastard, but good to work with, in his own way. I guess I stayed not just because I needed the stability for a while, but because it wasn't totally stifling. I had pretty much leeway to do what I wanted, even when he was screaming the place down. It involved a heck of a lot more office nine-to-five than I needed, but I did get to spend a little more than half my time out on the sites and travel around the country a bit.'

'We have a son, you know that, don't you?' he said abruptly.

'Marsha did mention that yesterday, yes,' I said, disconcerted. Later I understood that this was part of his illness, this sudden inability to concentrate, his mind moving from one subject to another in a kind of fog along roads that seemed straight to no one but him. That morning was in fact the longest he ever concentrated during the time I was with him, like the first gush from a hose that fools you that it is full of water or hooked to a tap when in fact it is only spitting out what's left between one use and the next. After the gush there's a slow trickle and then the drip drip, and you realize the hose wasn't hooked up to anything at all.

'He stays with his grandparents up in Amherst. Marsha's parents. She goes to see him at weekends. It's the only time she'll let the nurse stay alone with me. She doesn't think she can bring him here. She thinks it will hurt him to see me like this. She doesn't want to risk it.' He was talking as if he was repeating himself, though he wasn't; he hadn't said a single unnecessary word but it was as if he was talking to himself, trying to process a hurt that was both his son's and his.

As if on cue, before I could answer, Marsha came in and offered a drink. I opted for coffee. Denton said he wanted coffee too and she looked disturbed, as if he wasn't supposed to have it, but she didn't say anything. I felt awkward, guilty even. I was sitting on the hassock and he was half sitting up on the chaise. He had moved while we were talking, impatient with lying down, and his legs were half against my knees. I don't know how it had happened, I don't think either of us had noticed. It was just the kind of thing that happens when people who have known each other a long time are talking closely. If she noticed, which she must have done, she didn't say anything.

An awkward silence fell after she went out; I found myself thinking crossly, 'What's with her? Couldn't she knock?' although the living room door had been wide open. I didn't like the way my thoughts were tending, because I hadn't done anything or thought anything. This was too bizarre for words.

She brought coffee for both of us. 'I'm going out for a while,' she said. 'I have to run some errands. Normally I wait till the nurse comes but I thought since you're here... Will you be all right?'

'Of course.'

She smiled, that butterfly quivering on her lips again.

I didn't watch her go, I watched the coffee cup steaming in my hands. I didn't look at him.

'She gave up her job to look after me.' He said it like someone announcing they had won a magnificent prize they didn't really want. 'She said the hospital was totally out of the question.'

'Oh,' I said.

'She's a good woman.'

'Yes,' I said.

When he tried to drink his coffee his hand shook and it spilled a little on his dressing gown.

'Damn,' he said, mopping the spill with the comforter while the cup shook like a fever.

I steadied the cup, then put mine on the floor so I could help him drink by guiding his hand with both of mine. He smiled at me over the steam and between sips he rested his hand in the cup of mine, which had never seemed so big before (I have huge hands) or so like gloves. His eyes were dark, liquid and shadowed, a little bruised, behind the smile. The dressing gown was thickly padded so the spilled coffee didn't seep through and burn his skin, and anyway we mopped it again with the edge of the comforter and put a paper towel underneath. Marsha was very efficient. Everything was provided on the bedside table.

When she came back he was sleeping. She stood beside me for a long time watching him breathe. We stood together watching him breathe, as if he was doing something he had never done before and it was somehow down to us that he was doing it.

She and I had lunch on the patio overlooking the flaming hills. She was a tasteful cook. She served baked salmon seasoned with parsley, garlic and thyme, a mixed salad and fresh fruit juice that she had made with oranges, strawberries and passion fruit. She served it on a white tablecloth on a new oatmeal-coloured table top – carefully cultivated rustic. The house belonged to a friend who had loaned it to them for six months. I was glad it wasn't theirs or her idea, though I couldn't have said why that mattered.

.....

It is the pain that I remember. The long nights holding him while he twisted in my arms in the grip of restless dreams by which I knew he would not stay. The hole in my belly the morning I watched him walk through the barrier of the train station after the smartslot ate his ticket 'snick' and spat it out again so he could take it with him as he walked through. He didn't look back. The high cheeks of his buttocks moved rhythmically like a dancer's and women turned to look at him. It is the pain that I remember.

No, that's a lie. We had a heck of a grand time. I taught him sailing. We had long mornings roaring down the wind on the Bight and then way out into the Atlantic, the sound of sea dogs barking and his face wild and laughing as he ducked under the boom when the wind changed direction. He was a natural, as if he had been doing it all his life. We roamed the theatres, book-stores, nightclubs tucked like secrets in the quiet, narrow parts of the town, discovering each other. He had never read *Moby Dick* and I asked him if he was a madman, every seaman worth his salt had to read *Moby Dick*. All right, all right, I surrender, he'd said laughing, though who the hell wants to read a book about a whale – I'll read it only if you agree to read *War and Peace*. I read *War and Peace*. He read *Moby Dick*. If truth be told I read it quickly because I skipped all the heavy philosophical passages, so damn *Russian*. He started carrying *Moby Dick* around like a bible, though I felt sure he was mocking me because we had such fierce arguments about it. He made me read the poets from his corner of the world and in turn I forced him to go with me to the cinema. He hated movies; I said, man, you grew up under what the Aussies call a bloody pommy stone, how come your tastes are so bloody backward highbrow; this is what it means to be colonized. I made him watch every conceivable kind of junk, even things I didn't particularly go for, just to civilize him a little. We watched *My Best Friend's Wedding*, *Pretty Woman*, *Titanic*, *Gladiator*, Martin Lawrence, *Chicken Run*, *Agent of Death*, *American Psycho*, Eddie Murphy, any number of kung fu movies, everything Batman and Spiderman. We fought about me calling him colonized and afterwards fell into bed and on each other with a hunger and greed that exhausted itself and then repeated and exhausted itself every day. The only places we didn't do much were restaurants; I was used to cooking for myself: fresh food from the sea and dried herbs, and he turned out to be a connoisseur who cooked with a fastidious elegance like a French chef. We did eat out, but rarely, and then mostly sinful junk. This was on the days when we rented a car and drove for days into nowhere, stopping wherever we stopped, discovering cities, marinas and farms, eating and sleeping wherever we were, once even sleeping in the car. We went to Vegas, lost a lot of money and decided we wouldn't do it again; that was our Casino Experience for old age reminiscence and we didn't need another.

I knew from the beginning that it was a holiday because it was too intense to last. Parts of him were tightening up more every day, and I could feel that it wouldn't be long before he was unable to continue making himself forget the things he had put aside on shelves.

But I hadn't expected it to be so soon. It seemed to be over before it began.

Still, I felt I had known him for a long time. I keep thinking of that time as a lifetime, or at least five years. I say 'the time with Denton', I say 'Denton as I knew him,' as if it was a very long time and time enough to know someone, but it was really no time at all. I scarcely knew him.

After that first night there were things we never talked about, though they were always there, like a worm under the skin.

We had a bang up incredible grand time. My body opened like a bloody well and I fell right through it, down down down to a place full of stars.

....

Marsha and I fell into a kind of routine that neither of us had planned but that seemed to happen as naturally as the decision that I would stay. I didn't make that decision so much as it was made for me, and I couldn't say it was made by any pressure from either Marsha or Denton, but more by some force that seemed to be operating between us all with the vitality of an organizing will. She stayed with him in the mornings, I in the afternoons. We agreed without words to stay out of each other's way; she left the house to run her errands or went about her business inside without disturbing us. She was a woman who moved with a great deal of lightness.

'Thank you,' was all she said when I told her my intention to stay. Her eyes were very bright. Later, as I was leaving, she said, 'I can't thank you enough that you decided to stay. He needs male company – any company, but especially male company. We don't have friends here, and it is kind of rough on him that the only people he has to talk to are Nurse Padmore and me – it's dreadful, really.'

I wondered if she meant dreadful for her or dreadful for him. Nurse Padmore, though, was another story. She came twice in the week and at weekends, staying overnight Saturday because Marsha went to Amherst to visit her son. She was a mountain of a woman with a voice like a drum, and a brisk, bullying manner when she was talking to Marsha or me. I wondered how on earth Denton stood her and why Marsha didn't get somebody else, but after I saw her with him I understood why: she was extraordinarily soft with him, almost like a lover, but at the same time so efficient and businesslike that I thought she must have been a welcome breath of fresh air from the close domesticity of a shared small room and normal woman's things. There was no 'normal woman' about Nurse Padmore, she was a female Shrek. The thought made me think of her and Trevolt McClettie together and I couldn't help laughing.

At first I thought he was glad for my presence because it would give his wife ease. He kept saying, 'I'm so glad you're here. Marsha… she stopped doing anything, you know? She has her whole life revolving around me. At least now you're here she can go to the library, her Thursday evening church…' I wasn't amused. I felt that my free decision was being drafted into some project to provide his wife with relief on shift, an alternative Nurse Padmore. I began to feel again the sense of being the object of conspiracy between them, only, this time, a conspiracy on Marsha's behalf. Marsha the golden girl of sacrifice.

One afternoon he was particularly exhausted. He wanted me to read to him from *War and Peace* but fell quickly asleep. I put the book down and watched his breath going in and out through his slightly open mouth. The angle of sunlight suddenly shifted and bright shards, lit with the red gold glow of the burning hills, fell on his chest and his face. I rose with the intention to draw the window blinds a little. At my movement he woke with a start and cried out, flinging his hand over his eyes. I stood still. After a moment he removed his hand and looked at me. 'You're here,' he said with a curious sigh of relief.

'Yes,' I said, wondering what nightmares he had been having.

'Thank God,' he said. Then, 'You don't have to be here. You don't know what that means... how much I am glad that you are here because you want to be here.'

I didn't know if that was true. I felt I was there for other reasons that I hadn't yet worked out. Honesty compelled me to say, 'Marsha doesn't have to be here either. She could have left.'

'Marsha is my wife,' he said enigmatically.

'There is something you have to understand about women,' he added, abruptly. I was worried about his breathing, he sounded like someone who had been running. 'They... give everything. Even if it kills them. Even if you don't treat them right.'

It was then I had the first inkling that he needed me to be there not for Marsha but for himself. My presence eased what he felt to be an intolerable burden of obligation to an attachment – what he thought of as a love – that he was not free to refuse, and I could only imagine the sense of undeserving that made him say to me once, days before he left, 'It might have been easier if Marsha was the kind of person who bore a grudge.' Each day I was there he looked forward to my coming, because for the time I was in the house he was free.

Yet he talked about her a lot, obsessively. And his son. They consumed his whole world.

Sometimes, when he could manage, the three of us ate the afternoon meal together and watched TV or played cards in his room; sometimes we were very relaxed and made a great deal of noise, laughing uproariously. He had sudden wild bursts of energy. Inevitably, though she and I managed with uncanny skill to keep the lines of our separate interactions unentangled, I came to know little things about them, what went on in the house when I was not there. People leave traces in conversations, opened books, soiled plates and cups, even dust on the floor, that you can read like hieroglyphs in sand, especially if nobody is really going out of their way to keep secrets. He kept a Bible on the night table beside the bed, open to a page with the red words of Christ. I never read them. He never asked me to read them for him and since his eyes didn't allow him I deduced that she read them for him after the blinds were drawn and the houses closed and folded down for the night.

I stood for a long time at my motel window, looking out towards those shuttered rooms. I would wake in the darkest part of the night and hear its long, abandoned keening, the drawn-out distant hum that from childhood I had thought was the sound at the heart of the world, but it was the sound of my own loneliness and smallness, a tiny beating metronome lost in time and space. I thought of the two of them waking like this. Did they hear it, that sound at the heart of the world that was the sound both of life and the moment of its death? Did it make them afraid? Was he, in particular, afraid of what awaited him at the end?

It was he himself who told me that he liked her to pray with him every evening before he went to bed. He had always been attracted to the confessional, the mantras with which he had been circumscribed from a child. I'd thought that she would have been the religious one (my image of her as fanatic – her hands), but she wasn't. She never talked religion to me. He said she went out to her church meetings but she never mentioned them and no church people came to the house. Nobody except Nurse Padmore and me, and occasionally the doctor.

She always invited me to have lunch with her, unless we were having it with Denton. The lunches on the patio became part of a pattern, a piece in a mosaic we were making. Sometimes, and then more often, I helped her fix the meal. She was surprised and delighted that I could cook.

I watched her a lot, as I am sure she watched me, though I never saw her doing it. I cannot say that I liked her, because I didn't. I didn't dislike her either; my feelings were more complex than that: I think I wanted to catch her out in something, but also to believe that she was on the level. Obviously I wasn't jealous –the time for that had passed. You could not easily read her surfaces; oddly, if I were asked to define her aura, I'd say it was courtesy; in fact there was in her manner an almost courtly style, an effect of *giving way*, that reminded of Arthurian tales of chivalry I read in my uncle's library as a child. Marsha, a white knight? I laughed to myself but I was wary of the odour of sanctity that emanated from the Marsha of my imagination, a version that slid in and out among the spaces of the other. Throughout those ritual lunches, I looked for clues to the enigma of her act that had drawn us together in this strange alliance around the bed of death.

'We're very quiet here,' she said, almost apologetically, passing ice in a bowl. 'I guess you must have exhausted what there is to explore in no time at all.'

'The pharmacy, the deli, the grocer's, the fruitseller's, the bus stop across the street,' I said, smiling and helping myself to ice.

'It's that bad.' Now her eyes crinkled in amusement, the butterfly hovering on her lips that never quite broke open in a spontaneous smile.

'Actually, no. You'd be surprised what you find in some of these corners.' I told her about the rare edition of *Gulliver's Travels* I'd found in the back stacks of the used book store on Odyssey Street. 'I've been up on the Trail quite a bit, as well.'

'It's great to walk in, especially at this time of the year. But I don't go much now – I find the hunting hard to cope with.'

I looked at her and she was nice and manicured and her lipstick before she had eaten it off with her meal was the colour of blood. Now it was a washed pink.

I didn't tell her that I had rented a car and on some days I took long journeys in search of open roads and spaces. I had begun to know that part of the country like a song, and every nuance of the fall: its wild prolonged shouts of flame such as those that scored the hills on which we looked out every day; the long lonely trebles of empty bleached roads inside yourself; wayside inns, travel stops (in England there would have been pubs, smoky inside with noise and warmth); laden trailers; hidden creeks running low; garage sales and wide-eyed children on cluttered lawns; and its abrupt evenings choreographed in blue.

'Why are you staring at me like that?' Marsha said suddenly. 'Have I got mayonnaise on my lip or something?' She wiped her mouth with her napkin, smiling.

I came back to the present with a start. I was still looking at her but now consciously and deliberately, in a different way, and I said, quite suddenly, without any inkling I was going to say it, 'I don't understand you, you know. I mean, what happened between Denton and me – it's totally outside of your belief system, and moreover, let's face it, I am like the other woman in the story, aren't I? Only worse, in your way of looking at things. So why did you send for me – why do you have me around?'

She was very still, and then she looked at me with a kind of wary irony and the slight smile on her top lip. 'And what is my way of looking at things?'

'Denton told me about you – about your part of the world. You don't approve – you think men like us are wrong – wrongly made. Anathema.'

'I am sure Denton didn't tell you that I considered men like you – anathema.'

'Ok, maybe not. That's my interpretation then, if you like.'

'I see. So why did *you* come, and why did you stay, having come?'

It was a reasonable question. I shrugged. 'I have done stranger things. It's the way I grew up.' Her eyebrows raised a little so I explained, 'I didn't have a very orthodox upbringing.'

'I see. And yet you have very… orthodox views – about people.'

So underneath that calm exterior she was stung by what she had sensed was my opinion of her.

'Sometimes,' I said. Perhaps my orthodox views about respectable people were strongly held, because crudely held. I hadn't grown up among them and so what I had learnt I had learnt in the way people learn a foreign language, with a lot of emphasis on accent and correctness and getting it right.

She looked away over the Trail a long time before she answered. At last she sighed. 'It wasn't… easy. But it's very simple, really. It's nothing more than I told you at the beginning. I felt – call it an irresistible compulsion if you like – that he wanted – that he had something to say to you, and that it was more than simply "please get tested", because, of course, he knew you would, it's only common sense – but he wouldn't say what … because he didn't want to upset me. I didn't think I had the right to deny him something that seemed fundamentally important to him, not when… not when…'

'I see,' I said, suddenly losing my appetite. I pushed my half-eaten meal away, scrubbed at my face with the napkin. 'You were playing the good guy. That's rather a lot of righteousness, isn't it?'

She looked away over the hills again and when she turned back to me her eyes were vague and remote. 'Maybe.' She pushed back her chair, rose to her feet, quite gracefully, in the circumstances, and walked back into the house.

'You should have let him go,' I said after she had gone, and I am being very literal when I say I didn't and still don't know if I meant it for her or for me. Or what I had wanted or expected her to say.

But I thought that I began to understand her as I had begun to understand him. The two understandings were of a piece, really. I thought that she might really love him, and if this was the truth of her motivation as she saw it, then I saw that for her nothing existed beyond her husband; she had already sacrificed herself – pride, shame, belief; I saw that in her scheme of things I was nothing so long as I helped him die in peace. I glimpsed then the formidable ruthlessness of her protection and thought of the cold flame that ignited the heart of a suicide bomber, the one love against which you can't impose sanctions. Later Denton said no, was more like the love of a mother bear for her cubs, but I wouldn't know, I am not an expert on the subject of mothers, and as for bears – I dislike hunting as much as Marsha does.

But it was much later than that that it occurred to me that she must have had an enormous amount of confidence, a total belief in her hold on him and her place in his regard, to have done a thing like that.

And if, even later still, what I thought I understood then, about them, about us, about why any of us is here, came up for question and turned out to be only a small part of the truth, well, that was still a long way away and I had no idea of it then or that it would change what I was looking for when I put to sea again.

…..

We played dominoes on the Edwardian coffee table, whose pristine top we often stained with our mugs. I put the dice down gently, not with the exaggerated slapping noise Denton said was the way to play the game ('That's half the fun, man').

'Marsha said you had something you wanted to tell me,' I said to him abruptly that evening.

'She said that?'

'Yes. Something apparently so large that it constrained her to send for me.' I didn't try to disguise the irony in my voice.

He smiled, amused in spite of himself, but said nothing.

'Well, did you?' I prompted.

He hesitated, let out his breath in a 'pfhhh', threw his dominoes down and lay back looking at me. It was a peculiar expression that he had on his face, quizzical, speculative, enigmatic, secret, even sly, as if he was searching for the answer to my question in my own face and was slightly amused about it all. It was a look I was to surprise on his face again and again as he watched me when he thought I wasn't looking, and it was a look that I learned to associate with the approach of death.

'To tell you the truth, I don't know,' he said at last, slowly, half speaking to himself, as if formulating the answer as he went along. 'Marsha said I kept calling you in my sleep. I don't remember – I have faint recollections. I think I wanted to say I was sorry.'

'Sorry?' I echoed.

'Yes. Yes, I think so.'

'For what?'

'For what happened.' He was no longer looking enigmatic, but troubled, as if he felt pain, and doubt.

I had this feeling – what Marsha had called an irresistible

compulsion – that there was some truth at stake here, a truth that had to be established by being spoken, and that if I didn't ask certain questions it was going to be denied in silence. 'Which part of it?' I asked. 'What happened between us or the fact that you left? Us or the leaving?'

His eyes widened as if I had slapped him.

'There was no us,' he said. 'Not really.'

'You liar.'

'I'm not lying. It's true. There was no us, Alain. I never gave consent to it – not with my will, not –'

He sounded weak and sentimental and blustering; I was seething, I forgot that he was ill and I shouldn't be doing this.

'You bloody hypocrite. You bloody religious hypocrite. You gave consent to it, body and soul. Your soul gave consent to it. To us. Jesus Christ, you're worse than your wife. Why can't you admit, why can't you admit, even now, what you are, who you are?'

His pupils were wide and dilated, very dark; they filled my vision until I could see nothing else.

'Oh God. I'm sorry,' I said, appalled.

I stumbled to my feet and left the room.

The next day Marsha said he had developed a cough. The doctor had been. I felt like a convict, awaiting execution; I wanted to weep but I couldn't. When I saw him I said, 'I think I should leave.'

'Because of us quarrelling?'

'Yes. That sort of thing can't do you any good.'

He hesitated. Then he said, 'I'd like you to stay. It's hard on Marsha; you help her a lot. And I – you help me a lot, too. It's dreadfully selfish of me to ask, but if you can stand it, I would like you to stay.'

He saw the doubt on my face and smiled, that rare, lopsided sweet smile that made you think something was singing somewhere, angels perhaps. 'You keep me on my toes, Alain Lockheed. Yes, I'm sure.'

He coughed a lot that evening. I held him while he drank water from the carafe Marsha kept on the side table. Afterwards he lay for a long time breathing quick and shallow, his face, a pale but true replica of itself, exhausted, and then he slept.

I tried not to think about my fear, which had entered a new dimension.

.....

That Friday Marsha decided she wasn't going to Amherst to see their son; she would talk to him on the phone instead. She didn't want to leave Denton since the cough had developed. But the child cried on the phone and Denton was upset. He insisted that she should go, and moreover that I should accompany her. 'You know I'll be all right,' he said. 'Nurse Padmore is always here on the dot of duty and she never lets me out of her sight.'

He was the weakest I had ever seen him and yet he had discovered this ruthless authority that made me feel he was planning our lives and deciding how we should live them for our own good, and we went along with him as if all volition had been taken from us. In a strange way it made the two of us allies. The tyranny of the terminally ill, I thought, half in helplessness, half in terror. Marsha tried to be cheerful but she was drawn and anxious-eyed. He himself was very calm.

I thought his motives were a mixture of self-interest and concern for us, especially Marsha. I felt sure he wanted to get rid of us, that he sometimes found our presence oppressive, not half as welcome as Nurse Padmore's massive efficiency; but he was worried about Marsha. 'Marsha's very intense,' he'd said to me the day before, and I knew him well enough to understand what was not spoken. Moreover, he had said it in the tone of one making an appeal, and though when he was most himself he had far too much delicacy of feeling to say outright, 'I want you to take care of her,' I knew what was being asked of me, and I had gone past resentment.

.....

On the journey out she asked me to drive. I glanced at her in surprise but I took the keys and the driver's seat. We rolled smoothly and soundlessly out of the driveway. We didn't speak. On the motorway she laid her head back against her seat rest, closed her eyes and sighed deeply.

'You do too much,' I said impulsively. 'You should let me do more. I hardly do anything. I don't have anything else doing – I can come earlier, more days...'

She smiled faintly, and suddenly her hovering butterfly smile reminded me of Denton's lopsided grin, and it occurred to me that in some ways they were more like twins than husband and wife. 'No, that's not true – you do do a lot. I couldn't ask for more.'

'I'm his friend too, you know.'

'I know.'

'But you're very tired,' I insisted.

'Not much. It's just these last couple of days – I sat up a bit because he was coughing quite a lot. Normally I'm ok, and I will be again, just as soon as I find a rhythm in this.'

It was true. She was generally a calm, even restful person to be around, quite remarkable in the circumstances. The intensity that worried Denton was kept tightly under the wraps of what I recognized now was a formidable discipline.

'You know of course what the coughing means,' she added. 'His lungs are going. It's the beginning of the end.'

'I know.'

Something fell apart – I don't know how it was – something gave way. Suddenly there was a huge relief in being able to talk about this openly, not in suggestive phrases or half finished sentences of innuendo, but quite naked and raw. When I look back, I don't remember the whole of that journey. A lot of it is blurred and kaleidoscopic, as if my mind doesn't want to remember. Yet it was one of the most important journeys I made in that long winter and fall. I remember that we talked, and talked, and talked, headlong and with great and inexpressible relief, about our feelings about what was happening to him, about when it might be, about how he probably felt. Later that night, when I was alone, I cried the tears I had not been able to cry for so long. I don't know if anyone heard me; I hope nobody did.

. . . .

It wasn't a successful visit.

The grandparents lived in a house near one of the universities at Amherst. The father was a retired professor of something. They met us at the door, a grey-haired couple who reminded a great deal of their daughter except that the father was very light-skinned, almost white in the pale light of an afternoon in fall, and that his reserve lacked her courtesy. Marsha introduced me as a friend of hers and Denton's; they received me politely. Neither of them spoke to me; when they had anything to say they looked straight at Marsha, but in the manner of people saying in parentheses 'and he, your friend, we're talking to him too', only they weren't.

Marsha said 'Dad, why don't you show Alain your orchids? Alain, they're the loveliest things – you won't believe it' – and indeed it was almost true. The old man took me through the rows of rare and astonishingly beautiful plants like a tour guide in a scientific establishment, giving clipped, precise information about age, type, origins, botanical names, taking refuge in the lesson, and I saw that unlike his daughter he was not simply reserved but shy. I wondered how on earth he could have taught any class. Maybe he had worked mainly in labs, doing research.

The child, Christopher, was beautiful. He flew out of the house at the sound of his mother's voice, screaming, 'Mommy! Mommy! Mom!' She held out her arms but he didn't run into them; he flung himself on her so fiercely that her limbs were bound by his arms and legs, and he wouldn't let her go for nearly half an hour after we arrived. When he was introduced to me he looked at me with eyes that the light seemed to go through – they were the colour of sea water – and said politely, 'Hello, Mr Lockheed,' pronouncing my name very perfectly, but he didn't see me.

Later, while his mother played with him and his toys on the floor I looked at him properly. He was light-skinned and light-eyed like his grandfather. The rest was Denton. Completely. I saw no trace of Marsha in him otherwise. I felt pain in my stomach, the vegetable shredder working overtime.

His mother went to make coffee. The grandparents were watching the news. It was a little while before I realized that he had stopped playing with his toys and was sitting back on his heels, watching me. I smiled at him, tentatively. I haven't had a lot of experience with children.

He didn't smile back. His look was grave to disapproval. 'Are you my Dad's good friend?' he asked, sounding exactly like a judge at a tribunal.

'Yes, I think so,' I said, feeling like a guilty witness.

'My Dad's very sick. That's why he couldn't come and see

me.' He gave this information in the same grave, slightly challenging voice, as if daring me to dispute it, but also as if hoping I wouldn't.

'I know,' I said, feeling helpless.

'I can't go to see him either.'

'I know. Not for now anyway. But soon.'

Surprisingly, he repeated my exact words. 'No, not for now anyway. But soon.' He seemed to think about it after he had said it, because he was silent for a while, and then he nodded his head vigorously up and down, as if satisfied. 'No, not for now anyway. But soon.' He had turned it into a kind of slow chant, talking to himself.

'Do you want to play? I can show you how to play with my trains.' He walked towards me on his knees, pushing the train set with them as he came. We were down on the floor in a tangle of lines and exaggerated noise which the grandparents were politely ignoring when Marsha came back in, and he went to her at once.

Afterwards I went for a walk to see the town and stayed away until it was night. When I came in Marsha was carrying her son to bed; he was flushed, overexcited, disturbed all day by his mother's presence.

'I want Uncle Alain to come too,' he said suddenly, holding out his hand to me. I was more than a little shocked. I hesitated, my eyes finding Marsha's over Christopher's head, but she nodded and mouthed silently, 'It's ok.'

He was already sleepy, and heavy for her, I thought.

'Let me,' I said. 'If it's ok with you, Christopher?'

Wordlessly he held out his arms. He was so light and delicate I felt he hardly existed. His arms were around my neck and it was hard to put him down. I stood awkwardly while he said his prayers in a rushed singsong, 'Bless Granpa and Granma and Mommy and please make Daddy better soon' but suddenly he paused and said very clearly and quite slowly, as if making sure I understood, 'and please bless Uncle Alain Mr Lockheed.'

'He likes you,' Marsha said afterwards, explaining. 'I think you represent a kind of safety for him, because you're someone who knows his father. Your presence reassures him that his father will be all right.'

I had never wanted to leave anywhere as much as I wanted to leave that place at that moment.

I said, 'But he won't be. Why let him believe a lie?'

But I too had told the lie. 'Soon,' I had said. 'Soon.'

She looked at me sharply. And we must have come a very long way in that one day because she laughed, reached out her hand and ruffled my hair. 'Poor Alain. He's only a child, you know. Don't be so intense about it.'

…..

Denton

Memory was a funny thing. He couldn't remember if all these things he remembered happened all at once, or if they happened in stages or in a completely different sequence from the way he remembered, or perhaps none of it was remembered at all and all of it was dreamed.

Sometimes he knows when he is hallucinating.

Alain at the end of a winter of walking days. Alain at the end of a long drop of brown land that fell away to the ocean on the other side of a long white road where a bus he had taken to nowhere disgorged him and a flood of picnickers at a touristy place called 'Portland, Maine.' Picnickers… so it must have been summer then, not spring as he remembered. He remembers that though the ocean seemed quite near he had to walk a long way around a headland to get there. *He walks very fast past a lighthouse and down the dips and humps of a hillside dotted with goldenrod, beach grass and sedge where sometimes the land hides the ocean and at other times reveals it to sight. He walks until at last he falls down into a kind of hollow in front of a fence and a sign that says 'Danger: Do Not Proceed Beyond This Point', and he sees that the land has indeed disappeared into a sweep of mudflats and ocean, but in the distance behind the ocean is a new rise of land, high brown cliffs that fall clear down to the flats. He sees that the water has two tones, brown near the flats, like weak tea, and after the tea great wastes of polished gray, as if the ocean has had a wound that has been sutured and imperfectly healed. The place is drowningly peaceful; he fancies he has reached the end of the world. And it seems to him quite prophetic in the most banal kind of way that he should have found Alain in a place like this, near the ocean, when he wasn't looking for company but wanted most of all to be by himself. He stands there hearing the ocean bark under the rock, watching how the birds in the cliff remain clinging to the rock face even after the spray rises up in towers and pounds it and recedes, hundreds of birds, huddled like slick black parcels tied with string. And he thinks how wonderful it would be to be silent like this, in a place like this, forever, at the centre of the earth, where it stands still and wheels or crawls in perpetual motion, never having to think, forever.*

He is standing here at the end of a long walking. All through the streets of America's capital, a long stretch of winter days, up and down, Connecticut and L, Massachusetts and H, Pennsylvania and Constitution, Dupont, 19th and K, and L again, 7th and R, Florida and 7th, 8th, 9th and New York, walking as if by walking he could shed a life like autumn leaves. Through all the long walking trying to cut himself off from the memory of duty, the tyranny of life lived among expectations, trying to remind himself that this waste he is wasting is on the university's sabbatical, the taxpaying people's time, rehearsing the words until he hopes to say them without a stammer: *I am never going back.*

He longs to hold on to this and make it a permanent freedom. The hunger comes with an intensity that is brutal. He has given coins to vagrants huddled in clumps on the covers of the steaming manholes hugging each other for warmth; given coins and looked directly into their faces with a wistful smile because he thinks theirs is the most enviable of states. He longs to shed his neat clothes and join the ranks of those that are outside of expectation, who will receive coins without connection because people will be kind to them with eyes averted, giving coins with hands that do not touch.

He tries to touch this pending freedom, but is unable, because he cannot imagine it. He imagines its consequences, the whisperings, the speculations, the questions. Was it drugs, marital disorder, AIDS? Why does a man in the best of society in the best of jobs, the best of wives, of reputations, disappear so soundlessly and so well? He sees the tabloid headlines of that small place screaming, and he sees Marsha's face, puzzled, wounded and accusing. But Marsha does not accuse. Marsha's wound is an accusation. Marsha is a compassionate woman who never screams, never berates, forgives. Marsha's forgiveness is so powerful. So cruel. It is so cruel to have so much power, and he doesn't know who is burdened more by it, Marsha or he.

At the fence by the ocean which he has found this morning when he boarded a bus that would take him nowhere in particular, a bus to Portland, Maine, when he had thought he might go to New York, or New Orleans, or New Jersey, but he boarded this bus because it was the only one on the ramp when he arrived there going nowhere in particular, after another night of walking, and saw all the people waiting, drinking Starbucks coffee out of cardboard cups in the morning that was so fresh the steam came out of their breathing mouths – at this fence this morning, he thinks about these things, though he does not want to think at all, forever, in this place, in this now, and he doesn't know where the voice comes from that says quietly, 'A bit of ok, isn't it?' because it is such a quiet voice it seems to have come out of himself.

He turns his face but not his body, wanting to screen this intrusion that is so quiet it is not an intrusion. Khaki-coloured eyes set deep, a bush of beard, red and sprouting, luxuriant around a blunt, rough-and-ready face. Inside the bush a thick, sensuous mouth that awakes a vague disquiet.

'Yes,' he says, turning back towards the fence to refuse this encounter. The man stands unmoving behind him, and he feels the familiar tightening of his body that tells him he is being watched, *in a certain way*, sized up in a slow sweep from legs to buttocks to waist, to shoulders to the back of his head that his wife says is not a head at all but a Benin carving. Blood crawls along his veins in a slow river, beats up against his pores. He turns around quickly and catches the fleeing edge of an expression on the face of the other. The look goes rigid, blanches itself out and disappears in little runnels and wrinkles that trickle down into the flow of beard.

A hand like a football glove thrusts towards him. 'Alain Lockheed.'

He takes the hand but does not say his own name. 'Hi,' he says. He has fought so hard for a cleansing anonymity that he will not give it up easily. Though he feels it is ok to say his name in a place like this, he does not say it.

'You're not from here.' The stranger makes a statement, in a matter-of-fact way that does not demand an answer. But now he is annoyed. He does not want to be forced into a meeting, where personal facts are to be traded and exchanged. He distrusts the leaping desire to say his name, and the look he has surprised in the eyes of the other, seconds before it was wiped away.

'You neither,' he says, and wonders why he bothered.

'No. New Zealand.' The khaki eyes have narrowed, quizzically, noting his reticence and refusal. 'Came here two years ago because I heard from a friend the fishing was good. Fell in love with it for other reasons and decided to stay. Been here eighteen months now. Intend to stay at least another year.'

He is a big, blunt man, not tall, but broad and thick and splayed, like a carpenter, or a fisherman, or a woodcutter. He says the sentimental words 'fell in love with' without any trace of self-consciousness or apparently any thought that he has chosen an odd or unmasculine way of speaking

…..

'What is your name?' Alain cried above the beating roar of the surf and the long keening of invisible seals just before he drowned.

'Denton,' he groaned, 'Denton Trent.' And fell into darkness so deep that it filled his mouth when he opened it to contain his last cry.

…..

They lay on their backs side by side in the hollow darkness, breathing dreadfully and then not breathing. Not speaking. But he could hear all of Alain alive beside him, could feel the pulse of blood under the other's skin crawling along the open channels of his arteries and veins. The beat of blood seemed to be a continuation of his own. Tenderness and the desolating joy of discovery clotted in his throat like tears and he reached out to clutch Alain's hand and they lay like that, fingers entwined.

…..

When the pictures returned he felt them in his body like a pressure of welts. His arms reached for the stroke of beauty that he felt was himself discovered, but his body with its weight of memories had become his own enemy and it opened gates and poured out visions that he could not withstand and from the beginning he had been lost; it ended before it began.

99

It was incredible to him how long they had talked, and how completely. Hour upon drowning hour, sharing the most ridiculous of secrets, the most mundane of stories, the deepest unasked questions, things they had told each other not because they were strangers meeting and needing to get acquainted, but because each felt he had entered into the most complete knowledge that he had ever had of himself.

.....

Truth was a mangrove with visible and invisible roots. He had never met anyone who fit him so closely. He had never loved himself so lustfully or so well.

.....

He had never dreamed the question at the base of his belly all these years would have been answered in this way, so fluently and so long.

.....

He had never known he would know at last, at the last.

.....

The sky was so thick with stars that their bodies appeared as bluish silhouettes interrupting the dark ground. The picnickers had gone. The other felt the turbulence of resolve in him and sought to bring it to closure by giving voice to his own question. 'What happens now?' he said, quietly.

He did not answer. Alain waited and then touched him on the shoulder and when he still didn't answer, made a quick rolling movement like a fish and, placing himself on the other side, lay looking directly into his face with that frank, direct look that had so delighted and startled him because it made him feel free to say anything he wanted to say.

'Well?'

He thought of the letter in his pocket. His hands tingled with a sense of its imprint where he had fingered it until its edges wilted and it looked old and washed.

'I'm going back,' he said.

Alain didn't speak for a long time. Then he said, 'Just like that.'

Again he didn't answer, but the other felt at last not his thought but the finality of his withdrawal. 'Ah,' Alain said, in a voice cruel with understanding. And again, 'Ah.'

He had never met anyone who fit him so closely.
'What are you thinking?' Alain said, after a very long time.
'Nothing,' he said. 'Nothing left worth saying.'
'Ah,' Alain said again. 'Then there's nothing to be said, then.'
'No, nothing.'

.....

But he had not followed through on that grand pronouncement because a week, was it a week later? – he didn't know – he was sitting across from Alain in a bar smiling at the bearded face in front of his and thinking how easily they shared the smallest of things, things that added up to more than the sum of themselves, more than the sum of acquaintance.

The things that separated them were also the things that made each see the other in himself. Both the children of islands, one surrounded by oceans, the other by the living sea. He had grown up in a village under his mother's stern protective eye, stoning mangoes and pocketing coins meant for the offering plate in Sunday School; Alain had grown without a mother or religion, with a wandering father on a boat on the high seas saying, 'Heed the song of the birds and the wind talking in your rigging, those are the true gods.'

Alain had knotted rope, trimmed sail and hauled rigging from when he was old enough to be standing up. He, on the other hand, had known only the immediacy of the sea, raw waves beating on his back when he dived, and his mother quarreling that he would drown.

Alain had never flown a kite until he was thirteen years old, while he had never been without one – from as far back as he could remember he had been a tatter of wind at the end of a streamer sailing up over the treetops into the limitless sky, his shirt tail flapping loose over the twin globes of his bare behind. At first, Alain had not even been to school. Schooled on the boat by his father, the only homes he had known had been the boat and the marina in Wellington where once a year they docked for their own version of thanksgiving and rolled on sailors' feet into the city to sample the bars, the markets, the astonishing Maori shops and, his father, the raucous, melancholy whores.

At seventeen Alain had lain on his belly counting springs in a bare mattress while his first lover cut notches in a piece of driftwood for trophy and for luck.

Alain had always known.

For Alain, life had been very simple until his father died. His law up to that time had been the law of the ocean and its untrammelled ways, and it had marked him for who he had become. His father was a boat engineer who had given up engineering for the love of the sea. The old man had died in the night of Alain's thirteen birthday and Alain buried him at sea and brought the boat in by himself with a sure hand.

'And that was my bar mitzvah, I guess,' Alain said, smiling in the easy way he had of making large things ordinary, manageable and small.

He looked at Alain's broad sleek muscles under the brown shirt and imagined the slight lad braced for purchase against the taut rigging as he pitched the wrapped canvas package over the side of the boat, reciting in his high, thin unbroken lad's voice the words of the Maori blessing he had learned from an old man in a shop. That was the only prayer he had ever prayed, this prayer on the night of his father's death, his thin body a dark leaf in the wind under the starless sky.

An uncle had taken him in and sent him to boarding school 'to civilize him after thirteen years with that shiftless man', 'but by then it was already too late,' Alain said, laughing.

The boy had grown into a man with rust-red skin, warmer to the touch than summer rain.

Both of them had shown off in the boys' toilet at school, seeing who could piss the longest and farthest. Alain had won his contest. He and his friends were not so lucky; they'd been caught almost in the act by the bilious housemaster who hated all boys and had caned them all thoroughly enough to last a week.

The housemaster is punishing them for wasting time in the bathroom, but he feels with an unnameable, exhilarating terror that he in particular is being punished for something else that lurks in the curves of other boys' spines. He wants to ask a question, so many questions he wants to ask, but who…? The question is not permitted and there is no one to ask.

The morning after the incident in the toilet is the last day of term. The headmaster calls the whole school together and gives a speech, as he always does on mornings of ceremony, the rituals by which one school session ends and another begins. 'Remember this, gentlemen, as you pass beyond these august walls and go out onto the streets and into your various abodes to enjoy the freedoms of the holidays, and be of some more than dubious use to your parents: it is the choices you make now that will determine whether you will derive any true benefit from the experience of being a student of this illustrious institution. Remember the motto of this school: *Choose with Understanding*. Gentlemen, you must understand. Everything hinges on choice. And no choice is an individual choice. Every choice involves the lives and destinies of others. No action is a private action.'

.....

There is an email from Marsha. She is worried because he has not answered his phone in days and she has something important to tell him. She can't wait and she's put it in the email. He prints the email off and wears it in his pocket. The paper is worn and washed where he has fingered it trembling for many days.

He thinks Alain was in the summer but he can't be sure, because he remembers walks on winter days.

The sun was blazing when the plane landed at St Georges and he saw Marsha at the barrier waiting for him, smiling in pink. The sun blazing; that was not hard to remember; he was sure it had been.

He is ten years old again. Tasting the scent of calla lilies and beeswax in the Pentecostal church where his mother took him to the altar and said he was saved. He sees himself like a lamb to the slaughter. He is frightened and excited, dressed black and white in the circle of women who surround him like a flock of birds, women who carry pain in their bellies like sacrifice:

Take me to the water
Take me to the water
Take me to the water
to be baptized…

He hears again the low hum, the hung stillness of the sound of holiness and the susurration of tongues above which the minister's voice intones, so that the small boy trembles and, watching this scene from his past, the man on the bed weeps. *'Dearly beloved…'*

'Dearly beloved, sin not… but if we sin, we have an advocate with the Father…'

Marsha backs the silver BMW out of the driveway with one hand while with the other she searches in her handbag to make sure she has her cell phone so she can call him later – on impulse, always on impulse – 'I love you, baby.' The dew-wet lawns flanking the driveway of his sleek house are silver and green, like a lady with diamonds.

Marsha, her heart in her eyes in the white wedding veil in the Catholic cathedral. At first he had gone there with her because that was where she liked to be, and later because of his own desire:

Kyrie Eleison
Kyrie Eleison
Kyrie Eleison
O Lamb of God
That taketh away
That taketh away
That taketh away…
Kyrie Eleison

In the end, he had been afraid to speak the question, turning away from the confessional because he was afraid the priest behind the grate would recognize his voice. But the unspoken thing that had made him wake up sweating in the night had stayed with him throughout the years. It lay in dark coils of sediment at the bottom of his heart; it lay at the root of himself where his trunk sprouted in two and made a tree that anchored his footsteps when he walked. Appalled, he turned his eyes away from the secret warmth in certain men's eyes and in shame from women's appraisal. There was no one to ask; they were not questions he could ask of his own self. Everyone whose opinion he valued knew the answers, but they were not answers that permitted the asking of such dark questions as he had. Questions that had made of his entire being one large unspeakable question sign.

He had not thought the question would be answered, at the last.

.....

Tonight he dreams of Geneve. She is standing at the end of a tunnel of light, smiling sweetly, welcomingly at him, looking so different from the old Geneve he had cared for as a child. Looking like somebody clothed in her right mind. Alain knows about Geneve, poor retarded Geneve with her bat's eyes and clinging hands of love; Geneve yelling when it wasn't him feeding her her supper from her special bent spoon of blackened silver, scooping the soft mush into her mouth and making threatening faces at her not to spit it out, grotesque faces that made her squeal in horrified delight; Geneve throwing her rag doll in a tantrum to the floor because he wasn't there to play with her; Geneve singing songs to herself in a tinny monotone, songs she called without exception 'Geneve's Secrets', all of them on one note only – G minor; Geneve sleeping, smiling sweetly on his shoulder where she had drooled a bucket and he would have to shower and change before going on the street with his friends; and Mammy saying, how she takes to you; I don't know what would have happened to her otherwise when I am gone.

In the end, Geneve went before them both, dust to dust, ashes to ashes in the purple shade of a June evening. The doctor said her heart gave out because in her condition her age was thrice what it was in normal people; at twenty-three years old she was really sixty-nine.

He had said to Alain, urgently, 'You understand, don't you? Don't you?' These things he had told Alain – narrative fragments of himself that he had given into the other's keeping and closed his fingers over like a gift – he wanted Alain to understand without the need for explanation.

'You come from a hard country,' Alain said, hurt and angry.

'Yes, that is true,' he said, not knowing how to say, truth is a tree with mangrove roots; the place I was born in is a small place, where no choice is an individual choice, and not to think of others first is taboo. How can he say, out of this experience grows a conviction – the choices you make are never wholly yours, but they decide what you will become, and sometimes you cannot take another direction without breaking. He wants to say, you learn that there is a small place inside your multiple selves where there are no multiple selves, only a single hard diamond that is as cold as a star.

He does not tell Alain about Marsha's letter and the baby coming. He feels that that has not altered his choice, though it has pushed him into making it sooner.

Smiling, he tells Alain about the old people in the village, 'Boy, when you grow up you go look after your mammy; she work hard for you, you know,' because he wants Alain both to understand and to laugh. Alain says this is crazy, this is damn crazy, tells him that he has no balance, that the essential him, the essential desire for life, has been sacrificed. You bow to authority, the collective, appearance, reputation, too much, Alain says. The integrity you guard so fiercely has become a lie. How can you live for others when you have not learnt to live for yourself.

I can't look in the mirror, going your way, he says to Alain.

Life is a season of revolving mirrors, Alain says. And every one in that mirror is you. Yet you sacrifice them all, for one, a root without leaves, without branches.

My mother took me on a ride once, in a hall of revolving mirrors. It was in a playground, at Hope Gardens, in a section with a big white sign: 'This way to the House of Horrors and the Toot Toot Train to There and Back Again.' They set the mirrors up so that in every direction I went, I saw myself facing the same way; only it wasn't me but many distortions of me. I got confused and frightened; I screamed and screamed until my mother came and took me away.

…..

Tonight he wants to tell Alain he is sorry, but the words have stopped coming. His stomach heaves in his mouth, in his nostrils, in hot spurting gusts like dragon's breath. What he remembers now is Alain's pain, and he knows it is his fault for not having left in the beginning, when he said he would, in the hollow by the ocean when there was nothing left to say, and Alain was willing then. He made Alain cry with an anger and scorn that shamed them both, because he had known Alain as a man defined by stillness, who was quiet because he had found where he wanted to be and simply stood there, inviting others in. Alain's quiet self-knowledge had given him an area of peace and he had robbed his friend of it. And, of course, as a robbery it had not been worth it, since for him the peace had been temporary.

But in the morning Alain drove him to the airport and they shook hands like cordial friends, Alain's body still and closed again, as if impatient to go.

He can hear people talking. The sound is far away, at the end of a tunnel. Faces hang anxiously over him… growing, shifting, drawing close and receding, running suddenly into each other and breaking away like paint that water has touched. They are too far away to matter; he really doesn't hear.

Kyrie Elieson
that taketh away

He finds himself looking eagerly into blinding light.

A light comes up as on a dark stage. Alain is standing in its pool in the Trents' living room, or rather, the small downstairs living room of the house the Trents have borrowed from a friend for six months from the summer. In a shadowed corner, on a bed up right, Marsha and Denton are embracing. Down right, a liquid dark shimmer against the long French window, as if the world is dissolving and slipping down the glass in dark clots, reveals that it is raining outside and that it is night. Alain stands arrested, taking in the embrace, and makes quickly to leave the room, but Marsha looks up with a kind of relief on her wet face and speaks soundlessly to him, Don't go. We're all right.

…..

Marsha

'War and Peace,' Alain said, holding me tight against his stomach where I had completely ruined his shirt with tears. 'Do you remember that part in *War and Peace*, where Prince Andre is dying and he sort of goes far away from the living, to another place that he's impatient to go to, and he's got this irritated look on his face as if to say 'What the… what have I to do with any of these trivialities…'

'Yes, that's exactly the way he's been looking at us,' I said, rescuing my face and scrubbing it with the handkerchief he so gallantly produced out of his pants pocket. Alain is the most unlikely carrier of large, clean, nicely-folded linen handkerchiefs, or rescuer of damsels in distress you could imagine: a blunt, rough-and-ready sort of man with a really prickly exterior. I don't know how Denton could ever say he's a still or a quiet man, but I think inside he really is, you know.

But still only a man.

Saying that makes me wonder if I am bitter. I don't know. There are a lot of things I don't know. Their doubt has made me doubt myself. I ask myself the questions they asked about me, the ones that they never asked out loud (except that once, when Alain accused me at lunch on the patio) but were in their eyes.

I am not crazy, neither am I a fool, but I know I do things that people think don't make any sense at all. I do the kinds of things that people study enthusiastically in graduate classrooms, Oh, great, oh wonderful, alternative knowledges, don't you just love the way they subvert reified rationalisms. But afterwards, after the class is over, if they went outside and saw a gipsy hawking ancient parchments on which was written the story of the one world or saw an eleven year old girl really carrying her parents' dead bones in a bag that rattled, they'd look at each other askance and shrug and say, knowingly, with little secret smiles, Ah well, what can we do, the world is full of mad people, or Why doesn't someone take custody of this child and put her in care – as if the child were someone else's business and not their own, and moreover as if it was very clear to any halfway thinking person what should be done with the child.

If I said 'I was guided in this,' nobody would believe me. They would believe exactly what Alain came to believe once he saw that I was not mad: they'd say I acted out of a perverse self-interest. They'd say I wanted to prove a point, how righteous I was, forgiving all, putting my husband's desires above my own. They'd say, you see how bad this can get, this definition of a doormat, women like this betray the sisterhood all the time, all the time. Can abasement be so utterly internalized, they'd say; what a really finely wicked woman; can you imagine a more subtle, more honed revenge, to be confronted at the point of his death by his former lover, the visible accusation of sin? (Though please don't forget that Alain, having come, stayed. That must count for something).

And because it all sounds perfectly rational – after all, who does any of this sort of thing for love (which in a case like this could only be interpreted as a want of proper pride) – I gave consent, I said yes, maybe, perhaps that is how it really was. No one really knows his or her own heart, not in the end, not really... all sorts of dirty secrets hidden there; wing-splayed vultures posing like messengers of light over the murky abyss, you know the kind... I went along with it to see where it led, this journey of speculation through my own heart, but when I reached the end of the road what I found there wasn't me. I didn't recognize any of those persons they said. None of them was me. So either I do not know my own heart – though, you know, all my life I've scoured roads and quarries searching, obsessed like a madman with his navel, counting each whorl over and over in case he misses one – you see them sitting on the streets, on the sidewalks of St Georges, Kingston, New York – either I don't know my own heart, or something else, bigger than the sum total of who we are, demanded it... If I said I was led in this, everybody would say I was mad. But God knows.

One thing is certain: like Job, I had to face my own fear. But that wasn't anything difficult; I found in the end it didn't even exist. How could it, when five years ago I'd already faced the worst fear that a woman living in the twenty-first century can face? And anyway, when you're facing an issue like death, you know you don't really own anything. What could I possibly have gained by holding on to safety, pretending that Alain did not exist in his heart or couldn't be allowed to mean more to him than I did? The questions that a man asks at the end of his life are not about that sort of alliance. They're about how to cross Jordan, Phlegethon, Styx. The computer underlined Phlegethon in red and Styx in green, though the spelling is right and there is no extra space between the words. You see, those words frighten even the souls of machines.

I don't want to be doing any of this, not here, not now, answering other people's questions, manufacturing a guilt I do not feel. And in the end they were both glad that he came. Surely that counts for something.

Denton wonders why I give so much; he cannot bear it. Women's things, he says, you break a man's heart. Is it any wonder we are afraid of you. But when he looks into my eyes he sees the truth, himself reflected there, and my helplessness, my longing to go with him the whole way, for company, safe passage, not just his, but my own. When we are together he forgets the questions, because he can see in my eyes that there is nothing to understand. In the end it is he who has comforted me.

Out here it is so dark, the hills are raining, how slick and smooth the darkness looks, like the back of a fish, what is Christopher doing now, is he sleeping yet, Mama will give him milk laced with chocolate, it puts him to sleep quickly.

I wanted him to be all right, is all.

Come in out of the rain, Alain is saying, his wet hand on my shoulder, my back. He wants you again.

[Out of the darkness, a choir of women, carrying pain in their bellies like sacrifice:
hmmmm
fix me
hmmmm
Oh fix me
fix me, Lord
for my journey
home]

In the night sky, witness Aluin, wanderer of the seaways, sky-traveller, who has followed these journeys, bearing record between heaven and earth, grimacing with one side of the face, always smiling with the other. The angel, not a creature of interiors, hovers vastly, everlasting wings lifted as in the conducting of an orchestra, the crashing cymbals of the dark rain.

SAY

From the moment she get off the taxi I know something wrong.
Is the Monday she phone me, say Gan Gan, I coming Wednesday.
I send Jew Boy taxi to pick her up at the airport, I couldn't go
myself much as I long to see my darling because the arthritis was
on me worse than usual. I sit on the verandah whole day straining
my eyes to see as far as I can see, till at last I see when the taxi breast
the bump in the road and drive up in the yard and Jew Boy come
out with her suitcase and bring it in the verandah.

Him is a mannersly young man and he give me good evening
and say, 'Mammy, I bring her safe. Where to put the suitcase?'

But I not hearing him for my eyes on my darling as she come
up the step looking so big young lady I can hardly believe is the
little scrawny something I bring back to life from three months
premature when the mother thought she would died. She say,
'Gan Gan', and I hold out my two arms and she walk in them and
hold on to me with her face hide in my shoulder, and is then I
know something really wrong. You see, I live on this earth by the
grace of Massa God eighty-three year now, and I practically grow
that little girl, for every Augas holiday the mother uses to send her
to me, put her on the plane from Castries to Bridgetown and from
Bridgetown to Montego Bay, from she small till she big and they
go away to America. So I have a good understanding, and that little
girl especially, much as she go away from me to foreign when she
twelve years old, I know her through and through. So from that
minute, I knew. Oh yes, I knew.

But I don't say anything. I leave it to her to tell me.

She ask for her old room and she don't even look surprise to
see I keep it just the way she leave it all those years, like it waiting

for her to come back. She sit in that room for three days looking out the window. What she seeing I don't know, for all that is outside there is the same banana tree with beard like old man wanting a trim, and the canepiece and the hill-and-gully ride and Moutamassy Liza housetop at the bottom of the gully where is only Jesus know how Liza climb up from it every day to mind people business and trace them. Nothing new that she don't know already, but she looking out like she searching for something that her heart break from losing.

But I don't say anything. I leave it to her to tell me. But I pray. I go down on my knee inspiten the arthritis because I realize is principalities and powers not flesh and blood, and I going have to storm Massa God throne, hold on to the horns of the altar.

I cook all her favourite food to tempt her appetite, corn pone, duckunoo, roast breadfruit and gumma, ackee and saltfish with hardough bread and avocado, rundung and salt mackerel with green banana. I make toto and bammy and drops and grater cake with the red colouring just how she like it, I even call Jew Boy to make mannish water as only he can make it, but though she try hard she don't eat much, she jus sit in the room searching the window for thing that lost. Finally I can't stand it no more, for is flesh and blood, so I go to the room door and I say dou dou? Mi binny? and she come out of the room and stannup there looking at me with her eyes far and her body naked as the day she born, and I see that she black and blue all over like tie-and-dye.

I cry out, Lawd Jesus, mi pickni! and I feel somebody shaking me and is Jew Boy stanning over me on the verandah where I doze off in the sun. He shaking me and saying 'Mammy, you awright? Mammy you awright?' and I realize was dreaming I dreaming and is a terrible dream.

But this time as I wake so, I get down on my knee in truth, for of a surety I know is not dream, is vision, and my one darling in trouble.

I can't manage the phone thing but I give Jew Boy the number and ask him to call her but him don't get any answer, so I ask him to call her madda and fadda and they say she alright as far as they know, she in school in Iowa and she keep in touch with them every two week. Jew Boy try plenty time but don't get her.

'Mammy, I think she awright you know,' he say. 'Maybe her phone just out of order or maybe she don't feel to answer. Dem American young people very different you know. Dem have mood.'

'My granddaughter not no Amurcan young people, you hear me,' I tell him. 'She wouldn't not answer her Gan Gan phone call. Something wrong.'

Next day Jew Boy come running like him mad cross my yard. 'Mammy, Mammy, she call, she lef metches,' he shouting pon the top of him voice.

I say, 'Jew Boy, stop mekking up dat ruckus in my yard,' but I so glad to hear she answer, I don't really vex with him. He do whatever he to do with the phone to make it talk and put it in my ears and I hear my darling, 'Gan Gan, I can't write now. But write me, please. I soon come.'

I play the metches over and over to see if I can catch anything in her voice but all I catch is the foreboding of my own heart that know trouble, but I say I give everything to my God, Massa Jesus take the case and on top of that I give you the pillow.

I write her. I write, I say, My dou dou I don't know what happening to you I trying not to worry, I say to myself maybe you busy with school work for I know how it go sometimes, I hope you are drinking plenty carrot juice for the eyes so you can see to read the words sharp and I hope you are taking your cod liver oil to keep your pretty skin smooth like how it used to be when you stay here with me when you was a little girl and bathe in the river. Your cousin Celeste say to tell you howdy, you remember Celeste? The jokify one. She uses was to go town to buy and sell but now she stop and gone back to her sewing, for the other day when she go to town big riot, and police tear-gas her and some other people and she lose all her goods. Celeste say ascorden to how it happen, a sewer main burst on King Street, and the vendors had was to heap up their goods on sidewalk so they wouldn't get soaked in the sewer water. One woman name Corpie who Celeste say is some kind of joker sit up on her mountain of goods with big placard telling everybody who pass, 'Danger! Filth ahead!' Filth is not the word she use, she use another word but my dou dou I shame to write the word, that is to show you how big people disrespect themselves these days. Things not what they uses to be. Jamaica change a whole heap since you gone. Anyway as I was saying, this Corpie woman there with her out-of-order announcement and some uptown young people pass and see it and start to laugh. The long and the short is the vendor dem get vex for they say the uptown young people disrespecting them, laughing when they in such a plight, so they make to attack the young people with stick and stone and is so police come and scatter them with tear-gas and rescue the young people dem. You see the sort of hooganeering? That is what is happening here these days, Lord have mercy on us. So now Celeste catch her fraid, for she say it could have been real gun the police shoot and nobody to tell the tale or perhaps the young people could have got hurt and murder commit. So Celeste staying at home now doing a little sewing, and Massa God is good for as I pray for her I see that she making it, not as much as the buying and selling but she making enough to send the children to school and buy book for Junior. My dou dou I telling you this to let you know that no matter how a situation hard, God find a way to work it out, so you must carry on and have faith. Your loving Gan Gan, Mimma Barclay.

Yesterday Jew Boy come and help me in my field and we plant a new row of tomato for her. I water it and I say the Lord's prayer over it. Jew Boy say, 'Mammy, if you so concern bout her, why you don't go out? Madda Penny can read her up and tell you what wrong. Is plenty people I know go to her and she help them.'

That Jew Boy is a nice mannersly boy, a God-bless boy, really helpful to me a old lady that he don't have to bother with for he young and have him taxi to run to make a living. He is not my relative but every week as God send, if is even two hour on Thursday, he come and help me, whether him bring my groceries in him taxi from Browns Town or help me weed out the field. I give him a smalls for him time, is true, for reward sweeten labour, but he don't have to do it so I thank him. Yes, a God-bless boy, I pray for him every day. But sometime he talk nonsense just like a lot of the heathen people around here. I say, 'Jew Boy, shut you foolishness. I not going to no guzzum wukker, you hear me? I pray to my God and Him wi take care. If my mouth bruk and I cannot say to God what I wants to say, I know who to call upon to travail with me.'

The boy look in my face and tell me, 'But Mammy, Madda Penny is not guzzum wukker. She say the Lord's prayer same like you and when you enter her balmyard you have to spin three time and say the Lord's prayer to show you is not a evil wukker. And anybody who don't do it, you hear Madda Penny start trump "hu-hum, hu-hum, hu-hum, somebody in here not clean. Come outa mi yard!"'

'Ah say stop the foolishness.' I rebuke him strong for I don't want my God to vex with me that I don't warn the young people when they going astray. 'All that is obeah wukking – why you want to spin three time to say the Lord prayer, ehn?'

'What it matter if you spin one time or three, Mammy?' He looking innocent but I know he trying to make fun of me. I tell him you not suppose to spin no time at all, let your communication be yea and nay, no spinning, for whatsoever cometh of more than these is evil, and I stop the conversation right there before he blaspheme and is I who encourage idle chatter.

In the night I write her name on a piece of paper and I spread it out before my God, just like how Nehemiah did spread out wicked Sanballat letter and God destroy Sanballat evil plan – *Nehemiah* Chapter 6 verses 14, 15 and 16 – so I plead with my God to destroy any evil plan that plan against my darling. I bow myself to the earth three time like David bow and I call out her name and I see when my God hear for lightning flash and thunder roll and the rain come down that night. Is long time we waiting for the rain for the fields well dry.

I write her. I write, I say, My dou dou how you manage with the bad food over there. You mustn't eat too much of it, don't make them kill you off. Take your cod liver oil and drink salt physic once every three weeks. If you can't get salt physic, take castor oil with plenty plenty water. I wish you was here so I could fix you some strong cerasee and noint you down with olive oil, give you some good ground food and some fresh fish to eat. When you coming to look for your Gan Gan? But I know you have to finish your studying first.

116

I write and I tell her everything that going on in the district, just to keep up conversation, but I don't hear from her. In Almighty God name I just keep on praying and saying my psalms.

I don't hear from her but I don't call the parents again for I don't want them to say I harassing them, especially the father for he and me don't get on, he say I don't like him for he come from St Lucia, and I think only Jamaica man good enough for my daughter. What a big woman like me doing disliking people because of they race? Some people is just like children, talk foolishness when they don't want to face they own fault. He don't treat my daughter good and when I talk to him about it he say I don't like him. But I a woman who talk plain. I say is not only your wife, is your daughter you damaging with you foolishness. You is her father, you is the first man she learn to trust or not trust and if you don't set her a good example she won't know who to trust and not trust.

Two nights now I dream her, I see her standing in the river bed with the moon in her eyes. I say Dou Dou why the moon in your eyes. She say Gan Gan my soul gone in hiding, is a lantern I holding to take it out. I say why you skin black and blue? You not using the olive oil I tell you to use? She say something that I don't hear but in my dream and when I get up in the morning I putting her name before God.

I don't hear from her but I keep on writing, for I says sometimes when you down and out and you hear a voice, a voice of somebody who love you, even if is from far, it hold you up like a rope that somebody string cross a precipice, and you begging Massa Jesus not to let them pull the rope up before you cross, though you not saying anything with words. I know how it happen when you can't speak but you hope somebody speaking for you. So I write her a letter every week. Can't do more because the arthritis, it on me real bad now.

Grandma, my mouth is broken. My mouth is full of sores. Gan Gan, I fraid of my own mouth, my own body. A stranger come in there and invade it and I feel so unclean. Grandma, I running fast from myself, I am running on a long white road to come to you but there is this thing running inside of me, I am inside it. They say it is my body, that is what the counsellor says. She says this thing running behind me catching up with me, so dreadful and horrible, is my body. But that thing is so dirty and ugly, Gan Gan, I don't know it from anywhere.

Grandma, do you remember the story you used to tell me when I was a little girl, about an old man called Hungry? He would look at you pitiful in the market and beg you to take him home, but he wants you to take him on your back because he is so thin and hungry he cannot walk. And when you feel sorry for him and take him on your back, you cannot get rid of him because he grows heavier and heavier and eats more and more and will not get down off your back.

Grandma I am going to be well. I was glad to get your letter yesterday. But I can't write you now.

My dou dou, why you don't write. Even a little card to let me know you alright.

I write, I say, all sort of things happening in the district now. Hattie gone, take the plane yesterday, and Missa Miller and Totol finally married, after living in sin so long. Forty-three years, till people all forget they not married. Their grandchildren was bridesmaid and flowers girl. Say they want to get in the church and make their way right with God. Well, it is never too late for a shower of rain, and those who are laughing had better stop laughing for they have not made their own way right, and while they are laughing, the opportunity might pass them by, though God forbid for the Saviour is merciful unto all. But if He call and they don't come, what can He do? All I say is dry stump a cane piece mustn't laugh when cane piece catch afire. Two of the little children in the district, you might remember they parents, Sam and Louise Lue, pass examination with the highest marks in the region. Not just Jamaica but the whole Caribbean region. I praise God, for the parents poor and humble and is try they try. God is good and the whole district proud. As if they was we own.

My dou dou, I dream I see you again standing in the river with the moon in your eyes and your body looking black and blue. This time I noint you with olive oil and I sing the songs of Zion over you and you lay down in my hands and I let the river water run over you. And I see where you fall asleep with the river singing over you. I goes on my knees and I says to my God, Massa God, is life or is death? She fall asleep to come to you or she fall asleep for she find peace in this life? My dou dou, I cannot even say these things to you, I has to ponder them in my heart like the blessed mother of the Saviour, for I don't want to make you fret. Some things I write, some things I only say, and I says them to myself and I pray.

Grandma, I don't go to school three days now. The counsellor says I am improving and she thinks it is her skills. But it isn't. I am getting better since I get your letters. But sometimes when I am inside a building I hear funny sounds in my head, bell a-ring, cement a-mix, like an election calling (Do they still ring bells at election time, Grandma?) or a cement mixer churning up inside my head. I go to sit in the park sometimes. I don't do anything. I just look at people walking their dogs and leaves falling and the way ears look funny coming out of the sides of faces – Gan Gan an ear is a really funny thing. I laugh both because it's funny and because I can imagine telling you this when I was little and you understanding exactly what I meant and laughing. I thank you for the letters and for planting the tomato row for me.

She sits in the park and she rocks herself and she rocks herself until her body feels wound round in a tight cocoon, and she is a little girl again crawling into her grandmother's lap in the rocking chair or hiding from her friends, laughing in a hollowed rock by the sea at Anse La Raye.

Grandma, I wish I could tell you the truth. But it cannot pass the sores in my mouth. I don't know how to tell. I told the counsellor but mostly it was she telling me, she made up the words when I nodded in answer to her questions. Grandma, can you imagine someone could look at you and think you were nothing, and smile with you and lie to you when all the time they were planning to cut you down, to tear you apart like you were a piece of rag, as if you were nothing and did not come from anywhere? At first after it happened I wrote a lot of poems, but I can't write poems any more. I had to throw them away. The counsellor says I should not have thrown them away but she says it was good that I wrote them because they probably saved my life, getting the poison out. But Grandma I still feel poisoned, I feel as though my flesh has rotted. I do not even like to touch my own self. Grandma just hold me tight with your rope of letters across this precipice, till I get over. Grandma I would like to come to you, or go to walk on the beach at Anse, but I have nobody left in Anse. Everybody is here.

My dou dou, I write, I say, Celeste happy as a lark. She have it hard, especially since she stop selling the goods and the sewing slow because of the competition from Half Price Depot, you know people go there and buy things cheap that come down from America, so they don't too wait for the tailor and dressmaker any more, so plenty tailor and dressmaker gone out of business, but those who selling the foreign goods, they prospering. Ah, my dou dou, the falling of a old mule is the rising of a john crow. Up to yesterday I see Mr Vassell Forbes, who they say was the best tailor on the ridge here, catching bus to go to his security guard work in Montego Bay, for that is what he doing now to make a living, had was to give up the tailoring. But God is good and He hold strain with Celeste and she able to send the children out to school in them new khaki this bright September morning, and the best of all is Junior, he pass the GSAT and going to high school. You should see the boy, bright as a new quattie. The boy say, Gan Gan, Mama, I go work hard in school and make you proud of me. Watch me and see. When I see him my heart full. I say Massa God, praises be to you, You give me not just the bare seventy years that You promise Moses but you give me thirteen years reason of strength to see my great grandchild come out to something. And you let me still be able write letter to my dou dou in foreign, though the wicked arthritis trying to hold me down.

I write, I say, Your granduncle, I forget to tell you about him, he here boasting up himself same way as he used to do when you was a child. Old age on the man and he still carrying on like he is a child. He going around telling everybody how Junior pass the highest in the country and is his family side of blood Junior inherit why he so bright. Well you see, the Almighty have a sense of humour for he was there telling that to the man whose daughter come first in the class, beat Junior, but he don't know is the man daughter, so the man just let him talk and then he laugh behind his back. I say Cecil, you talk too much and you talking embarrass the children, that's why they don't like to go anywhere with you. I say your enjoyment is their grief, what feed him wife, kill Jack Sprat. You must stop it. But he don't pay me any mind. The boasting just in him like that. You remember the time when you were little and your other cousin Manfred get the teaching assistant job at the primary school and he went around telling people how Manfred get job as headmaster at the school? Some people did believe him and come to tell me congratulations. I had was to pray for Cecil same time. You would think a big man would sit down and talk to his God and prepare himself for when his time come, but no, not Cecil. Jus like a child. Ah my child, it take all sorts to make up this world.

I remember Uncle Cecil. I used to be vexed with him but when I got older and understood him a little better he used to make me laugh. I think he was just living out his own unfulfilled dreams through our success. But once he was cruel to Celeste. I remember one summer when I was there, he had to take her to the doctor. Celeste didn't want to go because she said he was always saying things to embarrass us in public.

'Lie, lie, lie dem a-tell pon mi,' Uncle Cecil protested, and Celeste's mother Aunt Vie counselled him very strongly, hushed Celeste and sent her off with him.

They were standing at the bus stop and getting along just fine, until a lady came along, who Celeste said was looking very smart, dressed like she was going to a wedding. Celeste notices after a while that Uncle Cecil is looking at her, Celeste, and looking at her and looking at her and his eyes are narrowing and becoming critical as he looks her up and down.

Feeling uncomfortable, Celeste says, 'Uncle why you looking at me like that?'

'Why you comb you hair in that ugly style to make yourself look so ugly?' Uncle Cecil says. 'Don't I tell you not to comb your hair like that? It don't look good."

Celeste said the ground just opened up at her feet and took her in. But the dressed-up lady looked around and said, 'But I think she looks lovely! I always do my daughter's hair like that.'

Celeste was wearing corn rows, which Uncle Cecil hated, and that was the whole trouble. But from the lady opened her mouth, Uncle Cecil changed his tune. The lady was not only well dressed, she was brown and spoke English. Uncle Cecil saw the chance to social climb, even if it was only for a few minutes till the bus came. All of a sudden Celeste hears, 'Yes is a nice hair style, fit her, but she don't do it good this time. See some strands hanging out the side there.'

Celeste said she was so shocked and angry she couldn't speak.

'Oh no,' the lady exclaimed, 'Not at all. Just a strand or two, and it makes her look so cute.' Celeste didn't like cute, but she was so glad for the lady, she wasn't quibbling.

Before she knew it, Uncle Cecil and the lady were in big conversation which continued till the bus came, Uncle Cecil boasting about all his nieces and nephews, including Celeste, who had become the mayor's daughter by the time the bus reached its destination. But the best part was when after they got off the bus and Uncle Cecil and the lady waved goodbye, Uncle Cecil went in his pocket and gave Celeste a hundred dollars to spend for herself for creating the opportunity for him to talk to 'that nice brown lady.' He was always doing things like that. He would make us feel bad because of the ways he used us to make himself look good, and then he would feel awful and try to make it up to us by giving us presents.

I understood afterwards what was wrong with Uncle Cecil. He would do anything to reach the moon. Celeste told me in a letter, when we used to write, before I got used to being in America, that he mellowed with age and stopped embarrassing people with rude remarks in public, though he has never stopped boasting. The world as it is has never been good enough for Uncle Cecil, so he makes it up as he goes along.

Today, Gan Gan, your letter made me smile. It hurt to smile, my mouth is so full of sores, but at least I did. Smile. The therapist says it's a good sign.

But Gan Gan, it comes and goes. Some nights I dream I see you in the river, holding out your arms to me and smiling, the river running so sweet and free, and other times I dream like I dreamt last night the terrible dream that I cannot tell you. It is like touching my body that I don't want to touch any more.

The dream she don't want to tell Gan Gan is the one where she wake up to find herself heaving and humping on the bed like she lifting weight, her face wet with sweat and tears from her eyes squeeze catatonic shut, one grotesque caricature of the act of love, one desperate bid to heave herself out from under the flood of sewage that pouring on her head. Somebody open a sluice gate in a silo of filth and the nasty water pouring out on top her like Joseph in Egypt pouring grain. She say Gan Gan, the sewer-water washed out Celeste's goods on King Street, and it is washing me out same way in America now.

But she is dreaming that dreadful dream less and less these days now. More and more, it is the river dream that she dreams.

And Gan Gan, last night when I wake from that dream I read your letter about Maisie buck down the big bull cow, and I laugh till I cry.

And after she has finished laughing, she says she will go to her grandmother, she will walk through the district on glass nails till she comes to the tree where her navel string is buried, she will make lightning flash from her wounds. Miss Mimma will give her peas soup and beverage with lime, will noint her down with oil.

'See I wash you in the river.'
'Yes, Gan Gan.'
'I noint you.'
'Yes, Gan Gan.'
'Drink the peas soup.'
'Yes, Gan Gan.'
'You revive now.'
'Yes, Gan Gan.'
'Try your tongue, don't you feel the silence breaking?'

This morning Jew Boy come in my yard asking me if I going to Curly funeral and I don't know if is because of that why I see what I see in the dream where, as I lay you in the river, a big black man looking just like Curly standing on the bank, watching and looking dead. When I wake up from the dream I don't feel good. Who is that man, is Curly or who?

I say, I write, My dou dou, I hope you well, in the Saviour precious name. I longs to hear your voice, hope you write me soon. My binny, all kind of wickedness going on. In these enlightened modern times, when people should look to their God, you still have people practising back-o-wall wickedness. You remember Maas Curly, the deacon that work as overseer at Hampden sugar factory when you was a little girl? He die yesterday. Strange and sudden death. Ascorden to how Jew Boy tell me, he pay D Lawrence to tell him how to hold on to his position at the factory till he die. And the D Lawrence man tell him he must throw the big Bible off the church podium into Pan Swamp and as long as it in there, nobody can take him out of the overseer job. And all these years Curly is in the church preaching from the pulpit, and all these years at the factory disadvantaging the young girls that come to look work, and everybody know, yet nobody do anything about it for Curly put spell on them. And Curly never need to do it for he have a wife. But he do it because he feel he have the power. Dog have money, buy cheese. Yesterday a cow fall in Pan Swamp so they had was to dredge the swamp to get it out so it don't stay in there to rotten an pollute the atmosphere. Jew Boy was there. Jew Boy say people stannup on the bank looking to see the cow come up and instead what come up is a big black leather case cover over with weed and slime, eh, eh, then is what? They zip it down and lo and behold, Satan is the father of all wickedness. My dou dou, not the Bible that missing from the church pulpit all these years? That was what was in the case!

All this time I in the house sweeping out as best as I can with the wicked arthritis riding me, and sudden so I hear a mighty scream, as if all the demons of hell let loose, and when I run outside, what that? What that? Is Curly drop dead in him house at the same exact moment that the Bible raise up out of the swamp, never to rise again. Dead as dead can be. The scream I hear is the sound that Curly make as he see the pit of hell open at his feet and himself falling down in it. Now all the church people who should have rebuke him long time, gone on fasting and praying, sweeping out and repenting. Massa God is merciful but sometimes I wonder how people take chance with Him and call themselves Christian, and who to blame, if is only Curly or is the whole of them.

Grandma, your letter cut me like a knife. Gan Gan, I think I am going to hell. I prayed against a man and he died. He killed himself. It was on the news this morning. He was an important man. It came on the international news. Grandma, he hurt me so bad, so bad, I didn't do anything to him and he hurt me so bad. I prayed to God to do him something bad in return, and he died. Gan Gan, he hurt me in a place I cannot tell you where.

My dou dou, I have a strange dream in which I see you crying crying crying, saying Gan Gan I make a man die. A man that hurt me and I pray to God to do him something bad and he take his own life. I see you bend in two like a thing that break and when I grab you suddenly I see you in the river and your body slip through my hand and I fall in the water with you and I swim with all my strength gainst the current till you reach a culvert where your body can't go through. I don't know where the culvert come from in the river but I thank God I grab on to you and I hold you and I wake up from my dream. Sweet dou dou my binny, what kind of thing is happening to you? You don't know that you can't make God follow you to do bad thing? God make up His mind what He will do. No prayer you pray make Him do evil or change His mind. It only change you. Man kill heself, is not God or you. Man do such a thing to himself is a man have more pain inside of him than Job read bout, is a man that turn his face away from his own self in folly. Every dankey have him own cubby, every tub pan sit down pon him own bottom. Man deal with him own life, you have to deal with fi you. My dou dou, rise up and live. Come let I noint you with olive oil and wash your batter-batter in salt and rub you down with blue.

Eighty-three year now I eating salt on this God's earth and never, I tell you, I know pain till now. I see clear clear now that my dou dou in trouble, I see it, Lawd. I see at last what the man do to her and I bawl. I hold my womb and I bawl. I ban my belly and I bawl. I hold her bend-in-two body under the river water and I bawl. I travail in the spirit three night and day, I call upon the sisters to travail with me, forty days and nights seven times round I spin, I groan, I trump – Madda Penny couldn't show me nothing how I trump. I say hu-hum, hu-hum, hu-hum, hu-hum, mercy Jesus, mercy Lawd. I flat on the ground, I see nothing, I eat nothing, I cannot talk. I lie on the ground like Saul.

All night she vomits, she sweats; rolled tight in a ball, she moans, as if in the morning she will die. When the pale sun falls in the room, the counsellor looks at the doctor and says, 'She has passed the worst. She will recover.'

The doctor smiles. 'I commend your skills.'

The counsellor gives a modest answering smile.

Grandma, I see myself on a minibus driving to come to you. It is day but the moon is shining. Apocalypse in the sky. The road is long and white and you are a tiny dot at the end of the road. It seems that I will never get to you, but I know I will and I say to the driver 'Faster! Faster!' and he speeds up the bus until it is flying. I can see ahead of me what is going to happen. I will step off the minibus when it reaches the district square, right in front of Mr Wycliffe's shop (Does Mr Wycliffe still have that shop, Gan Gan?) People in the piazza, sitting on the stone wall, will call to me and say, 'Miss Mimma granddaughter, pretty girl, you come to look for the old people? But you look nice, how nice you look, foreign gree with you!'

I will be glad to hear their voices, even though I know it is not true. Foreign don't 'gree with me.

They will look at me funny because I came in a minibus and not in a Bimmer, they will say (but not so I can hear) that I am not supposed to be coming from foreign and riding a minibus instead of driving a Bimmer, they will say I must travel in a way that will lift up my grandmother. Grandma, I would not be able to explain to them that I came in the bus because I want to ride with real, with glory, with judgement, with the smell of kerosene oil in pan in the minibus-back and yam, patty, cocobread, skellion, thyme, life and red peas, sun smell and people cussing, mercy Jesus! That I come that way because I want to ride with body self.

They will whisper and then they will say, when I call out good evening, some brazen boy will say, 'Hail sister. So what you bring for the poor?'

And I will say, 'Ha! The poor – don't you know I am the poor? What you have to give me?' and they will say, 'Nah, man, you is not the poor, you is the rich, you coming from foreign, you must have something to give.'

I will pass them, the boys on the corner, complaining, 'Cha, she too mean.' They will kiss their teeth in disgust, and I will be laughing in my sleeve, because I am so glad to be home and hear their foolishness.

Grandma, I get excited thinking how I will walk fast past them to come to you, and I get back in the minibus and say to the driver 'Faster! Faster, don't stop!' and Gan Gan, when I look it is me alone in the minibus. There is no driver and no market people, only the wind driving through a blackness in the trees. I see myself and I am not a real person, but only a ghost that the wind driving through. I calling out for you and I calling out for Anse La Raye, and is not my voice I hear, what I hear is a wind off a overturn boat in Castries.

Gan Gan, I fraid, I so fraid. I turn right and left for help and instead I see a big duppy man laughing at me and I realize is the wind I hear passing through his bones. And just as I am about to die a second time, I hear your voice calling me, Gysette, Gysette! I look up and I see you clear clear at the end of the road and a whole set of other women holding their bellies like coalpots full of sacrifice standing up straight behind you. They look like a wall, and I don't know where the words come out of my mouth but I hear my self say, 'Retro me, Sathanas!' and I cross my two hands 'Pow Pow!' and the man disappear and I see that he and the wild wind was a lie. When I look again I see a girl walking naked into a green river and her skin shine and I see an old lady looking at her with deep smile and I cry out, 'Gan Gan! It's me, Gysette!' And I go in the girl and the girl go in the river to the old lady, and is me, Gysette.

She strike her two hands sudden so, 'Pow Pow!' and the man disappear. She cry out 'Gan Gan! Is me, Gysette!' and she wake up.

She feel weak weak weak and she don't know what it mean. She put her head between her knee. She say, Gan Gan, what does it mean?

Late in the night she see a funny thing in the sky. She standing up at her window with the lights out, for she like to watch the night in the dark. That way she can almost see heaven behind the electric light. She see a big stain like a sheet in the sky, and while she watch, the stain shift shape and resettle and turn into two big angel wing, spread out. She see things write on it like rune, and she straining her eye to see what the writing say but the cloud reshuffle itself so fast, it disappear, and she find herself watching a rainbow like a arc in the sky. She say to herself, I am really hallucinating now. This is the kind of thing that used to happen to people who went to England in the old days – you know England is a place that used to make black people mad. But I am not in England, I am in America, and this is not a dream, so I must be mad. I am standing at this window going mad, after coming through hell in such wringing wet dreams, quietly stark staring mad, for where does a rainbow come from in the night?

But see ya, sah. Big shining rainbow, colour of the sun just set, or rising. Blue green yellow orange red, look it there, it stain the sky. And sudden so, she feel the weirdest hope taking wing in her heart. That is how she know prayer answer, benediction come. She decide that she going to find back her body, live in it again, and she hanging on to the navel string that connecting her 'cross the rainbow to Gan Gan, Mammy, Miss Mimma Barclay letter dem. In a funny moment, she feel to say after all she could fly.

She will write to her grandmother in the morning.

The one Jew Boy is a real Godsend. He cheer up my spirit. This morning he come in the yard looking at me and smiling. Not saying anything, just smiling.

'What you looking so please with youself so for, Jew Boy?' I ask him.

'Is you looking please with yourself, Mammy,' he say. 'I here looking at you looking please. Is days now I don't see you looking so please. So don't I also mus please?'

I just look at him and laugh, I don't answer him.

'So, Mammy. Tell me the truth. You go to Madda Penny?' That boy don't stop.

'Madda Penny? What I have to do with Madda Penny?'

'But you granddaughter awright. I feel it.'

'Yes, my granddaughter awright, praise God,' I tells him.

'So how you know? You get letter?'

'No, but I dream her. And I see where she don't black and blue any more.'

He don't say anything, but I can see he think I don't get enough surety, I should still go to Madda Penny. I pick up the watering can and I says to him, 'Son, you coming to help me weed the tomato this morning?' For I done with this conversation.

He stannup there a good while studying me before he smile and say, 'I hear you, Mammy.'

I singing serene and he walking behind me. Nice God-bless boy.

NOCTURNE IN BLUE

In the summer of 1995 I was offered a position as writer in residence at a small liberal arts college in the American Midwest. My job was to teach two six-week poetry workshops in addition to giving occasional public readings from my own work. At that time Marina and I had been married only two years; I was just three years out of a rather nasty divorce, and so the security of the relationship mattered to me a great deal. I was also very much in love with my wife, with a kind of passion I had never before known, but which I was warned by well-meaning friends was the definitive sign that I was terrified of growing old. Marina was twenty-five years old and beautiful in a wild, Irish kind of way with her red hair, green eyes and pale skin like white opals. We looked well together: her dramatic colouring against my dark skin and brooding blues kind of face.

I was lucky to have found Marina. She came into my life at a time when I badly needed a reprieve from the storms and hurricanes of five years with Majda, my first wife. I came out of the experience totally exhausted and at first I hesitated over Marina, but once I realized that her looks belied her true character, I knew what I needed and I did not hesitate.

Majda, ice-blue as the northern fjords of her Scandinavian homeland, had had many lovers. I was Marina's first love. That both humbled and terrified me. 'I've always preferred older men,' she insisted, when I told her my fear that soon the thirty years difference in our ages would indeed make a difference. She would reach the full bloom of her womanhood and I, hungrily coveting her youth, would almost certainly begin to fail.

'Youth!' she cried scornfully, in her soft, womanly way, smiling. 'What is it with you and this youth? It is you I care about. Only you! Always!' and she showered me with kisses until I drowned again under her spell.

I didn't tell her my other, secret, fear, the one I kept hidden even from myself, though Majda had known it and mocked me with it at every promotion I got, every new honour I gained for my teaching or writing.

Marina is extraordinarily proud of my success as a writer, even though I am really just a lesser light in the literary galaxy. If there is any kudos to be had from being awarded an M.B.E., it is not the kudos of being thought major, which I am not, but of being recognized at last as a British writer, no longer merely a quaint outsider scrabbling on the margins of the nation's literary life. I struggled to achieve this for a long time and I feel like a voyager who after many years at sea has finally come home. The year of Marina's advent, coinciding with this enigmatic arrival, seemed a kind of omen – the turning of my life towards a new beginning in which anything was possible.

Marina is neither ambitious nor literary – the national honour excited her because she loved me, the invitation from America because she liked to travel and the idea of America fascinated her. 'Of course you must go! We must go!' She launched herself in my arms, persuading me with kisses, but I had already decided; my whole life was dedicated to her pleasure. When she was excited her red hair forked on end, crackling with static, while her pale skin grew paler and more wan, as if all her body's fire was caught up in her hair.

Between the hectic preparations for leaving and my own self-conscious exercise regimen, I shed fifteen pounds at the start of that summer. We arrived in America young, much, much younger than I knew myself to be, and full of hope.

America proved to be more civilized than I had expected. We were received and treated like royalty, if the American way of thinking can concede such a thing. The Accommodations Officer met us at the airport, an impossibly blonde woman who did not bat an eyelid when she saw me and my wife together, though I wondered if she could have known what to expect; perhaps she had seen photographs of us at some public function in the newspapers and was well prepared for us in the flesh. But I am told the Americans are more tolerant of these things than the English.

The house they gave us was a huge, colonial-style affair with shining wood floors, and high-ceilinged rooms that we soon learned to consider a blessing in the Midwestern heat. Marina was totally taken with the place. She flitted from room to room, her squeals of delight so reminiscent of other, more private encounters, that I found myself brutally aroused and as soon as the Accommodations Officer left we made love on the dining room table in a short, sharp burst of exhilaration that was more mine than hers, but in which she acquiesced in a surrender more total than mere abandon. This capacity for surrender, this utter, quiescent giving of herself, so that you felt her body opened was the gateway to her soul, was Marina's true genius. In two years with her I had laid my ghosts; I felt that I could be whole again.

Even if it is only for three months, Marina is looking forward to putting our stamp on these beautiful rooms, each of which is big enough to be a house by itself. 'But we have already put our stamp, darling,' she croons, laughingly blowing a kiss to the exhausted table top as she shakes her glorious hair back into place. I think for the millionth time how lucky I am to be alive, in this place and time, to be married to Marina, and I tell her again how grateful I am to her and whatever gods there are for this second chance. It is the kind of thing I could say about myself only to Marina, the one woman in the world without guile.

Settling in has been fairly easy and I'm comfortable with the class. At first I anticipated problems, teaching in a culture so different from mine, but it seems to be true at a certain level that students are the same everywhere and there have been no surprises. A very average class: most of them willing to work, most reasonably, none spectacularly talented, all taking themselves more seriously than warranted either by their ability or the importance of the workshop itself.

At my first seminar I sought to deflate overweening expectations by pointing out that there was nothing particularly special about this occupation called Art, it was an occupation like other occupations, and if any of them had a gift, it was a gift like other gifts, to be compared with teaching, or farming, or running a shop.

'Writing is no different from these; it takes the same daily death – the same scrabbling with mediocrity – the same dogged scraping at the earth for roots to eke out a living,' I said.

They stared back at me with blank faces that spurred me to expand my homily. I said there was no such thing as inspiration, and if there was, it did not run down in everlasting streams, but furtively, barely, behind the back of sweat, and moreover, in the unlikely event that any of them became writers, they would not be privy to any special insights that were denied to the rest of humankind. 'All you have, if you're lucky, is a particular relation to words – and if you think I'm talking about art for art's sake, forget it. What you're doing had better have some material use in the world. Otherwise don't bother.'

The response was mostly the usual nervous confusion; someone asked his neighbour in a loud whisper, 'What's with this guy?'

A few smiled to show they had got the joke. One hardy soul ventured that he wrote mostly under inspiration. When I asked, 'How often do you write?' he said, 'All the time'; I replied that what he produced was probably self-indulgent verbal diarrhoea, not art, after which they realized that I was serious and the class was silent.

They didn't believe me, but it may be that a few of them were a cut above the ordinary, for they turned what I said into irony, that is to say, into fiction, a way of looking at things in which there is nothing that cannot be turned to advantage. Which is just to say that they went on believing themselves to be special and me a mere strategist trying to do his job in an interesting way, a crock who could be transformed by words to look better than he really was. So, to my amusement, over the next few weeks I was regaled with the occasional attempt at verse in which I was the undisguised butt of satire.

This was the formula with which I approached all my classes; I found that it worked, energizing them either to prove me wrong or, more usually, to prove me right, though my secret hope was always that my expectation would prove untrue, and one day a star would burst in my brown classroom. I would open the pages of someone's portfolio and there I would find it, the perfect gift, the pupil who would teach me more than I could teach him, who would do nothing and everything I wanted him to do, who, for one perfect moment lifted out of time, would turn the drudging clothes of everyday into the plumes of estridges. I longed for the perfection of art, a chance to hold it, touch it and feel it under my hands, through someone else's words because, in my heart of hearts, I knew that my own gift was small.

Later, I was to look back and think that this was a hope kept so secret, even to myself, that it surprised me when I realized it was there. Even Majda had not discovered it and dragged it mocking into light.

Marina meets me for lunch at the staff bistro and afterwards we stop at the supermarket for wine and steaks. Marina plans a romantic evening. She has been arranging romantic evenings since we arrived, 'to show ourselves worthy of the ambience,' she says laughing, pronouncing 'ambience' with a deliberately mock French intonation. 'One can hardly guzzle fish and chips within the precincts of a manor like this. Caviar and croissants, yes – fish and chips, oh darling, *definitely no*!' I like fish and chips, am in fact a regular customer at Addison's on Piccadilly Road, every Friday night at eight unless we're going out to dinner. But Marina's *esprit* is catching, and she's right of course, the place does demand a certain style (which I doubt the Americans give it) – not to mention that this is America, not Piccadilly, and fries are not half as good. So far, in deference to *ambience*, we've had French, Italian and Greek cuisine and Marina is experimenting; she cooks well and her pleasure in the whole thing takes the exhaustion out of dining *cordon bleu* three evenings a week at seven.

'A girl joined the class today,' I tell her casually as I put the car in gear while she settles our purchases between the back seats. The car is another American statement that the university has put at our disposal, a Cadillac Catena, the last word in oiled silk.

'Oh really,' Marina says. 'But darling, can they join so late? I mean, it is all of two weeks!' She settles in her seat, her body leaning towards me so that I find it easy to touch her while I drive. Her tone lifts my own speculation and makes it legitimate, important.

'Three weeks, actually. Seems she had some problem and received a special dispensation to register late.' I swing the big car out into the road that is really too small for it and think how much better it would look on a runway.

'What kind of problem?' I know Marina isn't so much concerned with the girl as in letting me know she continues to be interested because it is about me.

'I have no idea. She presented some paper from the Chair asking me to waive the ninety percent attendance criterion for passing the course. She hadn't submitted a portfolio beforehand, so I have no idea of her capabilities – but I sensed she was a special protégé and no questions to be asked. The Chair does have that way of letting you know her power and what she wants. I went with the flow.'

'Hmm, sounds like a real murder mystery,' Marina said, smiling at her own small joke. 'But you'll know in time whether she's any good,' she added, in that way she had of consoling me, her sympathy not in proportion to the occasion, but to her sense of our solidarity as a couple.

'Hmm. She handed in her portfolio with the note, so I'll know tonight, when I've read it,' I told her.

From the beginning, I thought of her every day. Even if there had not been the obvious reasons that made her conspicuous, her behaviour would have seen to that. She chose a seat by herself in the back and sat there, unsmiling, not speaking, looking at everyone else with wide open eyes that reminded me of places I had deliberately left a long, long time ago. She seemed unmoved about being late, or by the animated discussions going on around her; her silence was not the silence of discomfort but of extreme self-possession, as if she were a favoured visitor or someone sent to evaluate my class.

The silence was unnecessary. She stood out because of what she was. I disliked having her because from the beginning her presence forced an inevitable speculation of alliance between us from the other students and raised the possibility that she had expectations of me that I was on principle bound to frustrate. I felt an undirected anger at finding myself in this position.

'So, is she any good, darling?' Marina called from the kitchen, her voice wrapping itself around the fragrances of grilling steak (lightly seasoned in garlic and chives) and the clink of ice in glasses.

I didn't answer. I reached for another cigarette which I knew I shouldn't be smoking, my right hand fumbling with the lighter while my left turned the last page of the folder on my lap. I closed the folder and sat with the still unlit cigarette in my hand.

'What was that, darling?' Marina drifts into the room, bringing my replenished mug of beer. She is wearing a Japanese kimono, silk, in misty shades of mauve, blue, aqua and green. Marina likes to wear other cultures. Her hair flames another light above the robe's translucence.

I take the beer and move to stand at the windows. Marina follows me and lays her head in the small of my back; with her mouth she nuzzles into my shirt and kisses my left shoulder.

I'm holding the mug of beer in my right hand; with my left I cover her two hands which are crossed around my waist. 'She's all right. Not any worse than the rest.' My left hand is cold because I'd taken the mug with it at first. I rub my fingers to and fro over hers in apology for making them cold.

'Hmm,' she murmurs, our fingers playing tango. She asks me to lay the table for dinner and kisses my hand before going out.

The silver and white candles in Marina's cupboard are bright and winking over a thick layer of undergrowth in a green forest dripping with rain. A boy is swinging on lianas roped among trees and calling down to other boys standing on the ground, watching and laughing, while he looks at me directly with indecent eyes. *And I watched the vowels curl from the tongue of the carpenter's plane,*

resinous, fragrant
labials of our forest …
no day breaks without chains,
bent like a carpenter over the new wood,

a galley slave over his scarred desk,
hours breaking over his head in paper,
even in his sleep, his hands
like lolling oars.
Where else to row, but backward?
Beyond origins, to the whale's wash,
to the epicanthic Arawak's Hewanora,
back to the unimpeachable pastoral,
praying the scales would flake from our eyes
for a horned, sea-snoring island
barnacled with madrepore,
without the shafts of palms stuck in her side.

These are not lines from her poems, which are rough and raw, not this silk and elegant grit, but they are lines from another nurtured in that place that I do not care to remember and this is the fire with which she writes. Not yet this flame and strength, but the promise is unmistakable.

It doesn't occur to me to wonder if she wrote all that stuff herself. I know that this is new and different; plagiarism doesn't enter my mind, because nobody is going to do something like that for anyone else, and if it had been published I would have known.

On the third day she spoke, as if deliberately timing a resurrection. The class is animatedly discussing a poem a boy with pink and blue hair jelled and arranged in spikes has written – not a bad poem, and the class is being generous. The consensus is that the piece hardly needs revision. We're moving on.

'It lacks soul, though.'

An abrupt silence descends. Eyes swivel towards her in the enigmatic quiet. Most of the class hold themselves with care, their backs to her, as if waiting for the stone inside her words to break out and fall, fracturing skulls.

In three days, she has not turned in an assignment, nor offered an excuse, nor uttered a single word. It is I who break the silence, brokering the class's anger. 'Yes, really, Miss Henderson? And can you explain what you mean by that?'

She doesn't respond to the sarcasm. The frown on her face tells me she has taken my request seriously and is searching for words to convey a legitimate meaning. 'It's technically a fairly good poem,' she says, speaking slowly, as if making thoughts out of words rather than the reverse. 'But I think it can be better. There's no real feeling – it's too crafty, too bent on being poetic –' Her voice falls away; she looks at me helplessly, 'Do you understand what I mean?' and it is only half a question; it is also a statement and a demand that I play the assigned role of professor-in-charge and put my superior understanding and larger grasp of words to work on her behalf.

The pink and blue boy is frowning; the silence becomes dreadful. Animosity rises thickly in the room. Her explanation hasn't helped her, and more especially because she is right. But this is a class of everyday people, not geniuses, and this boy at least understands something of the homage that language demands for itself. She could have given him that.

'I'm afraid I don't know what you mean, Ms Henderson, unless you can find words to say it.' I turn from her to the class. 'Perhaps Ms Henderson can elaborate on her opinion at the start of the next session. But for now we have to move on. We can take one more reading, and at least start the discussion on it in the few minutes we have left.' I allow an effective pause before addressing her again, and this time I look at the class, not at her. 'Ms Henderson, I presume you do have something to show us this time around?' I put a very slight emphasis on 'this time around' and some of the students giggle. The tension among them eases.

She looks fiercely embarrassed, and her voice is trembling, but today the gods are on her side. Yes, she has brought a poem, and she will read it.

She reads it. Ah Christ, she reads it.

I had no reason to lie that first evening I asked her to stay behind.

'Yes, Professor, you wanted to see me?' Again her intonation made the words a question and a statement. It was the way she spoke, partly, I came to learn, a personal quirk, but partly also, the island lilt I had forgotten. It was, if anything, the most disturbing thing about her, apart from the poetry.

'Please have a seat, Ms Henderson.' She crossed her legs at the knee and her long skirt fell away at the slit, leaving her thighs exposed. She quickly uncrossed her legs and sat straight up with her feet placed correctly side by side. As if in obedience to her will, they immediately looked disembodied, like a painting of feet with shoes.

I moved papers on my desk and extracted the poem she had read that afternoon. 'You're quite a poet, Ms Henderson.' The lurking sarcasm that followed behind my words was not my intention and I noted its presence with a certain amount of regret.

'Thank you, Professor.' There was such a total absence of irony in her voice that I was startled into looking directly at her. It did not occur to me to think then that she was naïve. Her self-confidence seemed to be of such an order that it enabled her to ignore or misread every kind of challenge. By taking all utterances at face value, she allowed her belief in herself to remain intact. I could see that, as a result, the power in every conversation already belonged to her.

It took me a long time to realize that she was in fact impervious to the sinister (in the sense of 'the left side') undercurrents of ordinary speech, and incredible as this seemed to me then, I came to think that this verbal blind spot must have been the mercy by which she survived life in the Midwest of America's salt red neck. But hers was a schizophrenia I never truly understood – what the relation was between such a bald and naked innocence and the stunning, even brutal capacity to tunnel in the veins of words on paper that she displayed. Ironically, it was this contradiction in her that allowed me to go as far as I did, and it was my going that far that closed the gap of innocence and made her, I believe, a more whole person. And yet there were times, even afterwards, when I felt that the innocence belonged not to a boundless naivety but to a level of subterfuge, unsuspected even to herself. Each time the thought occurred to me, a chill went down my spine because then the person she most reminded me of was my ex-wife Majda – Majda of the serpentine heart.

Her eyes, wide, dark, the pupils endlessly dilated, gazed directly into mine. 'It's my whole life, you know,' she said, in the tone of someone confessing a fact. 'I've always known I'm a writer. I cannot be anything else.'

How old was she? At most, twenty. And she's always known she cannot be anything else but a writer. This is either crass self-regard or pure truth. I hold the evidence of her poetry in my hands.

I lean back in the swivel chair and look at her assessingly. She meets my gaze without flinching or embarrassment, her face open, alive, inquiring. Her face could have been a painting, instinct with the utmost blaze of feeling. Sometimes in the class she has had that arrested look, as if truly listening. Hers is an extraordinary face. She has near-perfect bones, the smooth matt of the skin like jade.

'Tell me about yourself, Ms Henderson,' I say abruptly. 'Where you were born, went to school, what you read, who you read – in short, what produced you, Ms Henderson.'

The question is brutal and invasive. She has no hesitation, and that lack of hesitation – which with a pang of guilt I recognize as an unconditional willingness to believe in my sincerity – lends her a dignity I had not foreseen. I watch the flame in her face while she speaks.

'I grew up in St Lucia, in a place called Anse La Raye. I lived there until I was twelve years old…'

I disguise the start of surprise and compose myself. I do not tell her that I know the place she names and I am surprised at how much my unwilling mind recalls of everything I have striven to unremember. The small boy among the lianas betting with his friends how high he can climb, laughing because he has not yet understood the soul-destroying limits of his circumference, malcochon, the six of them in the rain… The smell of the sea where the fishermen wash their nets at dawn. Large women waiting on the beach to haggle over the morning's catch, their patience the patience of a thousand hills, so fated, Jesus Christ, so fated. How could they accept that life as an article of fate? *It is God's will, Miss Rouse, Miss Lalee, God's will!* How I hated that acceptance, that poverty of spirit; how cursed are the poor in spirit; the boy with his naked backside on the beach – *Maman, Maman, the flying fish! That's the one you must save for me! Volant! Se sa la ou ni pou sauve ba mwen!*'

She fumbled words with the headlong abruptness of love;

everything she said pained and irritated me. Didn't she know it was all bosh – that in the end she would have had to leave, that in her backwoods paradise there was no way she could have written as she did? It was the leaving that had set her words free.

I let her run on for a while and choose to interrupt at a point where the question is irrelevant; I want to be rude. 'What are you doing here, Ms Henderson?'

'Sir?' The question startles her, the widened pupils flare even wider before narrowing again. She has a wild aura about her, like a woodland animal – a squirrel or a rabbit, I think, uncharitably.

'I meant, in this country. What are you doing here?'

Before the week is over I will have learnt that the widening eyes, followed by the looking away into space and speculative frown are characteristic responses to questions. Every word spoken is given intense contemplation, and yet it leads her attention not back to the questioner, but to a complete immersion in her own thoughts. She becomes so absorbed that nothing else exists but the question; I too am erased.

At last she says with a sigh, like a child who has drunk water without stopping, 'I don't know. I guess the easy answer is that I had no choice – my parents moved here when I was twelve. It's become where I live now, until I finish my studies and can go back home.'

'Do you want to go back – home?'

'But of course.' She gives me an astonished look and continues answering my first question as if there has been no break in the conversation. 'But as to why I am really here, I mean really, in the sense of what is it for, I'm afraid I can't tell you. You don't always know the purpose of something at the moment when it's happening, do you?' The furrowed brow invites me into her thoughts, assumes a shared space of experience that makes the question rhetorical. She thinks of me as the teacher; the teacher knows, draws out and corroborates the student's thoughts, the teacher is a guru to whom all questions are as transparent as his intentions.

Yet there is nothing I can teach her.

'Don't you?'

'No, I don't think so, not even intuitively. Only God knows all the time, and he may have his reasons for not always wanting us

141

to know. Maybe if we did, we wouldn't –' she frowns, hesitates and changes her thought, 'There's so much that is out of our control, isn't there? But I think the secret is just staying in your place until you know in your spirit it's time – even if you don't have all the answers.'

I raise an eyebrow. 'Are you religious, Ms Henderson?'

Again she looks surprised, as if I've asked a non-question, or something she hadn't thought could be a question. 'But of course. Aren't you?'

In answer to my sceptical look she says, 'Do you think it is possible to be a poet and not be... religious?' For the first time she is almost timid, as if offering an apology, yet she is looking at me with a curiosity that places us on the plane of equals, stating her right to ask me the same personal questions that I have asked her.

'It depends what you mean by religious.' I am annoyed at how pompous I sound, and I become more cutting than I had intended. 'If by religious you mean believing in some anthropomorphic... person, for want of a better word, who sits up somewhere in the sky controlling what we do, no, Ms Henderson, I'm not religious. But if you mean do I believe that there is some meaning in life for each of us, for which we all search, whether we will or no, then yes, I suppose you could say that I am religious.'

'Oh.' Her tone is curiously disappointed

'Oh, Ms Henderson?'

'Well – yes, oh. I hadn't thought it could be so – simplistic.' And this ridiculous girl speaks in a tone of disappointment, reproof even, as if she is ashamed of me.

'It is your position that is that simplistic, Ms Henderson. Religiosity – the God idea. Perhaps "spiritual" might be a better word to describe my position.'

Her brow furrows again – she will have deep wrinkles before she is old. 'I don't understand that, you know. I don't think it is possible to be spiritual without believing in God. Religious yes, spiritual, I don't think so.'

'Indeed? And what exactly do you mean by that, Ms Henderson?' I am asking her the same question I asked her in the class, and my tone flusters her. (Later I realized that she became nervous, discomfited, whenever she was asked to explain her reasons for anything at a philosophical level. Her sense of what could be understood of the world existed in purely intuitive terms).

'Well... if you're saying spiritual...' She's begun to use her hands, helplessly, evocatively, 'you're really talking about things beyond the limits of the senses – and I don't see how you can do that without connecting to some idea of God. Otherwise it's not spiritual, it's still rooted in that material experience. Whereas you can be religious in a narrow sense – just seeking after symbols, for instance.'

This time I am openly mocking. 'Ms Henderson, are you, a poet, suggesting that symbols are empty?'

'No, but they can be, can't they?'

I decide to end the conversation there in order to have a reason, an excuse, for our next meeting, but there is no need because my telephone rings and it is Marina wanting to know if I would prefer salmon or shrimp for dinner. I tell her salmon, that I will see her in a few minutes, and hang up the receiver before glancing at my watch in dismissal. 'Delightful as I find this conversation, Ms Henderson, I must postpone its continuation until our next meeting. Until then, my dear young lady, goodnight.'

At once she gets to her feet, with a kind of obliging alacrity, and I think she is going through the door but instead she turns and says, 'May I ask you a question, Professor Naylor?'

'Certainly, Ms Henderson.' I push papers into my briefcase and snap it shut.

'Why are you here, Sir?'

'I was invited by the university to spend the semester here as writer in residence, and give a few seminars as part of my roster of activities.'

'Yes, but why, really, Sir?'

'Are you asking me a religious question, Ms Henderson?'

'Perhaps,' she says, looking uncertain, taking me seriously again. 'But I would really like to know, because I know you don't come from England, even though you sound that way – I mean, that you're not from white people's country, though your bios never say clearly where you are from. Are you African, Professor?'

'Shall we take a rain check on the question of my antecedents, Ms Henderson?'

She nods in that accepting, acquiescent way of respect, or naivety, or subterfuge. 'Of course, Professor Naylor. Goodnight, Sir. And thank you for talking to me.'

I stand in the doorway and gesture to her to precede me. The space is narrow and I smell her hair. It smells of lemon and ginger and her hips are soft, even though she is a thin girl. She has a fey look apart from the wide, endragonéd eyes and the hot, infinitely material bruise of her mouth that is much darker than the rest of her face. Her mouth stands out starkly. It is wide and carved, and purple black.

I don't know how many times we met in my room after that. A lot of things from that time are unclear. One remembers shifts of feeling, breath, the texture of moments, dust motes in corners, an eyelash's flicker. Heat and light, cold. The flush of old desires, and Majda mocking in the doorway in a dream when she found the last secret. These things I remember. Events are less defined.

I believe we met after every class for the next two weeks of the term. I could be wrong; everything in my memory has become so nebulous.

Marina startled me by asking out of the blue one day, 'Darling, whatever became of that young woman – the one who turned up late for the class? How is she doing?'

'Quite well, in fact,' I said, unguarded. 'She turned out to be the best in the class.'

'Well now, look at that!' Marina is as pleased as if the girl is a discovery she has made, and by herself. 'Isn't that something! I hope you are going to have her over for dinner.'

Have her over for dinner. Jesus Christ.

But Marina is not to know. Having the better students over for a celebratory dinner at the end of the course is something we've always done – a habit begun when I was married to Majda and continued after Majda left.

'Sweet, you haven't answered,' Marina's voice complains laughingly. 'You're off into space again. What am I going to do with you.' She has said this a lot in the past few days.

'Yes, of course, by all means have her to dinner,' I say lightly, hugging her, and suddenly my hug becomes fierce and I am whispering urgently in answer to her other question, 'Love me, that's all'. I want to hold on to this halcyon time, dear God. Then I find myself smiling wryly; I sound like the Henderson girl, dear God indeed.

'What's funny?' Marina turns her lips into the naked crook of my arm; the skin shivers at her touch.

'I was just thinking about Ms Henderson. Strange girl – has some weird ideas.'

'Don't they all?' Marina says lightly, losing interest, wanting me again to herself. But I have an inexplicable urge to confess, though I don't know to what, or why. We stand together in companionable silence and then I say casually, 'She's black. The only one in the class.'

'Oh, you didn't tell me that. Then it's great that she has you, isn't it? Can you imagine how isolated she must feel otherwise?' Marina is all softness and compassion. 'Is she from the same place as you?'

'Not really. I was born in England, remember?' But I feel an unwilling compulsion to add, 'But she tells me she's from some place in the Caribbean.' (How strange that Marina, after all this time, still skips over the story of my English birth, and insists that I come from that place, simply because I had told her my great grandparents were born there).

'Then darling, of course we must invite her to dinner! How lonely she must be, in a place like this! And for you – it must be quite wonderful to meet someone from your region, after all these years. Why, you haven't been back there for – how long is it? Twenty, thirty years?'

There were accusations, but I never touched her. My memory may have gone bad from the long practice of forgetting, but I am completely sane and I do know that at that time I was intensely physically involved with my wife, more so than ever before, and I may not remember strict facts and dates, but I do remember emerging from hot nights of love under mosquito netting and going outside naked, to smoke and watch the dawn come. Alone.

Increasingly, I found it easier to sleep alone in the rocking chair outside our frosted glass windows. Marina said she thought I had nightmares from the heat; I had begun to talk in my sleep, which was something she had never known me do before.

'You kept saying something like "my couch, my couch, she's in the rain," over and over again.'

Malcochon. Six in the rain.

Appalled, I left the bed; it was then that I started the habit of going outside after love. I was afraid of what I might say in my sleep and what I might have to explain. The girl was one thing, that ancient life I had buried deeper than memory was another. In thirty years I had become a completely different person; I was the person Marina had married; I didn't want to subject her to coping with a stranger from another life that could easily terrify her with its difference. It was a life that I had laid to rest, beyond resurrection, until this girl with her wild poems and feast of uncontrollable words in praise of a people in whose eyes I remembered seeing nothing but the docility of cattle. She spoke of a present – forty years on – that I did not know, and she valorized a history that was for me a tale told absolutely without meaning, a fantasy that had no relation to the nightmarish quality of my struggle to escape drowning in that place. I knew that nothing had been created there.

I did not think about that other, more recent existence, the one I had lived parallel with my marriage to Majda. That did not count, I had buried that completely since Marina, and though sometimes there were faint struggles in darkness, I knew I would not be tempted in that way again.

I am not able to explain why I found it necessary to provoke our meetings – because provoke them was what I did, though she did not know it. I provoked myself as a child provokes a loosened tooth – with both obsession and love. Creating the occasions, finding reasons why she needed to see me alone, away from the rest of the class, was not difficult. I spoke to her about publication, about ideas for improvement that could not be dealt with in the narrowness of the seminar. With naïve arrogance and simplicity, she felt her own greater gift and its need for a different nurturing.

Did she view my office as a haven in the sea of white in which we two were the only stains – a place where she could freely recreate her dream of home? I had confessed, without details, that I had lived in that place for some years and knew it intimately. Up until the end, she went on believing that I had lived there as an expatriate (I was born and mostly reared in England, I said, reaching for fiction) who had liked the place enough to integrate himself into its ways and its people. This led her both to seek me out and to welcome my invitations at every turn.

I know that she became an addiction, an energy I needed in order for some part of me to live. I was split down the middle, my body dedicated to Marina, and this other part of me thickly ambushed, entangled in dark undergrowth, elsewhere. Perversely, though I began to write again, almost from the first I was more dissatisfied with what I was doing than at any other time in my life. Though I spilled words feverishly on paper, I tore them up in an equal fever immediately afterwards. I took up running again, every morning across the lawns to meet the light, in the soft hours before the sun grew fierce. That sun was not like any I had seen – even in that other constantly heated place – at times red with eclipse, at others bleached whiter than the sky from which it had sucked all colour, its penumbra a ring of metallic blue. I ran from it backwards into the dawn. This became my routine – hot, feverish writing, and then languorous drowning in Marina's green pools, the tearing and scattering of leaves in the waste-basket in the early morning before smoking, running, watching the dawn.

One evening, it rained unexpectedly, and, as neither of us carried an umbrella, we waited on the steps of my office building, until the rain stopped. I invited her for coffee in the Starbucks café by the gates. Afterwards, I said, I would drive her home. She said she lived in the student hostel, a stone's throw that she could walk, as she always did.

'Yes, but it might rain again. Look, the clouds are still weighted down,' I said, showing her the swollen sky.

Over coffee she was very quiet.

'What's wrong?' I asked, placing my hand over hers, which were clasped in a nursing motion around her cup. To me my gesture was unexpected, and even frightening, but she scarcely seemed to notice.

She shook her head, mutely, but I didn't take my hand away, and after a while she said, 'Nothing. Just an odd feeling – do you get those sometimes? Like someone walking over my grave.'

I found myself trying to humour her. 'So. Does anything ever happen when your grave is... walked over?' I said, smiling.

The light teasing worked; the corner of her hot mouth lifted in a smile. 'Not really.' But she drew her hand away.

'There you are then.' I made to touch her again in reassurance.

'I'm going to the ladies',' she said abruptly, getting to her feet. I felt that she wanted and did not want me to touch her again. I sat there feeling frightened because I had not planned this. I had thought that darkness was over, but at the same time I was very calm, as I had been the first time. It felt good to be on familiar territory, in a place inside myself that I knew. And yet this was completely different, in a category by itself; I could not compare it to the former way, by which I had thought I would not be tempted again. I felt a sharp, fleeting regret, almost a flash of tears, for us both, as I realized and accepted what I was about to do.

She came back from the ladies' and we left. She still wanted to walk but I insisted, and then the rain came down again heavily so that when we got to the hostel she could not get out of the car; she would have been soaked to the skin. I drove away from there and we waited a long, long time behind the water that slid in curtains down the windows and blotted out the world outside.

I got home much later than usual that night. Marina was worried, and a little frightened by the rain, which was so different from London's negotiable storms, the predictably unpredictable rhythms of English weather. 'Darling, you really do need to get a mobile phone,' she said for the hundredth time, but she was relieved to see me, and relieved too by the rain. In the hot summer days the intensity of the sun drained her hair of light and left her feeling a little unwell; now her misty energy returned.

That night, for the first time since the beginning of this episode in my life, I slept without dreaming. But this is not strictly true, because when I woke in the morning I was looking out over a long hazy sea where fishermen were throwing nets and shouting in my direction, and a boy in khaki shorts and bare feet was kicking pebbles on the beach and turning away from his mother. It was Marina's voice calling from inside, 'Are you awake, darling?' that made me realize I was looking out not at the sea but at an Iowa landscape, and the human figures in my dream were not humans but shrubs silhouetted against the ambiguities of dawn. As I had come to expect, that fragility of the morning did not last beyond the time it took for the sun to climb above the horizon, trailing red flags in the sky.

Two mornings later the boy came, and at the end of the week it was over.

She brought him to the class with her, and he sat without explanation in the seat beside hers, not participating in the class but closing himself around her with the unmistakable stance of a bodyguard.

My agitation became indescribable. I knew then that I was a prisoner of my past, marooned among islands, aslant the whale's wash, in which, despite all my efforts over forty years, I would most certainly drown. Because of this boy, I became hopelessly ill, so much so that I could not pretend I was not, as I had always done. All my life I had been ill. I sought to find out who he was, invested a huge amount of energy and subterfuge in going over and over again this tight fistful of questions. Of what necessity was he to her? Was he also a student here, another of the handful of us that I saw dotted about the campus every now and then? Was he from the same place that she claimed as hers? She did not introduce him but brought him in and out of my classroom when she pleased, and the fact that I confronted neither of them but sought information elsewhere is the measure of how I came to distrust her and myself, and of my growing anxiety about the possible consequences of this situation. I knew that in this society one one could be taken to court or waylaid and beaten for almost anything, and I remembered that the corridors had been quiet and the door of my office closed on every evening that I had spent with her. I had no idea why she felt it necessary to make this threatening, or mocking, or self-protecting gesture of bringing her boyfriend into my classroom; whether she was brazen or afraid. I knew that it could be said, from the fact of those meetings alone, that I had breached the bounds of conduct between teacher and student, and I had no witness to stand on my side.

He was a fat, rough-skinned boy with splayed hands and an offensively unblinking stare. I began to see them walking about the campus, he with his arm around her, their heads close together. I was astonished that I had never seen them together before. It was clear that they must have been inseparable for a long time – they had that air of people who had become joined at the hip. Had they had kept themselves invisible until now, when she imagined hostility between us, or had I simply not cared to look? On those evenings when I kept her back after classes for the long conversations in my room, had he waited for her then, her patient lackey – or her knight – whose patience lay in the certainty that youth only called to youth and nothing about me could entice her to corruption? Yet, enraged, I wondered what she saw in him. It was only now I realized how little I had admitted the existence of a life she owned outside the hours when she was mine; I had thought the scope and circumference of her living began and ended on the altar of poems she brought me as a weekly token of the return I had refused every day of my life for forty years.

I realized I did not know her, except as a proposition. But my own life had come to define itself by the dreams and nightmares of the past she had induced in me. There were dreams of silken girls, acquiescent, my hands spread over them like a garment, like a threatening shroud, their bodies laid end to end like a jewelled archipelago. How many of them had there been, dear God, in those times of my emptiness? I dreamed of islands suspended in water, racked by chains, of myself impossibly naked on an auction block. I heard the curses of the damned hurled over the side of ships hung between continents. I had needed her to understand this, this link of chains between us, anchored undersea. I needed her to understand that she was my terror and salvation, different from the others in whom I had spent my seed, dying where it spewed on bare, infertile rock within sight and sound of the ships' wake. But when I tried to tell her this, foam rose to my lips; there were no words, and I resorted to an older darkness.

It was her youthfulness I yearned for. Because she was born young, as I had never been, she could have rewritten my knowledge through her completely different lenses, could have washed and sanctified the feet of places my memories had stained, her faith a libation warm as salt.

In the past it had not mattered. I had never needed more than a first encounter. Once I was done, I was done. It was as easy as hopping islands. Majda had faced me, her eyes glittering with my secrets, and made a lot of threats, but there was nothing she could do, because no one – or only a few – had been unwilling, and the few not for long, and even if they were, who would believe them? This girl of the islands had struggled and cried, unwilling; her struggle drew me into fathomless oceans – no, sargassos; my dry throat drank her cries. Her refusal made me cruel, though I had not meant to be. This I swear; you must believe me. She could not see that her struggle choreographed my own, under the dark fall of the rain turning jewelled seas to gray, and afterwards I felt that her tears were for herself and for her islands, not for me. At no point did she acknowledge or care to know that the struggle was also mine. This was the greatest loneliness I have known, that she fought me like a stranger.

I knew that in bringing this boy to my class, and in the red-streaked darkness of the poems she now wrote and read fearlessly in my class – once weeping so uncontrollably that she had to go outside, shocking the class into dumb silence and speculations of her madness, speculations that she must have been abused as a child – I knew she was declaring more than a challenge; she was declaring her victory and our alienation. I had carried her beyond innocence, and if it made her write better and more whole, it made me unconscionably afraid – not that he or she could ultimately harm me – for who would believe them, if they brought an accusation?– but that I had lost her forever.

One evening shortly before we left, the boy turned up in my office.

He sat uneasily on the edge of the chair I was forced to offer him and said his name was James Jasper and he had come to talk about Gysette. I granted him a raised eyebrow, pointedly ignoring the hand he stuck in my direction.

I sought to disguise my anger under slight derision. 'And are you Gysette's... guardian? You seem a little... young... for the position,' I said, staring him up and down, turning 'young' into a term of insult. But how young they were together, and how free!

The obsidian eyes glittered, registering the offence. Immediately I regretted my impulse, aware that I had cheapened myself to bandy words with this adolescent.

'We are the same age,' he said, the voice guttural, grating. 'And we have been friends for years.' He was raw and headlong, with the rawness of something not fully made. His hands were very big and splayed, as if still growing. He twisted them between his knees.

I waited without speaking.

'I do thank you for everything you have done for Gyssette, Sir. She... thought very highly of you and looked up to you a lot.' He spoke hotly, as if in defence. I felt the defiance and fear in him and I understood his knighthood and his youth. I also knew that whatever she had told him (if she dared, after my warnings), there was nothing he could accuse me of. But his words were ambiguous – why did he speak of her feelings in the past tense? What exactly had she told him? I decided to be bold.

'*Thought... looked*, Mr Jessop? You speak as if Ms Henderson no longer has regard for me, or is no longer alive.'

'Jasper. My surname is Jasper, sir.'

I let that pass. It angered him; the eyes flashed and were quickly veiled. 'As I said, I do thank you. But I don't know if you are aware… Gysette is not well.'

'Not well?' I echoed, startled in spite of myself. What was he pretending not to know?

'Yes. She sent for me. She said things were happening – she gets these – attacks, you know – severe attacks of paranoia.'

I held carefully still, while inwardly I let the tension flow out of me. He was concerned about some illness that he thought she had. She had not told him anything. They were not as close as he said.

'It shows itself in all sorts of peculiar ways. She keeps saying things like "Someone's walking over my grave" over and over. And bad dreams – she has bad dreams.'

'Why are you telling me all this? It seems to me that you need a doctor, not a professor,' I said, smiling indulgently, to appear to take the sting out of the words.

He went on as if I had not spoken. 'I thought it was over – that she was fully recovered. She hasn't had this for years. But last week she sent for me – I knew immediately, just from hearing her on the phone, it was bad. When I saw her I knew that she'd had a relapse. On the surface she looks quite normal – a stranger couldn't guess – nobody except us would know. But I've never seen her this bad before.'

'And you haven't taken her to a doctor?' I acknowledged that in speaking in this way I conceded his guardianship, the role he had assigned to himself, but there was at this stage nothing I could do about it.

He paused, as if considering what reply to make to my question. Instead, he raised his eyes and looked directly into mine. 'I think it didn't just happen like that. I think that she was interfered with. I think something happened to her. Someone did something to her.'

There was a long silence in the room. He waited with his hands between his knees and I knew that the time for sarcasm or banter was past because this was very dangerous. At last I said, speaking slowly, 'If you feel that way, young man, you ought to get her to talk or at least go to a counsellor – or the police. I admire and respect Ms Henderson, and I am very sorry to hear this, but I don't think I can help you. It is not my area of expertise.' I lifted my hands and let them fall in a gesture that spoke of my own appalled helplessness. 'I don't think I can help you.'

He rose as I did, but his eyes were still looking into mine when he said, 'I think that you can help me. She hardly spoke to anyone else here – hardly anyone else spoke to her. You knew her best.'

Rage seethed in my belly like a rising tide; anger at being forced to acknowledge his threat because I had no choice, when the threat had been made so openly. 'What exactly are you suggesting, young man?' I said softly.

Speech flew from him hot and headlong, not accusing but lost.

'That you might know who... might have hurt her. Maybe if you think very hard – about something she might have said – someone she might have mentioned. Because she won't tell me anything.' His eyes were suddenly blazing bright; he had begun to weep. 'She won't tell me anything, Professor.' I felt lost between his enigma and hers.

Marina has fallen asleep, her hair bright against the seat's leather backing and my arm. The flight attendant shimmies between the seats in first class, offering sherbet. I decline and she wants to know if I would like anything else from the choice of drinks on her tray. I say no and turn away towards the window. She realizes finally that I do not want to be disturbed and continues down the aisle.

It is near sunset and the sky is redder and more crucified than I had seen it even on those apocalyptic mornings that pursued my flight in the Iowa dawn. Clouds surround the aircraft in thick forests, so near they invade the cabin. If I were to look at them long, they would have the dreadful runic force of her last poems.

But my sight is elsewhere. I look out beyond sky and cloud and cabin compartment to another life, aeons before we boarded this plane back to London. I see her at the barrier at the airline desk and I can't believe she has come here and I think with a sickening jolt that she has come to make a scene. What is to be done if she makes a scene…? I do not see the boyfriend anywhere. Oh my Christ, Marina… how could she have known this is our flight, the day we are leaving?

Marina is engaged with a woman in front of us and her petty, demanding child. Marina wants passionately to have children; she thinks this one is cute.

'Where is your bodyguard?' I say, behind cover of fussing with the bags. My voice comes out furtively like steam, hissing, 'What the rass have you come here for?'

She does not reply. She stands and she looks at me and she looks at me until I am burning all over with embarrassment; without saying a word she is causing a scene – she who has tumbled words out of themselves and made them anew.

She looks at me and looks at me. I see the bright arc of islands in a jewelled sea turn dark under rain; I see a woman's back receding and hear a boy crying *Maman Maman*! I want to reach out and say 'forgive', but my hands are frozen to my sides with terror.

People are beginning to look. 'Who is this, darling?' Marina has turned from the child and stands with curiosity at my elbow.

'Nobody. A madwoman,' I turn away muttering under my breath, but her hand on my chest blocks me on the turn; she looks proudly into my eyes, her flower-bruised mouth so close to mine we could have kissed, and in that obscene intimacy she spits in my face and walks away from the barrier, away from the crowd.

It is Marina I must consider, Marina who must be protected from all of this, she deserves better than this, my Marina of the firelit hair…

The rumours that burst around the campus prior to our departure, fuelled by the wild poems and the boy's enquiries, could not stick, as none of the others before could stick, for even Majda in the end had had too much to lose by breaking her silence: most especially the illusion of her hold over me, because she knew that in the end I did not care. In a way I wanted to be brought to book since it did not really matter what happened to me – except death. Death was something that I would choose only if I felt it large enough to pay the debt of the life I had lived. It was the one free choice I felt I had left, and I would make it carefully, and intact. A superficial shame would never be enough.

Moreover, I had not felt guilty, even if they were students, because I had not really coerced anyone. Their own dreams of another life, the obverse of civilization, a fantasy place where life pulsed wild and free, had made them seek me out or accede to my seeking.

Now I thought of the irony of how in the end she had not needed to bring her bodyguard to my class for speech or protection. In truth, she was strong enough to come on her own, and even at her most wordless, her most wounded, she defeated me. What was more, I had known the instant when she wept, my hand bruising her hot and broken mouth – I had known that instant that my life was no longer justified by the weight of its own

155

struggle, forgetting, and guilt. I knew what I had to do, and I knew that she would see the headlines, even back in America, and I hoped in the name of the nebulous God she believed in that her understanding of what I would do would set her free. I wanted to give her something back, and I could think of nothing that could atone for a life, except another life. My Marina. At last I could do something truly important, the one perfect stanza of all.

The sunset has exhausted itself at last. Passengers are pulling down window blinds and preparing to sleep, blocking from sight the long fading wash over which the night will fall blue.

FOR ISHMAEL

He thought of himself as a magpie sort of person, a collector of small, ridiculous things. Most of what he had collected he kept in his head, so, trawling among the few material things he had gathered, or rather the things that had attached themselves to him, he had no difficulty deciding what he would discard and what he would keep.

The glass mug from his niece, engraved in blue 'to my one Uncle J, with love.' A battered, coffee-stained first edition of Edgar Mittelholzer's *My Bones and My Flute* (his other books had shipped, unaccompanied luggage). The prayer rug Ana had given him from Tibet – he would like to meet the Dalai Lama, maybe one day he would. His kette drum battered with travel and age, but still able to sing sound. His stash of CDs but not the CD deck. The antique brass telephone from 1933 that he had picked up among the trash in a thrift store. The hard-cover notebooks in which he had kept his journal, trailing behind his life in scattered tracks across the city's face. The pot of earth he had brought from home. He had nurtured in it a geranium, which bloomed bright red every year, like foaming blood.

He carefully lifted the plant, now without flower, re-potted it in the city's soil, and placed it on the windowsill. There was no sun, but the hard bright winter light and the fluorescent lamp he kept burning had kept it green. Carefully, he wrapped the original pot of earth in mesh and paper for safe travel in his carry-on luggage. He planned to pour it back in its own place, one day, when he got back to his own country, whenever that would be. He liked the idea of cycles, things returning to themselves, ritual. Ashes to ashes, dust to its own dust.

He looked with regret at the stack of postcards and letters,

fastened together by a rubber band, the are-you-all-rights, thank
yous, news, questions, exclamations, rehearsals from friends, co-
workers and family that kept him connected as often as he moved
from one posting to another. He would have liked to have kept
them, but if the city had taught him anything, it was the need to
travel light. This, for a man like him, spare and frugal in his habits,
had not been a hard lesson to learn. But there had been a time
when he'd travelled with a great deal of junk, for no other reason
than sentiment. He'd been a man whom it was easy to read, just
watching him across a crowded room – a rumpled man, with
pockets that often bulged.

Sighing, he pulled off the rubber band and let the cards and
notes drift down one by one in a slow cascade into the fire that he
had lit in the grate. Faces passed before him as the paper caught
fire and flashed red, orange, then crumpled black and gray. As if
in apology, he said each name associated with the card or note as
it fell, consciously locking into memory some particular scene or
thought that matched the owner of the name. For each he
whispered a prayer.

He stacked his pictures into a corner ready to be taken away,
a gift to the friend who would come in the morning. His friend
would take the geranium as well; he had green fingers. With neat,
economical movements he travelled between closet, suitcase and
bin, making quick decisions as to what clothes he would take and
what he would give away, rolling each with the same attention
regardless of whether it was going into the case or the bin. Three
days ago the Salvation Army had taken the furniture away; the
floors echoed under his feet with the desolate, inquiring sound of
emptied rooms.

There was one picture he would keep. Not the best one; in fact
perhaps the least. He stood for a long time looking at it in its cheap
plastic frame which he had deliberately not changed after he
bought the picture from the artist. The frame, the kind sold in
pharmacies for two dollars, was held together by frail white clips.
They kept popping out so that the picture loosened from its
backing and the glass was in danger of falling out. But though he
had bought it, he felt that the picture was not his to change; he was
merely its steward.

It was an impression of a young male dancer, done in the stylized form popular in the 1920s. The shimmering figure clad in black and red – rouge et noire – seemed strangely alive, as if it might actually shimmy down and out onto the living room floor. He danced with feet balanced on a yellow moon; around him planets whirled in shades of yellow and neon green. The face was featureless under a brown hat and a mass of dreads. The left hand tilted the brim of the hat, as if bowing towards his audience. But the dancer was alone, up among his stars, the audience excluded beyond the rim of the frame. The drawing had been done with cheap coloured pencils, but from a distance it looked as rich as oils on canvas.

It was signed in pencil: 'Samuel Reevers and Ishmael, August 2005', and to the right, 'For my son'. The artist had smiled apologetically when he told him the reason for the inscription, with the air of someone who regrets taking up your time but is compelled to do so. Ancient Mariner in blackface, he had thought, his heart moved.

'I lost him. Thirteen years ago.' He showed a photograph. 'So I sign my pictures like this, for him and me. His name's Ishmael. I have this dream, you see… One day he's gonna see me drawing, in a park like this, and I'm gonna see him, and recognize him. It's a hope I hold on to, you know?'

He said 'you know' as if needing an answer.

'Yes.'

The photograph is of a laughing child with a bush of hair, reaching fat hands to the camera. The child is naked except for diapers. The photograph is crisp and new, as if recently taken. No creases. It is in his wallet, in a compartment in which he keeps nothing else.

'I know I could recognize him anywhere.'

'He has a look of you,' he says, looking at the picture gravely.

The artist looks flushed, pleased. 'You think so? I always thought he looked like his mom.' There is a hesitation in his voice, as if hungry for this new possibility.

'Both is not unusual. But you're marked all over him, man. Xeroxed.'

The two of them laugh, the artist with relief.

He had watched the artist in that park for three days, without speaking to him. They sat on opposite sides, the one bent intently over his drawing, finished pieces set out on the bench beside him, his portable radio plugged into his ears, seemingly oblivious to those who stopped by to study the drawings displayed, the oblivion of a polite shopkeeper who does not wish to disturb his customers' browsing with crude offers of help. When they left without speaking, he merely carried on, occasionally pausing to feed the squirrels. It was early fall and acorns were thick on the ground, but these squirrels were used to people and liked bread. There was one in particular that ate from the artist's hand.

He thought that eventually he would walk over and inquire about that drawing. Its vivid red and black made the others seem faded.

One day when he came as usual to eat his lunchtime sandwich and be quiet, he was finally forced into conversation. The benches were full so he sat on the grass, which no one except himself and the homeless ever did. This was Columbus Park, at the backside of the Houses of Congress, between the metro station and the white dome of the Capitol. Most who passed there didn't wear the type of clothes in which you could risk sitting on grass. The homeless rested here for short periods with their belongings: bags on trolleys with strange, irrelevant things sticking out of the sides: dustpans, brushes for sweeping the floor, mops – it was astonishing how many men and women carried mops. What were they going to clean? The odd luggage, even more than the lost look on their faces, conveyed their sense of bewilderment. Apart from these, the ebb and flow of human traffic mirrored the city's ruthless, efficient core. Groups of native tourists, faces driven, intent on the monuments with their cameras. Dark-suited men and women, nervously confident, faces serious with the task of making a nation work. A few stopped to eat their sandwiches in the sun, if a bench was available, then hurried on.

He unwrapped his sandwich and paused with it halfway to his mouth. Two policemen, both white, were accosting the artist, black like him. The man got to his feet, courteous, or afraid; he imagined both. The policemen talked for a long time, earnestly, genially, one after the other. He guessed that the artist was being reprimanded for selling in the park and he was disturbed, though he had expected that one day this would happen.

Conditioned to the city, as he watched he supplied an imaginary dialogue to fit the expressions and gestures in the conversation he could not hear.

'You can't sell here, or paint here. This is a public park. A *non*–commercial park.' They would stress the 'non'.

'We're sorry.' The rebuke layered over with smiles, spread hands, disclaiming responsibility, claiming innocence. 'No offence meant, Sir.'

They would say 'Sir' – it was necessary for them to say 'Sir', always necessary to say 'Sir', and 'Ma'am.'

'No offence, Sir. It is the law.'

He thought himself a reasonable man, and a part of him thought all this was perfectly reasonable; after all the policemen were only doing their job, but a part of him, the part that supplied the unheard dialogue, was angry and disturbed.

The policemen left. The artist, without looking in their direction, stood for a while and then slowly packed up his drawings, placing each one carefully in a wrinkled plastic bag and put the bag at the side of the bench, out of view.

But then, instead of leaving, he sat down again and continued drawing. The traveller got up and approached his bench.

He had to say hello three times before the artist looked up, unhooking the radio from his ears. 'Oh, I'm sorry.' He gestured towards the black box. 'Was listening to the hurricane warnings. They think this one will be big. They're afraid the levees in New Orleans might break. But you know how it is with newspeople – like to make a fuss – sells, you know.'

'Yes, it does sell, doesn't it?'

It was a way to start a conversation, between strangers. But it made the traveller's question easy to ask.

The other's smile was ready and quick. His teeth, very white, flashed in his face. 'Oh no, they were very courteous, very nice. They said they didn't think it was allowed, but I should watch and see. All they said was I should leave the bench clear, in case others wanted to sit down. Not to give the impression I was hogging the seat, you know. Park crowded, you know. They were very nice, very nice indeed.' He repeated this as though niceness was unexpected.

He had done drugs. Whether as seller or taker, he did not say. Been in and out of prison. His wife, tired, had taken his son and left. At first she kept in touch with his mother, and he, telephoning his mother between jail terms, maintained a tenuous link with the life of his son. He often felt intrusive and impertinent, as if he had lost his right to contact.

Then his mother died, fulfilling her prophecy, 'Son, you must call more often' – but no rebuke in her voice – 'Mama won't always be here, son. One day I got to travel on home.'

After that, his wife and son disappeared into thin air.

'Nobody would tell me where they were. Maybe they didn't know; I don't know. I had a friend they used to keep in touch with, he lost track of them as well. He thought maybe she remarried and moved away. Couldn't understand though why she wiped even him out. Like she didn't want to be found.'

Later, he tried the internet. For a long time he'd done nothing. How could he? What can you tell a child you have not loved with a life pure enough for him to emulate? He'd had no wisdom to pass on, only his own shameful years. He'd waited until his son was maybe old enough to understand, old enough to forgive. He hoped the time was now. He drew and signed his pictures in the park, looking always at the faces that passed, though there was no reason why he should expect to see them here.

'They lived in Louisiana,' he said.

The sentence lay between them, filled with their unspoken thoughts. People move from place to place all the time; the traveller himself had moved between two cities and was packing now to travel to a third – but by what likelihood would this man's wife and child have travelled here, in answer to his hope? It was a large hope, larger than coincidence could bear. But to a man like the traveller, used to living his life on faith, it was not a ridiculous one.

'Come from Little Rock, Arkansas.' The white smile shows again. 'Like Bill Clinton. Could have been president myself, you know. Plan to go back. Actually came here to spend a week or two, now it's months. Things changed – you know how they do sometimes, when you're least looking for it.'

Every time he said 'you know', he stopped as though he waited for an answer.

'Yes,' the traveller said.

He was looking after his sick sister, who lived alone. Perhaps she would improve – go into remission – but he did not know. 'Multiple sclerosis,' he said. 'I do everything for her.'

'My last stint in jail, I decided to change my life around. And go back to my art,' he said.

They were still talking when two dark-suited men came, bargaining for a picture they said they'd seen earlier, before he sheathed them in their bags. He searched, unearthed the picture, a drawing of two nude women placed head to toe in a frieze. He said seventy-five dollars.

'Soiled at the bottom,' one of the men said. 'Half price. It's a fair discount.'

Peering closely, he found beneath the glass a long water stain that had him frowning. 'I had not seen that,' he said, taking forty dollars. Embarrassed, he took thirty-five for the dancer on moons, though he had previously said fifty. The traveller knew it was because he had witnessed the bargain with the white men. He wanted to say, no, I will pay the fifty, but he feared that it would cause offence. He hoped a profit had been made. He made quick calculations in his head. Perhaps, a little. The pencils were cheap, and the drawing was on ordinary cartridge paper. What price the drawing, he tried not to think.

'So,' he said, smiling to break the tension of the buying and selling as he watched his own purchase being slowly, carefully wrapped, 'What was it made you "change your life"?' Then, smiling to make it sound casual, like a joke, he said, 'Somebody talk to you in a cloud of fire?'

The white smile flashed. 'Not really. I think I just got tired. Maybe Somebody did speak to me (he said 'Somebody' like a name, with a capital 'S') – but I don't know. I just felt tired. Maybe that's a way of speaking too. You know.'

'Yes.'

He finished repacking the drawings, wound the cords of the radio around itself and put it with his pencils in the shabby leather pouch, zipped the pouch briskly, re-fastened it around his waist. 'Got to be going. Sister'll be needing lunch,' he said, reaching to shake hands.

The traveller caught the other's hand in his just for an instant but he could feel the lines on his own palm changing, as they had done on countless occasions before.

He stood and watched the other walk away, then looked down at his left hand. And saw that yes, the horizontal line near his wrist had grown another branch and a part of the long lateral one had worn away.

Every day now he studied what looked like writing on his palms, which had suddenly changed into a Babylonian stele. The writing changed after certain encounters, as if someone had immersed it in water to blur the lines and then written on it again.

Recently, it had begun to happen more often, and increasingly without warning. Yesterday an old Latino lady had stooped to retrieve a nickel he had dropped, and handed it to him smiling, 'God bless you, son' – though his hair was as grizzled as her own. The touch of her fingertips had moved him unbearably, here in this city where people jostled each other in public places but seldom met, kept firmly divided by suspicion, language and race. At the moment when his heart moved, he felt the runnels quivering in his palm, and had been unsurprised by what he later found, though he could not explain it. And there had been the time, on the train from New York to Connecticut, a day of eclipse when the sky rainbowed with wild colours, when he had looked into the face of a young man with death on him, and had looked away shocked. The young man, too, had looked away, as if ashamed. But afterwards they had spoken, and he, his heart burning, had offered the young man the only gift he had, the gift of the One Word, printed on a tract. The folded white tablet of paper screeled a trammel of roads in his palm as it passed from his hand to the other's. That night his hand had pained him, made him feverish so he could not sleep.

He wondered now whether, if he were ever to commit a crime, he could be found by his fingerprints, or whether he could be found guilty of a crime committed by any of the people who had changed the lines in his hand.

.....

It had started when, newly arrived, he rode the buses, at first because he had not bought a car and later because he could not imagine any other way to travel. On the buses he found another world: encountered the most spontaneous of kindnesses and struck up the most unexpected friendships, some fleeting and whimsical, others surprisingly strong.

He loved the seething chaos: the loud talking, emitting, preaching, easy-greeting, conversation struck with strangers, curses hurled at the unwashed, laughter rolling in waves from passenger to passenger and the drivers' voices freely adding to the noise. Anyone could ride the buses, but on this route, between Georgia Avenue and downtown, the buses were the territory of the poor and the visibly destroyed: the drunks, the druggards, the disorderly, the wild-eyed prophetesses, the unsanctioned magnificos disturbing the peace with their boastful talk. At first merely fascinated, he had moved slowly from observer to sharer, judging himself harshly for his own voyeurism. Here, as always among people whose only possession is hope, kindness was more ordinary than bread.

He felt with gladness that the world had not frozen to death, after all.

But often in the midst of that feeling, he had a sudden dreadful apprehension, of a great beast sleeping at the centre of the earth, a creature by whose every breath the earth, unconscious, drew its own breath and moved. Beneath the hot chaos of the buses' life, lay pulsing this terrible dread. The first day he glimpsed this universal beast in a vision was the day the lines on his hands, which had always been wavery and indeterminate, began to change.

Then more and more he found himself trawling the backside of the city, feeling less and less like himself and increasingly like a filament sucked into the city's amorphous core. Yet it was on these journeys that he felt most in touch with the part of himself he did not want to lose. The peculiar energy that he found in certain parts of the city made him feel less wasted, less like a hothouse plant than he did in the confines of the organization. He liked his colleagues, but breaching their liberal certainties had made him tired.

He had lived the same kind of schizophrenia as a priest in Kingston. For three and a half days he gave himself to his work in the prisons and their environs, where the lives of people boiled and seethed. Then from Sunday to Wednesday at midday – his week so neatly cut in half – he performed his service at the uptown altar, neatly cassocked above the polished pews. ('The Lord be with you'… 'And with you too' – placing the wafer on the tongues of the faithful, too many of whom had long forgotten its meaning).

His struggle was never free of guilt, the fear that he himself was the most patronizing liberal of all. For hadn't he let himself commit the ultimate fallacy – of measuring human pain in terms of haves and have nots, though he knew that need was everywhere, and no person more precious than another?

Still his heart, in spite of his thought, went its own way.

But though he was glad for the sense of relief that the world had not frozen to death, nor he with it, he found himself thinking over and over again, 'It may not have frozen, but it is surely rushing to death by fire.' And he felt his own helplessness and fraudulence like a weight.

The lines in his hands kept on growing, as thick and shifting as the city's Babylonian signs.

The place where he had met Samuel Reevers and Ishmael was part of an area less than two hundred square feet, between the metro's back and the dome of the Capitol – the statue of Columbus in his waterless fountain sandwiched in between.

Every Wednesday at noon he passed by Columbus and his flesh-and-blood fixtures. There were four of them who seemed never to leave the plinth or the shadow at Columbus' feet.

The man playing the soundless recorder.

The man playing the soundless saxophone.

Both with caps on the ground for pennies.

Both, when he asked, said, 'Yeah, I comes here every day, 'ceptin in winter.'

Their instruments were soundless because they had no money to tune them. 'What's it matter anyway? People still give money. A man gots to eat.'

The third was a man with the face of a Magyar from the Urals. He sang sad, melodic songs under a great white banner marked with a red cross and 'John 3:16' lettered in blue. Singing to strangers in an unknown tongue.

And then, Miss Rita, to whom he gave money every week, wondering how much went on drugs. Miss Rita, tiger-striped from face to foot in bands of pink and white paint, insisting, 'Call me Rita, I ain't no Miss Rita. Don't care about no mark of respect for old people where you come from. Call me Rita, I ain't that old.'

She painted without discrimination, mounting the colours over the tatters of her dress that she had not changed in a year (It was increasingly difficult to stand near her without holding his breath). 'Make-up,' she said, when he first asked why. 'Not paint. I ain't no actress. 'Tis make-up.'

She wouldn't let his institution or any other help her, and she wouldn't stay in the shelter. What she got on the streets from the kindness of strangers was enough, she said, no strings attached.

'Jus say a prayer for me, amigo.' She liked to say she knew Spanish. 'Jus a little prayer. Tha's all I need.'

He said a little prayer.

Two days after his meeting with Samuel Reevers and Ishmael, Hurricane Katrina devastated Louisiana. In New Orleans the levees broke; the city drowned. No one had dreamed that such a disaster could have happened in America. It was if a sleeping beast, unacknowledged, unrecollected in the absence of the ancient prophets, had suddenly awakened, opened its great maw, and belched its venom. Many people were evacuated to this city. The Red Cross, with which he had volunteered, had taken many in. Helping, he searched faces feverishly for the faces of Ishmael and his mother. He felt that if he saw them, he would know. But he never did.

He prayed that Samuel had better luck.

Standing now in his empty rooms, remembering, he made a sudden decision. He unwrapped his pot of soil from home and poured half of it back into the pot with the geranium. With his fingers he mixed the soil from home with the city soil in which he had replanted the flower. Then he pulled an elastic band and a luggage tag from his pocket, looped the elastic band through the hole in the tag, and wrote slowly and carefully on the tag before snapping it around the pot's perimeter. Then he pulled up the tag gently until it rested, writing uppermost, among the lush geranium leaves. 'For Ishmael.'

Tomorrow he would tell his friend to take especial care of that one, because it was planted in the name of a child.

It was only a gesture, but because he was superstitious, his hope was large.

In the night he dreamed of a beautiful angel drawing lines over and over on his hands, crossing them out and redrawing them. Who are you, he said. Aliun, Aliun, the angel replied, speaking words in a language he sensed he knew but which he did not understand. Afterwards he dreamed of Samuel, of Ishmael, of the dancer dancing, of drunks and druggards flowing off buses, of waves of people coming and going between Columbus Park and Columbus Square, of two policemen throwing their hands up saying no no no.

In his dream these faces gave way to others, the faces of his longing, of people who lived in the place to which he was anchored at the root, though he had traveled paths like rhizomes.

One particular face.

In his dream he sees her molding a clay face, he does not know whose, though he thinks it is the face of someone he has known.

When he was lonely for deep companionship, as he often was, he walked beside beautiful gardens at evening and thought of her weeding, sculpting, molding mugs between her small hands. He thought of how he had wanted to kiss, deeply, her mouth, on the day that he left, but he had not. And his longing was a longing for thick black earth and cities grounded, but also part of a larger hunger for rainbow, for sky.

REQUIEM

1979

Holy Mary Mother of God
pray for us sinners
now

A woman is walking among the graves. The small boy driving his flock of three goats past the tiny cemetery encircled by naseberry trees stops and watches with great interest, his left thumb in his mouth, his right pulling on the rope of the mother goat so that she lifts her head with a loud 'Maaay!' of protest as she jerks to a stop. The kids, seizing the opportunity, dart between her legs, nuzzling at her udders.

The woman is red and tall, in a polka dot dress and a hat. She is circling the headstones one after another with the intent, slightly lunatic face of people who talk to themselves. There are four graves; one of them is new, with the red earth still turbulent around the concrete slab. She picks up a fistful and inhales deeply; the boy knows from experience the exact smell she is smelling: raw depths, salt, and the indescribable fragrance of soil that demands to be eaten. He watches her scatter the clods in the ancient rite, ashes to ashes, dust to dust, and he thinks she must have lost the way of salvation, the way Miss Mabel in the AME Zion church declares when she rubs her hands together and gets into the spirit shouting, 'Yuh lose...yu looooose the way of salvation brethren!' The woman is pressing the fingers of one hand over the folded fist of the other, which is grasping a long string of beads like the ones the Roman Catholic ladies carry. The top hand rubs the bottom hand as if to dislodge the remains of the dirt while she sings to herself in a rough, tuneless voice; he does

169

not know what, but even with her lack of melody he hears the cadence of songs for calling up the dead. He has never heard such songs but he has heard tell of them, the songs of black wickedness.

The boy is waiting for the grave to fly open with loud crashing cymbals and the resurrection of the dead. He does not know whether the dead will emerge as a white vapour or a tattered skeleton clad in flaky cerements, or looking just like life itself. Torn between bravado and caution, he isn't sure yet whether he will bawl out 'Obeah wukker!' and run, or tiptoe silently away, or wait to see all that will happen, so he stands with one foot poised to fly, just in case. He is greatly disappointed when she lifts her head and calls out 'Good morning' in a cheerful voice and he sees she is not a D Lawrence but Miss Sybil's topanaris dress-up sister who visits from foreign all the time.

'G'mawnin.' He goes on sucking his thumb, scrubbing one bare foot across the other and regarding her with stern curiosity. Her eyes crinkle in amusement to which he is totally impervious. Finally, as if making up his mind about what is to be done, he removes the thumb with a loud pop! and asks, 'A wha yu did a do roun di grave? A obeah yu did a wuk?'

She laughs outright. 'Not quite. Just paying my respects.' She realizes that he probably won't understand so she explains, 'Just telling mi old people howdy.' She adds in a teasing way, 'Seeing as how I was late for the funeral.'

The boy considers this in ruminative silence. A very serious little man, she says out loud, inadvertently, and laughs again. The sound of her own voice startles her because it is a free, clear sound, and it matches the bright sharp blue of the sky and the sticky sweet smell of ripe naseberries hugging the air like a layer of memory. It astonishes her that she has laughed three times in a single minute, seduced by this grave boy in ragged khaki shorts with his rib-cage sturdily defined beneath his skin, which is silky and tender as flowers. There is a heart-tugging mixture of child and grown-up in the way he holds himself, with such innocent aggression. She thinks he has copied the aggression, if not the innocence, from young men playing dominoes on street corners or knocking back six in the Chinese rum shop in the village square.

With impregnable self-containment, he offers her information as if teaching her something she might need for a long time to come, 'Is Ole Uncle bury inna di new grave. Dem nuh tomb him yet. Di grave haffi sekkle fus.'

Instead of laughing at this, which ought to have been quite funny, she finds herself saying humbly, 'Oh. Oh yes, of course. So yu did know Ole Uncle?'

'Huh huhn.' He nods his head vigorously up and down, then, suddenly remembering his manners, as if he feels the shadow of an adult standing over him in strong rebuke, revises his answer, 'Yes Ma'am, yes Miss Lady,' then adds expansively, 'Dem seh a pisen dem pisen him mek him ded. But dacta nuh find no complain. Dacta cut him up, cut up him belly, mek him tripe drap out.' He contemplates the gruesome picture he has conjured up with grim satisfaction, and repeats his conclusion, 'But him nuh find no pisen complain.'

'Oh,' she says, faintly this time. 'Ah see.'

'Him a good duppy. Him bury laas week but up till now him nuh walk. Mi mumma seh is becausen him a good duppy. Only bad duppy walk. Yu haffi plant dem mek dem stop walk.'

She thanks him gravely for the information. The mother goat has begun to skip impatiently, jerking on the rope. His body curves with the effort of holding her, like a comma turned out.

'I think you better go on and tie out the goat for it look like she getting vex, an you mother soon start calling you an get vex too,' she advises.

'Huh huhn.' Entangled between more vigorous nodding and the irate goat's pull on the rope, he scampers jerkily down the hill, the goat and her frisky kids in charge most of the way. She watches him go, feeling something inside her delicately balanced, between laughter and a soft fall of tears. She wants to think of it as a benediction, the last in the sentences for the dead.

.....

It was said that the uncle spent the last day of his life telling stories, as he had always done. He had told them across three generations, to his brother's children, his brother's daughter's children and his brother's great grandchildren, weaving a long skein of tales like a rope, on which he hung the beads of the years the way people hang Christmas cards, stretching them on a cord across glass-fronted cabinets that are opened only on special occasions. (*You could string fee fee roses like that too, on a blade of grass knotted at one end and passed down their middle like a bone. Sometimes the flowers break, if you handle them too roughly or too fast*). All the uncle's stories were about himself, stories of deadly encounters that he'd had on lonely roads with succouyant, ol' higue, rolling calf, whooping boy, river mumma, deads and other liminal folk that we all believed in but only those with more than two eyes were able to see. In this occupation, this stringing of himself across generations, the uncle achieved immortality, though he had never otherwise been heard of and in fact it was known that he was not 'altogether here'.

A screw in his head was missing. This was what his brother's second youngest daughter told her children, and though the children did not find this difficult to believe, to them he seemed perfectly all right because they measured him by the thing he was good at, his stories. Furthermore, he was old, with an oldness that could only mean that in his lifetime he had acquired wisdom. At the same time, they were ready to believe he did indeed have a screw missing because he did not have a woman, had never had a wife, and had never been known to do any useful work. He lived on a government pension and his meals were provided by teams of relatives, as in a relay.

When the part of his life that is about to be told was happening, he slept in the house of his sister, Madina, but it was in the family house of his niece, Sylvie, his brother's second youngest daughter, that he spent his daylight hours and the haunch of the night, until the children, sleepy-eyed, reluctantly let him go. 'Till tomorrow, Uncle! When yo come, tell wi di one bout River Mumma an di sieve full of milk!' The thought of his bravery caused them enormous suffering. They dreamed him tall and strong, cutting through the fiery hosts, sheaves of deads strewn in his wake all the way to 'Ta Maddy's front door, and the thought was almost too much to bear. They surfeited on a pleasure accented by the fear that kept them from venturing outside to the well or privy once the uncle had begun to speak. They always made sure the front and back doors were securely shut. Often one or other of the children had wept because the mother wanted something at the shop that she had forgotten and would not take 'Please Ma, no Ma', for an answer; the thing had to be fetched.

And so they learned to race the wind past leering faces on bushes and awful choirs clustered keening at the feet of trees. Rocks and stones and smooth shop pavements were all the same beneath their flying heels. The uncle's stories were tapestries patterned with black holes through which you could fall, down, down, down to the other side.

The girl liked to crawl into the uncle's lap where, with her knees drawn up into his chest, her head buried in his shoulder and her arms clinging around his neck, she listened to him in a terror so joyous that it brought her physical pain. She was all wires and vines, her arms and legs double-jointed so that she was capable of the most fantastical contortions and could stay curled in the same position for a long time. The uncle held her cupped in the broad palm of his hand though there was no physical need, for she twined herself so tightly around him that no shock could make her slip or fall. She liked the comfort of his hands, which punctuated the joyous feel of terror with their touch and pressure, letting her know how safe she was.

Afterwards, in their daytime play and on the nights when the uncle for one reason or another did not come, she would terrify her younger brothers and sister with reconstituted versions of the uncle's tales, speaking in a hissing sibilant whisper for effect and accompanying her words with the most hideous twists of her double-jointed limbs. The uncle told his tales in a slow, drawn-out monotone with long ruminating pauses in between, sometimes even seeming to fall asleep between the most hair-raising portions. The girl picked out and rewove their fabric in patterns of modulation, staged pitches and rhythms, with a savage look of concentration as she woke the deads to another voice, to another life that she plotted in her serpentine body. With grimaces, sprawls and fantastical gestures, she shaped her weird choreography of unspeakable signs.

'This is how Whoop'n Bwoy go when Uncle lick him wid di supplejack!' she cried, leering with the occult power that had risen within her. The five and three year olds, DenDen and Sybil, shivered, their eyes rounder than moons, fixed on her and on the enormous shadows she cast on the wall. 'Tell wi how him go again, Girlzel!' they cried, entranced, terrorized.

'Like dis, like dis!' Jumping up and down like a jack in the box, the girl lashed at them with her imaginary whip, chasing them into corners and finally into terrified weeping until the mother came and sharply put a stop to the girl's tyrannical pleasures. But their sleep would be nightmared, disturbed not by dreams of the uncle's danger but by visions of dreadful living things. They woke up irritated, gritty-eyed and restless. When the uncle told his stories, it was only in the time between the story and falling asleep that they would be afraid. This, above all else, distinguished the uncle's stories from the girl's.

In certain moods, sometimes for days on end, she refused to be called by her own name, and terrorized the children in a different guise. 'Don't call me Girlzel! Call me River Mumma! Or else I go cut out yu heart when yu deh sleep!'

'River Mumma, River Mumma, do, nuh cut out wi heart,' the little ones obediently begged. She held utter sway. They adored her.

The older brother, John, however, laughed at her. 'Yuh a idiot. Is not River Mumma cut out people heart, is Black Heart Man!' And for days his voice rang in the house and yard with derision, 'Black Heart Ooman! Ol' Higue!' and the two of them warred.

Hush. Hu-sussuru, sussuru … The uncle is speaking. The girl is twined about his neck and the others are huddled close against each other around the table smelling of new pine shavings. All except John, who is seven and scorns the open fear of babies; he sits with a careful distance between himself and the others, nonchalantly building a new catapult as he listens.

One night after paybill. Late o'clock inna di night mi a-come home past Mammee River right where yu si it run pass High Guinea Road. Da's the part wheh dem say you no suppose fi walk after twelve o'clock fa is deh so River Mumma hide off when she want do smaddy someting, under di ole iron bridge. A deh so she draw 'way Sammy Look Up an keep him twenty-one days till Madda Roberts tell Miss Icilda wha fi do an Icilda do it, an a so Sammy get fi come back home.

'What she tell Miss Icy fi do, uncle?'

'Wha him tell him fi do?' The uncle had a habit of repeating questions and pausing before he answered them, as if to garner his thoughts, as if words in his mouth were choice morsels savoured and reluctantly let go.

Mi nuh really know wha him tell him seh. Madda Roberts nor Icilda never tell nobody, dem keep it to dem quiet. But a from dat time him a-walk an look up inna di sky like how yu see'm deh, like him a look fi rain. Is because River Mumma hold him fi twenty-one days under di bridge and when him finally let him go him have a mark. Everybody River Mumma tek 'way have a mark, whether is twist dem hand like dem a-wash, or look up inna sky fi rain or turn dumb at certain hours a night, ebery one get a mark.

The uncle pauses, falls into his characteristic reverie. The ring of faces is dim behind the flickering kerosene light. If he could have seen them clearly their expressions would have moved him, for they held the carved solemnity of masks, of bodies turned to stone by surfeit of feeling. The unmoving faces turn his tales into the highest of dramas. He receives back his scattered self, whole and transformed, from their five pairs of eyes that have swelled into one living eye. The huge pool of their composite eye widens and contracts in ripples of silver and black, in waves that break over the bleached rock of his voice and flow outside into the moonlit yard where every one of them can see, as clear as day, that other listening audience huddled hu-sussuru under the banana trees. Their widening eye ripples and spreads until it fills the entire room to the ceiling, taking this in.

Finally DenDen stirred and poked him impatiently with a finger. 'Uncle, go on.'

The cup of the uncle's hand moved itself up and down the girl, stroking; his body picked up the slow rocking of memory, of old age remembering.

Hmn hmn. Anyway, Busha pay late dah evening an a me one wen live a dat deh side a di district, so mi find miself pon High Guinea Road inna di night, me one pon di road. Di breeze fresh an di road quiet an mi goin on, goin on, goin on. So mi gwan so till mi reach a di foot a di bridge, an same time as mi ready fi cross it, mi see one light a-come toward mi, a-bob an a-weave like peenie wally, but mi know a no peenie wally fa same time so mi head start to grow big.

'So yuh never fraid, Uncle?'

'If mi wen fraid? No, mi never fraid. But mi head grow fi warn mi. Mi walk up to di middle a di bridge an mi stap. An mi ben down an mi draw one cross pon di bridge wid mi penknife an mi stick up di penknife right inna di cross wheh di part-dem mek four.'

'Wheh yuh get di knife, Uncle?'

'Mi always kyar mi knife inna mi pocket fi peel mi cane an eat mi food a day time.'

The questions are ritual, as are the answers, a call and response of delay and titillation, for the story is already well known.

So after mi draw di cross an stickup di knife inna it, mi stannup an mi wait. Di light come on an it come on an it come on a-bob an a-weave same way like flashlight so till it stop right in fronten mi an sudden so it out, so, poof! An mi si one tall tall red ooman stannup a-look pon mi, an mi stannup an a-look back pon him.

'But Uncle, how yuh see har widouten no light? No did dark night?'

'Pitch dark night. How mi see'm? [Pause.] Mi see'm becausen moon come out same time.'

'How near she come, Uncle? How near she come to yuh?'

'Near near.'

The uncle describes a space on the table smelling of fresh pine boards, and a ghostly foot miraculously appears in the space he has described, planted and firm in a shoe shaped like a mule's. *Yes, when him come near, him light tun smoke so, pooff! an disappear. An him stannup deh a-look pon me and mi stannup deh a-look pon him an di two a wi nah budge.* Columns grow like ghosts out of the shoe, which has split; they waver like water imagined and then slowly fill in, the way water seeps upward and turns an empty hole in the ground into a well, or the way a pencil shades in contours made merely to hold the shape to come. A tall woman appears, very red and very clear, but with her corners wind-tattered and where her face should be, no face at all but only a black hole, as if her eyes, nose and mouth and all the spaces in between have been blown away by the wind or a flying bullet.

The uncle's congregation shivers in the wind or the bullet that crosses.

The tall red woman cannot cross the cross the uncle has made at the crossroads by the bridge. The tall red woman and the uncle struggle there at the cross all night and the tall red woman loses. The tall red woman wants at last to run away but she cannot, the uncle is holding her by a tight long thread that is coming out of his mouth. Finally the cock crows and the tall red woman walks backward off the table, but she doesn't fall off. Instead she walks straight out on a plank of filtered light that is coming in through the spaces between the jalousies, and as she reaches the window she wavers and breaks up, like a picture flung under water, and disappears. Outside, a hu-sussuru rises under the banana tree as the duppies receive their dead. No one will go outside to the toilet tonight. The children huddle close together, the girl's arms tighten around the uncle's warm throat where a pulse is beating steady and firm, filling and emptying with tumescent blood. Johnny's new catapult is clutched very tight in his hand that cannot move. But the uncle will leave fearlessly on his way home, walking very slow and solitary under a sky impossibly thick with stars.

The morning brought reassurances. Rites of ordinary things, work, school, play and punishment, days whose boundaries were the familiar shape of bright sun; sketched chores; skinned knees; the smell of fruit half eaten by birds; the taste of rain-dampened soil (the soft *broogoodoop* kind); the schoolroom chantwell of hymns, 'twice ones two, twice twos four, twice n'n'are eighteen!' rising above blackboard partitions placed like dams to break the flow of congregational noise from Class 1, Class 2, Class 3, Class 8; the preacher preaching in the church on Sunday *Jesus loves the little children*; and the bellyaches from eating unripe mangoes, naseberries, guineps, starapples, cashew, june plum, sugar plum, coolie plum, hog plum, jackfruit, pomegranate, lime, wailing woie! woie, Ma! while their mother scolded and declared her intention of ignoring them and letting them die as they deserved, though at the same time she was heating her hand with the healing oil over the Home Sweet Home lamp and pressing it hard over the distended belly, so that they felt the exquisite torture of what it was like to be loved again, between one stomach ache and future ones loaded with tomorrow. This to them was what it meant to be saved, this return of love from one day to the next, scoring away the night shadows.

These days were as far removed from the nights of the uncle and their progeny – the girl's terrorist apprenticeship – as sweet childhood is removed from luckless dreams.

…..

The girl was taking extra lessons, studying hard. John was going to be apprenticed to Maas Ransford; it was all already arranged; John would be a carpenter, the best. No-one knew as yet what would become of DenDen and Sybil; they were very young and still in infant school. The parents worried about Sybil because she was born with a limp and would not get a man. Ma and Da said study yu book, education and independence is all. Buy yu own house, put on yu own pot, after that, when you have everything, you can think about looking man to marry. But they worried about Sybil because even with book and education Sybil would not get a man. Sybil, little and pretty and shy, sucking a little tiny part of her first finger, the top joint only, looking dainty like a high-class woman smoking a pipe. Miss Kayla, the infant school teacher, says Sybil and Den Den are both *so so* bright, but Sybil has the crippled foot and Sybil is a girl. Sybil is not going to travel.

…..

The mother and father are 'talking business' in their room across the partition. Lying in her bed between the sleep-tangled limbs of her brothers and sister, the girl can hear their hu-sussuru whispering that means children are not supposed to hear, and if they hear they are not supposed to listen. The father says, 'Sylvie, I have to go you know. It look like no help for it. The children growing big an Girlzel she soon pass scholarship fi high school an is plenty money fi board up a convent. Wi can't manage unless mi go.'

The girl's heart freezes, all of her stops, then beats in terror. She knows what they are talking about. For weeks now men have been leaving; her friend Moonie cried at recess in the schoolyard because her father had joined the slow trickle that was taking all the fathers away in an unknown stream.

178

'Ma say it not for long,' Moonie said, wiping her eyes on the sleeve of her uniform blouse and leaving a big dirty brown mark on the pristine white. Miss Mai is going to give her a buss arse for dirtying up her school clothes, but Moonie is too upset to care. 'Shi say him soon come back. Like how Rhygin come back. Shi say you can mek nuff nuff money quick quick over dere an come back in no time. She seh farm work is go an come, is not go fi stay.' She sniffed apprehensively. 'But is only Rhygin one come back quick, look how long Maas Charlie and Dado and Greasy Bwoy an Tata Paylo an Half a Cow gone an none a dem nuh come back.'

'Maybe is because dem nuh wuk fast like Rhygin, or maybe Rhygin get a good wuk that pay him plenty money quick quick,' the girl comforted her friend. 'Yuh know how everybody say how Rhygin quick wid anyting him put him han to.'

'Heh!' Moonie said derisively. 'Dem mean seh a tief him tief, him quick wid him han, like fingersmith. Ma say is prably tief him tief over dere an dem ship him back home in disgrace.'

The girl didn't know. Rhygin had come back with a lot of American one dollar bills which he showed to everybody, saying, 'Plenty more where that came from,' and bought rum. But she didn't want to hurt her friend so she kept silent.

She lay stiffly in the bed, not breathing, waiting for the mother's answer. But she could not hear what the mother said, her voice was a low murmur, not like the father's, who always spoke too loud.

The father sighed a long, drawn-out sigh. 'Ah bway. Dis is really di worst time, wid another little one on the way. You one going haffi tek charge, with all a dat.'

The girl's heart thumped. The next morning she stared piercingly at the front of her mother's dress, but could not see anything to confirm what the father had said.

…..

That was the summer the girl suddenly shot up tall. Her thighs and legs stretched so that the lower half of her body appeared artificially elongated. A shameful darkening like fine lint came up under her arms, which had also grown too long. Her breasts were swollen and made little round points under her dress; they became painful and made her cry. Her hair, always unmanageable, grew wild and it too became painful so that she refused to have it combed and wore it in a bush that flamed on her head. Instead of walking she lunged forward, with a peculiar grace and gracelessness, stumbling over things in her way, breaking them if they were fragile, with sudden, startled arm movements wide like a grass cutter, or short, sharp and abrupt, like cries bitten off. She had never been a child who smiled, and now her eyes darkened and receded into her head with a look of misery.

The girl felt that the worst part of this alien invasion of her body was the break in her voice, which grew rough and smoky like a boy's. She could only mimic the timbre of dead women's voices, while those of men came naturally. In a gesture of premonition, the girl stopped retelling stories. Feeling taken over, she bullied the younger children, whom she had hitherto fiercely protected from everyone but herself, and became rude.

The mother felt assailed by an ambivalence of feeling she had hoped was safely put away after the girl's difficult birth. But she felt caught at the root of a vague obscenity that she felt was the lot of mothers with their daughters. From the beginning the girl had been troublesome. She was a breach birth and moreover born with a caul over her face, one of the four-eyed, or second-sighted. Uncompromising, she broke her mother's waters a full night and day before she was born and it was thought the mother would die. She grew into a fierce, solitary child with a shadowed, scowling face that seemed ugly, though it was not.

After her, John was born, only a year between them, and then DenDen and one crib death and a year later, Sybil. With each birth the mother became ill and from the time she was four the girl was a little woman about the house. She fetched, carried, washed, swept, became adept at changing nappies and hushing babies when they cried. She knew a lullaby which she sang in a high falsetto that her brother said sounded like one of the uncle's deads.

Clap han clap han till mama come home
Mama bring cake fi baby at home
Baby eat cake nuh gi mama none
Clap han clap han till mama come home!

But the baby slept. She sang with her impassive scowl that rarely gave way to a smile. And even before the baby could understand words, she told it her awful stories, chewing and regurgitating the pieces from the uncle's memory and feeding them to the child like a bird feeding its young.

Throughout this last pregnancy, she kept staring at the mother's belly as if she saw something buried there. The mother regretted the child's involvement in the secrets of her body; she felt that never again would she ask this child for any help, no matter how ill this birth made her. Each birth was part of a cycle of judgement on the sin of her body. She had wanted to be a teacher. Her ambition stumbled on her father's contempt for girls – on whom he wouldn't waste a willix penny – and the tall, coolie-royal boy with his white smile and the part in his hair arriving at her sixteen-year-old gate too early for her to say no. Now the girl's unseemly, clairvoyant, equalizing-up-herself gaze, her rudeness and new secret smell of flowers made the mother ashamed and also fearful for her daughter, for she could see that this inheritance of female flesh was burgeoning in her much, much too early. She quarrelled inexplicably with the husband and spoke harshly to the girl.

'Yuh practisin to be a slut? Set yuh clothes properly!' The girl sat with her legs spread too wide, the crippled child's head balanced in the curved tent of her lap so she could manoeuvre the hair she was plaiting. Her dress rode up over her thighs.

The girl was a headlong, abrupt speaker; she trembled and cut her words short in anger and shame. 'Nutten wrong mi frock!'

'Yuh answering mi back? Yuh answering mi back? The devil sen yuh here to test mi, hihnnn?!'

'Devil?' the girl's eyes flashed with anger and shame. 'Yuh do all yuh badness, then is the devil!' Struggling for breath, she clarified her meaning, 'Blame devil fo yuh own work. Poor devil!' Her soul contorted with despair, wanting to hug her mother tightly, but she had lost her. Through her fault, this angry person had supplanted her mother. She did not know how she had come to do this, but still she had caused this angry person to supplant her mother.

The mother told her husband, 'She ha no manners. You spoil her.'

He, guilty with the knowledge that this was true and that he was expected to inflict some form of punishment, glanced uneasily across at the girl where she crouched over the crowded hall table, her lesson books warring for space with paper bags of foodstuffs, stacked enamel plates and a cut tin of condensed milk with newspaper stuffed into the cut so the milk wouldn't harden or attract flies. The girl was all ears and trembling, but she kept her eyes sullenly buried in her book to show she didn't care. He was afraid of the mother and the girl. So he called to the girl in a harsh voice and when she got up and came and stood before him with her crouched shoulders and drooping, sullen mouth, he said, looking away from her, 'Yuh faas wid yu modda, gal? Yuh waan taste supplejack? Hihn? Ansa mi!'

'No, Da.'

The acknowledgement that someone is talking to her, someone due the respect of an answer, however grudging and sullen, is all he requires. He sighs inwardly with relief, thinking how awkward this could have been if she had held out and refused to answer so that he would have had to beat her to save his face and the mother's. 'Don't benta it again, or yuh know wha yuh wi get.' He hopes his voice sounds sufficiently threatening. 'You hear mi warn you?'

'Yes, Da.'

The mother isn't satisfied, but it is the best he can do without beating her, and that he cannot bring himself to do. For good measure, as a form of conciliation to his wife, he repeats the warning in a louder, more threatening voice, and again the girl says 'Yes, Da.' He allows her to return to her corner and, sighing wearily, calls for his dinner. He has worked eighteen hours because the overseer is short of hands; more and more of the men are leaving. Eighteen hours in the sugarcane at two pence an hour. That is what your wages amount to, if you match time against acreage cut. Soon he will have to stop putting off the decision whether to stay or go.

......

The uncle notices the girl's new silences, the new excursions and mysteries of her flesh. She still attends his griot's gathering, but now she holds herself aloof, and it is four year old DenDen who sits in his lap, curled under his chin. Sybil doesn't like to be held by anyone except the girl, whom she has adopted as her mother, ever since the mother started leaving the little ones in the girl's care during the crop season when she goes to the property to earn a little extra tying the cane. Crop season is when the women go in droves to tie the cane. The men come home in the smoky evening wearing soot from the red fires that have sent black shards flying through windows to stain the beds. The women cover the beds with rags instead of pristine calico sheets until the burning is over. Sometimes the father brings molasses, sweet and wet in a bamboo gourd hidden under his clothes, where the overseer can't see. Sometimes they don't recognize him because the soot on him is like a uniform of black that includes his face and hands and only his eyes stand out red and burning.

It is to the girl that the uncle now directs his narrative; he finds himself beseeching, weaving his threads, recreating himself in the countenance of her eyes. He understands now that she has been his ideal audience, the only one in whose sight he has truly wished to be seen. He knows now why he used to love the way she listened, not like the others, requiring answers, elaborations or tessellated refrains, but quietly, with an intent, gleaming gaze as if she understood exactly where he was travelling from and would stitch the gaps and silences in for herself, or string them in without prompting, mending the breaks in the line of beads. Now that he is not sure if it exists any longer, he senses how much it is her apprenticeship that has made him grope towards his craft as a master storyteller. He recognizes her gift, as one passing his mantle on to another. He misses her trust, which has become lost to him in her now constant state of misery and rage with the world.

…..

now and at the hour
of our death

The father is going to America.

'Wi going to Kingston for yuh fada papers,' the mother said. 'Wi goin stay overnight with Aunt Katie in Denham Town. Wi comin back Thursday morning.'

The girl's face screws up into an uglier grimace than usual. She turns abruptly and walks out of the yard towards the grove of naseberry trees. Sybil screws up her own face in imitation, but when the mother adds, 'Uncle wi stay wid yuh' she cries 'Yippee!' instead of bursting into tears. DenDen cries 'Yippee!' and John tosses his catapult in the air, catches it before it falls and runs outside where he dances a jig. DenDen runs after him, grabs him by the leg so that he falls with DenDen on top of him and they wrestle like a big puppy and a little puppy, the big puppy rough but taking care. Sybil follows them out the door, limping.

.....

Some time during the night the girl stirred, pushing a heavy weight off her. Her dreaming eyes caught the dog's dark shadow; its outline, a moving blur, blotted out all other space around. Her mind groped for the words of enchantment with which the mother cursed her neighbour. 'Get thee behind me, Satan!' She muttered in guttural sounds. The weight hung still, shifted, eased. The girl murmured again and was still. The weight settled. A beast with two backs is on the bed. The girl thrashed in her sleep, her hands, fluttering like trapped birds, pushed at the dog's shaggy sides. She moaned a little. The weight grew heavier. The girl's body jerked in resistance. Her eyes flew open; from the bottom of sleep-laden pools she saw the thin gleam of the dog's gaze reflected. The girl's hands, cleaving the pool, cut a long swathe in the wave and she is suddenly sitting up in the bed and crying, 'Come offa mi, come offa mi!' The girl's voice has two sounds, one frantic and sharp, the other underneath and distant, like the echo of sound in a cave. Her hands beat with two rhythms, one frantic and tattered, the other in slow motion, like a swimmer's hands breaking dreaming pools. The occult thing pressing down on her fully understands the ambiguity of sound and motion and presses itself into the space between sound and motion; towards the unequivocal flowers of blood.

The girl was truly awake now, screaming in earnest. Her strong, tensile feet, seeking to protect her navel, remembered their ability to contort and jackknifed into something soft and solid. The impact drew a short, sharp grunt. Beside her in the bed DenDen cried out. Sybil sighed and twined herself more securely into his side. The weight lifts abruptly. A rustle, a shuffle of feet on bare floor, a door creaks open, creaks closed, the girl's breath wheezes in the silence.

The little boy stirs. 'What do yuh, Girlzel?'

'Nothing. Go back to sleep.'

'Yuh was a-dream?'

'Yes, mi was a-dream. Go back to sleep.' She pulls the ragged sheet over him, tucking it into his neck with a convulsive, kneading motion. The boy sighs, puts his thumb into his mouth, with his other hand searches under his nightshirt for his navel, falls immediately asleep, curled around his thumb and his navel.

The girl lies awake, watchful through the night. At first she holds her breath, releasing it slowly only when she cannot hold it any longer for the pain in her chest. Her eyes fixed on the jalousies where the ghosts climb out to colloquy at cockcrow, she waits for the morning.

…..

and at the hour
of our death

In the morning the uncle's face is pale, pale, pale, like someone whose blood has been drunk in the night. The girl's mouth has a resolute, cruel look, like someone who is not innocent. No longer loping, but carrying herself with a careful containment as if there is a breakable vessel inside, the breakable vessel of her essential self, she moves with the tightness and freedom of a woman a hundred years old.

The parents have returned. They have brought gifts for every-one, a special gift for the uncle for taking care of the household while they were away. Over the clamour of joy and welcome, the heads of the swarming children, the uncle's eyes are beseeching. 'Please.' The girl watches the way his throat works up and down, and she hears him as clearly as if he has spoken, begging her silence. Stiff with dignity, age and scorn, she turns away.

…..

The girl does not know what has happened, or if anything has happened. She searches and searches herself but does not know what she is looking for. No one has told her anything. She washes and washes herself until there comes a burning and when she walks past the mother the mother looks at her with suspicious eyes. In the night before climbing into the bed she bends down to make a cross on the floor and plants a knife in the middle where the four parts meet. She makes the cross exactly over where there is a crack between the boards (there are many cracks in the boards; she chooses one) so that the knife can go easily through. Sybil sits up in bed looking at her with big open eyes, sucking her finger like a dainty lady sucking her pipe. 'What you doin, Girlzel?'

'Nothin. Go sleep.'

Sybil's eyes grow rounder with a dawning thought. 'Yuh plantin somebody, Girlzel?'

'Come, go a yuh bed.' The girl pushes the little one down in her place in the bed and covers her up with the sheet. Sybil is wriggling with excitement. She wants to say her say before she obeys the injunction to fall asleep. 'If you plant him wid di cross an di knife him can't move, yuh know, Girlzel. Yuh know? Yuh know?'

'Shhh. Come mek mi tell you a story.' Sybil shushes quickly at the joyous prospect and wriggles up under the girl's armpit where she is sitting on the bed. The girl starts a soft, gentle story without contortions and the child, disappointed, begins to fall asleep with her arms clasped around the neck of the girl. The girl sings her tuneless lullaby, in her new voice full of smoke:

Clap han clap han till mama come home
Mama bring cake fi baby at home
Baby eat cake nuh gi mama none
Clap han clap han till mama come home!

She feels the warm breath grow sticky, the little arms slackening around her neck. She lays the child softly down and draws the covers up around her once more. She sits on the edge of the bed watching the three children sleep while, thinking, she moves her hands in that washing motion that she has developed since she started getting older.

The mother takes the girl aside and speaks to her in a cold, controlled voice, scrubbed of all emotion. She talks from a distance about something dreadful called becoming a woman that makes blood sprout between your knees, every month by the phases of the moon. You must not speak to boys or touch them with your hands. If you do, babies will come. Throughout, her eyes are averted.

When she leaves the room she has left on the white, pristine bed a pile of neatly folded calico cloths, like babies' nappies, which the girl had always hated washing. The mother's voice reverberates in her head. 'You will have to learn to wash them, when the time comes.'

The girl takes up the cloths, goes outside to the privy and throws them down its dark well, her mouth pursed and cruel with resentment. She makes sure her mother sees her passing with the cloths in her hand, and passing back without them. She knows that shame, the shame of being forced to bridge the gap between them, child and woman, mother and daughter, ruler and subordinate, will keep her mother silent.

In the morning the father goes to the wharf, where a ship rides at anchor.

1979
And forgive us our trespasses
As we forgive
As we forgive

In a minute she will make her way up to the house to greet Sybil and the children who are expecting her, but for now she wants to enjoy the cool quietness and the feeling of peace that is shifting in and out of the still clarity of her mind like the sunlight on the headstones. She wants to hold on to this feeling a little while longer until it becomes truly hers. For now, she tells thoughts with beads.

This circlet of trees has guarded the family graves for so long – even before there were any graves here, because from the beginning Da marked it out with an intention. Here is the most important spot on this two acre piece of ground he bought with the first money he earned in America. More important than the family house, with its gallery of photographs, black and white and faded sepia brown. There are more recent, glossy coloured ones whose glossiness will soon also fade, though more slowly than black and white. Only Sybil lives there now. Sybil, guardian of the home to which year after year we all pretend that we'll return for a bang-up pick-up lick-dung grand reunion but nobody except me has come, and me not since Da died, for what is the point, if Ma and Da aren't there any more.

Nobody ever really meant it. It was just a grand lie they told themselves so it wouldn't hurt too much not to come back. Because after a time there is no going back. Not in that way. But I think they were wrong not to come. One comes back to remember not what used to be but what will be, so that one is a part of it when it comes. Otherwise memory is just a false house of safety between longing and the temptation to despair merely because you can't have things any more in the way that a lost innocence demands. We are no longer innocent, any of us. I thought we owed it to Ma and Da to keep coming back so the place wouldn't die. We all say Sybil is here, but it isn't quite the same thing, is it? It's a bit like keeping the photographs together. Each of us has a part of the collection and it's ok, the collection exists, but still it doesn't exist, not really, except in a museum kind of way, unless we make the journey. To gather in the one place. The dead can't travel so well as the living. It is we who have to come.

Yet she had stopped coming for three years.

I couldn't keep it up after Da died.

She thought about DenDen's estranged American wife who thought Jamaica was a place where you lay under coconut trees, drank rum and scampered in the sun to the beat of reggae music, and where natives with happy smiles said 'yo, mon, no problem' in guttural tones and then migrated to other people's countries to fight them for their rights. She thought of John's dreadlocked daughter Monica, born in England, waiting for Babylon to fall so she could return home to the constructed memory of paradise that her father had raised in her for himself against the ravages of a chosen exile. Coralee, the youngest, to whom she had never really been close, was a jetsetter in New York and hardly kept in touch with anyone else in the family.

Each year, John and DenDen sent Sybil large barrels filled with things to eat and wear marked 'Made in the USA', 'Made in China', 'Made in the UK' or 'Made in' some other far away place, and in return, every Christmas, Sybil went to a photo studio with her seven children and posed and sent them each one copy of a new, glossy photograph with her and her children and no man. On the back she wrote, unvaryingly, and they could hear the laughter in her voice (Sybil had been the brightest of them all and the family wit) 'Keepers of the Graves', and the year of the photograph.

Every year they said half-heartedly, Sybil do you want to come? and Sybil who had stayed because she had started having children too early for too many men – though Ma would have kept the children – remembering past hurts, said pridefully, No, I am not leaving my children anywhere to be a burden to anybody or taking them anywhere to be where they forget who they should be. They may be the offspring of many fathers, seven to be exact – saying this, Sybil always grew offended, as if somebody was disputing her claim – but not a one of those fathers has been given jacket to wear. Every surname was legitimate, and her children were doing well in school. No, she said again; and anyway the barrels were more than adequate.

She who had kept coming every year until Da died (because, she supposed, she was the one who had no children, no family otherwise), watched Sybil's children growing up and knew that one day they too would move away and inevitably the house and the land would be sold.

Family houses and family lands are never sold. They keep the genera-tions together; from time immemorial we have done this.

But that was before we had enough generations, she thought, watching the photographs float away, the cabinet fronts falling softly downwards with a curious bow like a musician taking applause in an empty hall. The wood caved in with a clicking sound like musical sticks, then slowly dusted down in pools of eaten grain the way wood always does when there is chi chi behind the paint. The beige piles banked, settled, rose softly towards the jalousies. She watched the grain go out on planks of coloured light. The whisper of previous occupation, the residue of laughter in corners, of fights and scolding and the *hu-sussuru* of night stories told against tattered leaves; all these walked out behind the photographs in a pale procession of sound.

189

It was the graves that would remain. Closed in this circlet of trees, quiet and peaceful, marking time and standing it still. Here the ghosts would retreat, keeping the one space inviolate. But would they? How could anyone know? Maybe with the press of the years and new-minted people, the spirits would have to leave and travel far distances to seek a new peace. Maybe they would return at the close of every year to make sure the stones were still standing, and hopefully still cared for. In the end, it would boil down only to stone. This is all that would be left. Stone. In its neat rows in the shape of a cross.

Grampa Herman – Augustine Herman Sylvester Dullich, the west arm of the cross, in white enamel, 15th October 1872 – 1st May, 1937. The more elaborate double tomb of her parents formed the vertical body piece. White ceramic tiles lightly veined in blue and pink to distinguish Da from Ma. Rose Dullich Fagan, 30th August 1914 -10th October 1972. Ma had had a bad heart, like her father, Grampa Herman. Many people on her side of the family did not live long. Albert Roy Fagan, 3rd January 1904 – 11th June, 1976. May their souls rest in peace.

The east arm of the cross in its bed of red earth was still the light gray colour of drying concrete.

And light perpetual shine upon them.

With the others, she had long made her peace. Her father had been easy; there had always been a softness between them. In the last years after her mother died it was she who had sat with him between Grampa's and Ma's graves and exchanged stories about his picking oranges in Florida, and her in New York and Prague and all the places she had been, while Sybil's children on top of the hill joyously shrieked the house down. Strange, even though he had proven beyond doubt that he was strong enough to live by himself in a foreign country for months on end over many years, still they had felt that if their mother went first, he would go soon after, that he would not have been able to endure alone. But he had stayed behind five years, though in the end, his life, too, had been shorter than most.

'You stay same like me,' he used to say when they sat among the headstones. 'Strong. Tough as Jamrock. You wi live.'

She had not so much made peace with her mother as that her

mother had won the war, in the end. She marked this on the day she turned forty, looked in the mirror and saw that her facial features, always fine drawn and slightly hawkish like her father's, had rounded and broadened out and begun to set a little in the jaw in strips of disapproval the way her mother's did.

'I am becoming my mother,' she said, in bemused, amused irony, quoting the words of a poem that she hated.

'You *have* become your mother,' the ghost retorted, leering brassily beneath her supplanted skin.

'Go away, old woman,' she said, indignant. '*Retro me!*' Swiftly she made the sign of the cross.

'Retro yourself.' The spirit copied the sign, their arms moving in the mirror like twins. The effrontery paralysed her.

But long before this she had wept uncontrollably, in the understanding of her own coming of age, that a woman is not a rock nor a bankra full of clean and clear or black stones and white – but shoals of doubt and fear and frail navigation on watery ships of compromise. It was then that she had forgiven her mother.

'It is the children who are clear,' she said aloud, speaking into the shadows between the tombs. 'Only children are really ever sure of anything.'

The other had not ceased troubling her. If she came to help Sybil keep the graves, she came more so to close the lid of his grave.

In all the years, it was she who had carried the guilt. He, she believed, had carried the shame. She wondered how the weight of this expiation has been shared so equally between them – two halves of a whole.

She knew he accepted his shame by the way his head bowed in her presence, and it made her angry and cruel. His shame made her guilty, as though she had been at fault. She ruled him with his shame like a wand.

For a long time she hated him for this: she had not wanted to become his equal.

After she went to college, it became easier. She came back home in the first yearly break to find that to the village she had become 'Miss Girlzel', a title of respect that meant either you had achieved age or, as in her case, the hopes and aspirations of the community and now carried the whole village around inside you. (*In a culture without monuments, all titles were an ellipsis of ceremony*). Unable to bear the weight of such a conferral, grieving at the separations and the loneliness that came with it, she relented. Besides, she had had biology lessons at school and knew he had not harmed her (not really), and she wanted to forget.

She laughed and joked with him about things. He accepted her friendship with humility; she gave it with confused pleasure, self-censure and reserve. She sat and listened to him telling other children stories, and that made him ashamed and glad. But she never trusted him with the children; if any of them crawled into his lap, she looked pointedly at his hands, which he kept ostentatiously turned out and upwards, like open fruit. He always said 'Miss Girlzel.'

They said you slipped away quietly one forenoon, no warning. After a last lunch of green bananas, mackerel rundown and beverage made with sugar, ginger and civil orange. The children wanted another story. You said you had to lie down a little first, you didn't feel so well. They put you on the cool green sheets in Sybil's room and you didn't wake up in the evening. You were a hundred and one years old, by your own count, which was probably invented. I think you were older.

She touched the headstone facing east. 'So many stories you told us,' she murmured, keeping her voice low so he could hear. 'But we never knew which of them was ever your real self.'

She waited the minute or two it would take someone who was slow of speech to answer briefly. Then she added, 'If there ever was one.'

The therapist said what he had done was at the root of the problem in her marriage. She didn't think so. And after all he hadn't done anything, had he, not really.

Not really.

'Then why are you so much with him? How many books have you written?'

'Four.'

'And how many are not about him?'

She shrugged him off, thinking she wouldn't come back to waste any more of her money with this fool. It was all behind her.

The uncle was in her books because she heard his voice in her head when she was writing. No more.

But Jasper left, a very frigid man, saying she was frigid. She was frightened at how relieved she was to see him go.

She said in an angry voice, 'You know, I cannot understand why I should be the one who is sorry. You almost damaged me forever. You know that, don't you?' She repeated like her father used to do when he was threatening to beat, 'Don't you?'

She doesn't have to say any of this, she knows. She is just saying it as a ritual prologue to what she really wants to say. What she really wants to do is ask his forgiveness for never writing down his stories, as she had pledged to herself to do, before they were forgotten.

EPILOGUE

The landscape doesn't easily settle into quietness. There are other comings and goings. In this traffic among worlds, tomorrow a man will walk up this hill, shading his face from the sun. He will love the remembered warmth beating down on his shoulders, his skin, but he has lived for a long time in a different light; the brightness hurts his eyes. He will stop to rest just past the bend where the road runs between banks of shale, balancing his duffel bag on the twisted root of a guango tree that marks where the shale ends and the firmer, more clayey soil begins. The tree's roots run deep in the soil, but a large portion of each root is raised above the place where it is earthed, fanning in different directions like tributaries over the surface of the ground until they sink again underground or vanish in the overgrowth.

The man, resting, will observe these familiar things as though they are newly made signs that he has never seen before (it gives him delight to think of them as newly made, like fresh bread or the rain returning). He will think to himself about the journeys of these roots, and their anchoring. He will notice how they look like the architrave of mangroves. He will pour soil like libation from a jar onto the root of a shooting plant growing between the toes of the great tree, stirring his soil into the greater soil and mixing it in with his fingers until the line of demarcation between soil and soil almost disappears. He will wipe sweat from his forehead with the back of one hand, and, holding his tan polo shirt away from his back with two fingers inserted into the collar, allow the soft breeze off the sheltering leaves to dry his skin before heaving the duffel over his shoulder again and proceeding with a sigh. He does not know if he will be welcome or even if there will be anyone there to meet him at the top of the hill. For once again – returning to old habit, the habit of years ago, as if rehearsing the past will make it stay secure – he has not announced his coming. He will smile to himself, somewhat mordantly, somewhat whimsically, for he will think of himself as someone returning from his wars. In the old days, in places older than here, or now, the maidens would lead a song of praise to meet the warrior, placing garlands over his head with silken hands.

He feels that he has earned a modicum of rest, but if there is none to be had, he has no quarrel. He feels that life has been gracious to him, sparing him neither joy nor pain, generous with the cup it has asked him to drink. He is a patient man, who has grown more patient with the years, more grizzled in the hair, thicker in the hands and the waist. He is still a rumpled man, slightly askew, walking now with a limp because of the experience of feet in the cold. He is a man of great hope, and little expectation. He will be content, yet as he ascends, his pace involuntarily quickens and he strains his eyes to see whether there is anything to be seen over the brow of the hill. But the sun is blinding in his eyes (all he can see is the scar in the sky low to the west that tells him it might rain). He will have to wait until he has finished the climb.

At the top of the hill, a woman, startled, will shade her eyes from the sun, watching him come.

Aliun, watching, smiles, grimaces.

Aliun, world traveller, who smiles with one side of her/his face and grimaces with the other, true form of Orunmila sayer of songs, muse of Mbaba Mwana Waresa the Rainbowed One, Aliun, unperceived mercy of the God of Heaven, sweet Jesus, recorder of hopes and wrongs, s/he, Aliun, who has crossed continents through many waters, Oshun's wash, and hung crucified on bats' wings among islands, jewelled archipelagoes, spreads wings upward to the sky's deep, and dives.

THE END
Friday January 20, 2006.

195